A GRIFTER'S SONG

SEASON TWO, VOLUME FOUR

A GRIFTER'S SONG

Season One
The Concrete Smile by Frank Zafiro
People Like Us by J.D. Rhoades
The Whale by Lawrence Kelter
The Movie Makers by Gary Phillips
Lost in Middle America by Colin Conway
Losing Streak by Jim Wilsky

Season Two
Gone Dead on You by Eryk Pruitt
Upgrade by Asa Maria Bradley
The Money Block by Holly West
The Sound of Breaking Bones by Eric Beetner
Still Life with Suitcase by Scott Eubanks
Down Comes the Night by Frank Zafiro

Eric Beetner, Scott Eubanks,
and Frank Zafiro

A GRIFTER'S SONG

SEASON TWO, VOLUME FOUR

Series Created and Edited by Frank Zafiro

Down & Out Books
3959 Van Dyke Road, Suite 265
Lutz, FL 33558
DownAndOutBooks.com

Cover design by Zach McCain

ISBN: 1-64396-143-8
ISBN-13: 978-1-64396-143-9

CONTENTS

INTRODUCTION

When the green light went on for season one of *A Grifter's Song*, I was thrilled. It was the culmination of an idea that had morphed considerably from its initial idea stage, at least in terms of format. The core premise—the episodic tales of two grifters on the run from the mob—remained intact, but the shift in format made the stories much richer. See, originally, I was going to write each episode. They'd take place in a different town with a different con each time, and each story was intended to be self-contained with an over-arching meta story that progressed in fits and starts. Then during discussions with Down and Out Books (and thanks to a variation introduced by Gary Phillips), the idea of using a different author for each episode crystallized.

What did that do?

Everything. It did *everything*.

I was always excited about how a new con and a change in venue would keep the series fresh. But adding the narrative voices of different authors each time out? And allowing those authors to pick the point of view character and presentation? Yeah, that blew anything I could have done by myself right out of the water.

Season one saw our intrepid grifters troop through St. Louis, Raleigh, New York, Los Angeles, Lima (Ohio, not Peru), and Little Rock. Aside from my own writing style, readers got to experience that of JD Rhoades, Lawrence Kelter, Gary Phillips, Colin Conway, and Jim Wilsky. This is a stylistically eclectic bunch, who wrote some killer stories.

What could top that?

Season two.

No, I'm not saying season two is "better" than season one. First off, art is so subjective and individual that these terms are sorely lacking. Secondly, everything is "better" when it is shiny and new. And thirdly, even if I *did* like one season better than the other (I truly don't) or a particular story better than its sister stories (okay, I do have favorites), I wouldn't tell you that. As the editor, that'd be poor form. And since I have varying levels of friendship with all of these authors, that'd be an even worse thing to do.

So maybe saying season two "topped" season one is a bad choice of verb on my part. What it did do was continue the series in absolutely wonderful fashion. And in terms of author diversity, I don't think anyone could argue it stretched its arms a little wider. That's a cool thing, and something I was purposeful about in reaching out to and selecting season two authors (and season three, which is happening, so get your subscription, folks!). I'm not going to go over the box score with you on this count, but suffice it to say that I was pleased to get talented authors whose backgrounds were varied. These differences included gender, nationality, body of work, geography, age, and style, just to name a few things. These differences throughout this series go a long ways toward keeping it from ever becoming stale. Plus, like the first season, this season's authors are awesome people that I'm proud to be associated with (and call friends).

In the end, though, the story itself is everything. And this season's authors nailed it in that regard. The cons were inventive, the locations varied, and the stories took these two characters in directions and into situations that were new and exciting.

I enjoyed the *hell* out of this season.

Eryk Pruitt's *Gone Dead on You* kicks things off in episode seven. I was both thrilled and relieved when he agreed to join the project. His style of rural noir had an edge to it that I badly wanted to inject into the series. He went me one further by including some woo-woo in his episode that I think plays really well. I remember when I got back to him about liking what he'd done, he sounded as relieved as I'd felt when he said yes to coming on board. While the story isn't a massive departure from other work from Eryk, it does have some different elements that I think his fans will dig, and it puts a new wrinkle on this series as well.

I will admit up front that asking Asa Maria Bradley to pen an episode might have initially surprised some people. After all, while Bradley is a highly successful author, her work falls primarily in the paranormal romance genre. But there were two good reasons I had for inviting her. One, the woman can write. Just read her Viking Warrior series if you don't believe me. Two, I knew she was a massive mystery fan, and I believed she'd have fun stretching her wings a bit. You can see I was right on both counts, as *Upgrade* is tight, including a wonderful balance of mystery, intrigue, and an element of romantic tension that hasn't been heavily explored to this point in the series.

The Money Block has a few surprises in it that I won't ruin for you here. But I will say that some of what Holly West did in this story has etched itself into the psyche of both Sam and Rachel in a way that will follow them both throughout the remainder of the series. When you couple something powerful like that with a new and updated digital take on an old con, you know you've got a winner.

Eric Beetner actually got an invite to season one, but had to defer because he was overcommitted. If you take one look at his back catalog and check out what else he has going on, you'll see that isn't an overstatement. Thankfully, he was ready to contribute when season two rolled around. The reader gets some more lean, action-filled Beetner prose, and in *The Sound of Breaking Bones*, he finally got to use a title that had been brewing in his mind for some time.

I met Scott Eubanks through Asa Maria Bradley, who she introduced as a promising new voice in fiction. The idea of including a crime fiction debut in the series intrigued me, and once I read some of Scott's writing, that sealed it. Like the other authors this season, he brought elements to these characters that became indelibly printed upon them, things they will carry forever. A variation of the old fiddle con, the scheme in *Still Life with Suitcase* is full of intrigue and violence, all told in a spare, literary tone. It also provided me with a perfect jumping off point for the season finale.

Down Comes the Night closes out the season with Sam and Rachel trying to resolve their longtime issue with the Philly mob. The events of episode eleven give them the key to that attempt, and they have to decide how to use it. I'm edging close to spoiler territory here, but there is a betrayal here that hurts them, and sends them scrambling for money to lie low for an extended period. All of this really puts a strain on the sentiment you some-times hear one or the other of them express throughout the series—that it's "worth the stretch."

Depending on which version of this collection you hold in your hands, it may include the subscriber-only bonus episode, *The Reckoner*. This tale, much like season one's bonus episode, *Come the Apocalypse*, is told from the perspective of Rocco Tolenti. Rocco is Little Vincent's right hand man when it comes to enforce-ment, and he's been tasked with finding Sam and Rachel. The first season saw him attempting to do just that across the scope of all six episodes (he appears in episode one, though unnamed). It's an alternate view of events, and was fun to explore.

This season continues that tradition, as Rocco's pursuit of the pair includes culling through rumors of events that occurred in episode seven through eleven, as well as an alternate telling of events from episode twelve. Once again brushing up against spoilers here, I will tell you that everything you think is true in *Down Comes the Night* proves to be a little different when you see things through Rocco's eyes. I remember when I told a writer friend of mine over breakfast at a diner about the idea. He grinned at me and said, "You know what you're doing here, right? You're conning the reader."

"But in a good way, right?"

"Absolutely," he said.

I hope he's right. I hope you read the bonus episode and you agree. Because at the end of it all, I'm not only proud of the great work these authors have done, but also take some strange satisfaction in the fact that this is a grifter series, and the cons don't just come from Sam and Rachel.

These are the tales of season two, folks. New cities, new schemes, new authors, new voices...and some new meta to go with it.

Enjoy!

And keep both hands on your wallet (after you subscribe to season three, of course).

Frank Zafiro
May, 2020
Redmond, Oregon

THE SOUND OF BREAKING BONES

ERIC BEETNER

A GRIFTER'S SONG

BOOKS BY ERIC BEETNER

The McGraw Crime Series
Rumrunners
Leadfoot

The Lars and Shane Series
The Devil Doesn't Want Me
When the Devil Comes to Call
The Devil at Your Door

The Fightcard Series
Split Decision
A Mouth Full of Blood

The Lawyer Western Series
Six Guns at Sundown
Blood Moon
The Last Trail

The Bricks and Cam Job Series
(with Frank Zafiro)
The Backlist
The Short List
The Getaway List

With JB Kohl
Over Their Heads
Borrowed Trouble
One Too Many Blows to the Head

Stand Alones
The Year I Died Seven Times
Criminal Economics
Nine Toes in the Grave
Dig Two Graves
White Hot Pistol
Stripper Pole at the End of the World
A Bouquet of Bullets (stories)
All the Way Down

As Editor
Unloaded Volume 1
Unloaded Volume 2

THE SOUND OF BREAKING BONES

Eric Beetner

CHAPTER 1

Rachel hated straight-up stealing. It takes such little skill. It's brutish and simple. Anybody can do it, and they often do. But sometimes, you gotta do it. But even for Rachel, her stealing had style.

She stepped up to the counter of the fast food joint. Grease hung in the air like a foggy day. Her phone was pressed to the side of her face and she spoke in a deep southern twang. The slack-jawed kid behind the register watched her approach like he was eyeing a snake slithering toward him; a little leery, ready to jump if he had too.

"I am asking. I'm here right now. Gimme a goddamn minute."

Keeping the phone pressed to her ear, she first let out an exasperated sigh, then asked the kid, "Do you have a lost and found? My dumbass husband left his wallet here."

She immediately went back to speaking in the phone, her annoyance at the dumbass crackled hot as a live wire.

"Gimme a goddamn minute, he's gotta go check. Jesus Christmas."

The kid didn't leave his post at the register. He turned to the back where only one round-bellied guy could be seen standing next to the fryer.

"June? Can you check the lost and found?"

From the back office a young girl not more than twenty-two stuck her pimpled face out and called back like a pissed-off teen-ager, which she practically was.

"Okay, okay I will. Keep your panties on."

Rachel cupped her hand over the phone and spoke to the kid again. "Might as well get some food while I'm here. Gimme two double cheeseburgers, two fries and—" She took her hand away and spoke into the phone. "What? Fine."

She rolled her eyes so far up into her head she might have seen behind her. "Make that one fry and one onion ring. And two chocolate shakes."

She practically screamed into the phone. "Are you serious?"

With a huff of hot air she corrected the order again. "One chocolate and one vanilla shake."

On the other end of the line, Sam laughed at her, but he knew she wouldn't break character.

When in the deep south, as they were here outside of Starkville, Mississippi, you can affect any number of southern-style accents and get away with it. There were the newscasters who kept only enough drawl to seem authentic, the school teachers who polished their Delta roots with a smooth layer of East Coast grammar and flat vowels, and then there was the trailer trash—which Rachel had taken the guise of—who spoke with a broad *Hee-Haw* accent you almost couldn't go too far with. Oh, sure, an anthropologist could tell the difference between accents at every mile marker off Highway 61, but if anyone looked at her and said, "You're not from around here, are you?" All she had to do was make up some place like, "Nah, I'm from Hog's Head, Tennessee," and they'd nod and move on with it.

The pimply-faced girl, June, came out of the back holding a creased and worn cardboard box with L&F written in Sharpie on the side. Up close, she looked like a wet rag. Her hair hung like

10

overcooked spaghetti and aside from the red welts of the blemishes, her skin looked as gray and lifeless as a corpse.

Rachel, an expert at controlling a situation and the people involved, kept up the nonstop chatter and dove her hands into the box. Chances were there was no wallet in there. Ninety-nine out of a hundred times there wasn't. But it was the sport of it. She could have come in, ordered take out and left five minutes later without another word spoken to these minimum wage desperadoes, but what's the fun in that?

She saw a vinyl-sided wallet in the midst of three trucker hats, a hooded sweatshirt, a black comb, a container for a kid's retainer and a crumpled pack of Marlboros.

Into the phone she screeched, "It's here you dim-witted dipshit. I swear on a stack of Bibles if your own ass wasn't attached to you, you'd leave it behind on the toilet seat."

She flipped it open and thumbed out the driver's license.

"Of course it's yours, you bucket-head. Says your name right here, Cliff."

The slack-jawed kid held up a finger like he wanted to intervene but she was a bulldozer bearing down on him. Best get out of the way. The total for her food order, fifteen eighty-three, glowed blue on the register screen.

"What?" She held out the phone to him. "He wants to talk to you."

The kid drew back his attention-getting finger and let his mouth open and close a few times in mute protest. Rachel shoved the phone forward. He took it, set his greasy skin against the screen as he pressed it to his ear.

"Hello?"

Sam channeled Johnny Cash with his accent. He wasn't sure he'd be able to do it without laughing.

"Is that really my wallet you got there? Did you find it in the toilet?"

"Um, I don't know where—"

"What's the name? Is it Cliff?"

11

The kid read the name off the license, unknowingly giving them the answer to proving it was theirs. "Um, Cliff Hickman."

"Well, shit, son. That's me. Hot damn. Now listen, I want you to tell her this happens all the time. She thinks I'm some kind of dipshit, but I want you to let her know this happens every day, got it?"

The delay gave Rachel time to open the money section and check the contents. Three twenties, a ten and three ones. About all you could expect from a wallet lost at a mom and pop burger joint. She slid out the ten and handed it to the kid.

"Thank you so much. Praise Jesus we found it."

She reached for the phone. "What's he saying to you?"

The kid released the phone and she shoved the ten into his open hand. His jaw slacked open a little further. Share the wealth. A good grifter's trick. Make them a part of the windfall. Complicit. Ten bucks in this town could buy him a beer or two, maybe a toke of a meth pipe if that's his thing. Maybe a hand job from his stepsister if she's willing. Who knows?

"I'ma get you one of them chain wallets," she said into the phone.

A bag with a grease stain already spreading at the bottom landed on the counter next to her, dropped by the fat guy from the back. Rachel held the phone to her ear, but moved the mouthpiece away and spoke to the kid again. He had yet to pocket his ten bucks.

"That's yours, slick. A reward." She winked at him, but with no come-on attached to it. "Run and get that other girl, will you? I wanna thank her too."

The greasy kid didn't move. Obviously someone had told him on his first day to never leave his post at the front. Rachel knew how to make people do what she wanted, though.

"Go on. Go get her so I can say thank you. This means so much to me. You don't know how long I prayed and here it is, an answered prayer. Maybe a miracle? I dunno. Tell you what though, it's a miracle I stay with such a dumbass dipshit of a man who's also a lazy tub of lard most days. Now run on and get her so I can bless her day."

The kid moved just to get away from the machine gun attack of Rachel's words. With the counter abandoned and the blue numbers of her order total glowing in the grease cloud, Rachel snatched the bag from the counter and walked out the door. Free dinner and sixty-three bucks to the good.

Better than straight stealing, but only slightly. And way better than paying for it.

CHAPTER 2

When Rachel got back to their modest hotel room, Sam sat on the bed watching a preacher on TV. The man in the all-white suit let sweat run freely down his face, his eyes clenched shut as he practically swallowed the microphone for his soul-saving rant to the flock.

Rachel set down the bag of food. The grease stain had spread to cover the entire bottom of the bag now.

"Dinner's served."

"I tell you," Sam said, not taking his eyes off the TV set. "If we could figure out a way into this world, this is the original long con, and the most successful in history."

Rachel shrugged off her jacket and tried to watch a little of the preacher man, but turned away in disgust.

"Taking money from these people is like those hunters who go to some ranch in Texas and shoot a lion who's been chained to a tree. There's no sport in it."

"Yeah, but the money that's been taken from these marks for two thousand years would buy and sell every billionaire on the planet ten times over. There's more than enough slices of the pie for us to take a bite."

She lifted the remote from the bed and clicked off the power on the set. "You don't look good in white. Washes you out." She kissed him on the lips. The deep scar over Sam's eye had been healing well, but would always be a prominent new part of his face. It was the last of his injuries to heal after their previous job went a little sideways. No better place to recover than the back woods of Mississippi. New Hampshire might have it on their flag, but this was the real land of Don't Tread On Me. People minded their own around here. Live and let live, so long as you live according to the gospel.

"How much did we get from the wallet?"

"Sixty-three."

Sam gave a one shouldered shrug. Small fries, but better than nothing. He knew she did it to stay in practice and to alleviate the boredom that came with hiding out in a roadside motel while he healed up.

"I wish," she said, "that these people wouldn't be their own worst stereotype, y'know? I mean, some of the best people we've met are from the south. Then you go and meet some real mouth-breathers and you see why the New Yorkers have such an easy time tarring them with one brush."

"Yeah, but then you go up to New York and see how easy it is for Southerners to paint them all as mobbed-up mooks."

"Everybody likes to put somebody else in a box, don't they?"

"Sure do."

They ate sitting on the bed, dripping ketchup and milkshake onto the bedspread. Far from the worst it had seen, surely. Each one made different groans of satisfaction. The grease bomb burgers were lard-laden delights of decadence and gluttony. Worth every damn calorie.

Too stuffed to move by the end of the feast, Sam switched the TV back on. Rachel was too weighed down with fast food to protest. The preacher's hour of power had ended and a local news broadcast now played. This stretch of road, midway between Tupelo and Starkville, generated barely enough news to fill out a half hour local broadcast. High school sports, the latest from the Mississippi State teams and weather rounded out the headlines.

One story caught both of their attentions, even through the

food coma. The male anchor of the pair, one desperately trying to hide his Delta accent as he read the teleprompter, explained about a sad turn of events for some families looking for some good news.

"Almost a dozen families found out they'd been bilked tonight when the adoption agency they'd been working with to bring a new baby into their lives was revealed to be a scam."

It seems the group, working closely with local churches in the middle of the state, had started the process of adoption for these families, even providing them with pictures and fake backgrounds on the children, and then after payment was made to the tune of forty thousand dollars each, had declared a "financial emergency" and was forced to file for bankruptcy. The man at the top had been funneling off the money and using it to buy himself things including a boat and twin jet skis for his lake house. When his paperwork seemed off, the state agency looked into it a little deeper and they didn't have to dig far to find out this guy had been using desperate families to finance his lifestyle for years and now it had finally caught up with him.

The failed mechanics of it fascinated Rachel.

"It's like a pyramid scheme," she said. "He runs out of money for one group since he, y'know, stole so much of it, so he uses the money from the next group to pay for the first and now he's got himself in a spiral."

"Amateur."

"I do feel bad for the people. A little."

"You heard what he said, working with local churches. These are gonna be serious bible thumpers."

"Maybe. They still want a family, though."

"Only sucker more ripe on the vine than a parent, is a wanna-be parent."

The news report went on to say that the man at the top of this scam had bilked more than a dozen small church groups and religious organizations throughout the South. This time, he'd dealt directly with members of a group called the Shepherds of the Golden Lamb. The news anchor described them as, "a small group of fervent Old Testament worshippers who keep mostly to themselves."

As Rachel's empathy for the victims reached her throat and built into a lump there, one of the potential mothers was interviewed on the news. Her hair hung lank and thinning, her voice a gravel road of nicotine abuse, and her T-shirt stretched taut over her thick middle invited anyone to *Come Take My Guns (if you dare)*.

"This man will have to answer to God. He knows what he's done to our families and the others. All we wanted was to bring a little light in our lives. You got gays and dykes can adopt and that's okay? And look at us here, God-fearing people who get ripped off for no good reason."

Rachel turned to Sam. "Did she say 'gays and dykes'?"

"She did."

"Fuck her."

The next woman didn't help Rachel's attitude toward the victims any.

"I prayed to Jesus for them not to abort these precious little angels. And now what's gonna happen? These girls hear the adoption fell through, you know they're just gonna go off and find some radical liberal doctor to give 'em a procedure. Makes me sick."

Rachel waved an angry hand at the TV. "Don't they understand that there never *were* any babies? The scam got exposed and they still don't know they've been scammed."

"We also have science and they still believe in talking snakes and burning bushes."

"Okay, turn it off," she said.

Sam switched off the set. "Y'know," he said. "It does give me an idea."

Rachel saw a familiar gleam in his eye. She knew it meant he had a new con in mind, and had a good guess what it might involve. The gears were turning. The plan formulating. She bounced up straight on the bed, eager to hear what he had to say.

The grift was on.

CHAPTER 3

Sam found himself more energized than he'd been in weeks. During the travel to the South, the hotels and bad restaurants, the recuperation and mandatory rest, he'd seemed to lose an edge. It came back now, so sharp he could split a hair down the middle.

It wasn't easy to get the names of the victims. The Shepherds of the Golden Lamb were, as the anchor had said, a group that kept to themselves. In the end, they made progress by uttering those four magical words that get you through almost any door: I'm writing an article. Nobody asked to see credentials, or asked what paper or magazine you wrote for. They were blinded by the idea of seeing their name in print.

Some were eager to spill details about the Shepherds. The group numbered fewer than two hundred strong, but they'd been a fixture in the area for over a hundred years. Descended, more than one person said or implied, from a splinter group of the Ku Klux Klan. They believed in strict adherence to the word of God, no ifs, ands, or buts. And for God's sake, no queers, coloreds, or Jews. That part went more unspoken these days, but it seemed to be an open secret.

Through news reports and court records filed in an effort to recoup some of their lost money, Sam and Rachel soon had the names of eleven would-be parents who were still desperate for a baby.

They also did a little research on Golden Washau, the man accused of stealing their money. Golden, born Elton and called Goldie by all his closest friends and followers, was a preacher who had his hands in more cons than Sam and Rachel could ever hope to, all tied to the church he founded and the suckers he exploited in the name of the big man upstairs.

17

But Goldie hadn't thought ahead. Strange for a man who spent most of his life making promises about the afterlife and what a wonderful one you'd have if you only gave him a little more of your cash.

Then they worked on character.

They decided on southerners. These people would be distrustful of anyone else. Definitely people of God for the same reason. They were local, though recent transplants to the area, and they saw the story on the news and felt they simply had to do something for such good, God-fearing people who got just plain ripped off.

With eleven names they decided early on not to put the hard sell on anyone. Best they could hope for would be maybe fifty percent of the group. A much higher percentage than an ordinary fishing con.

They showed up to the first house and gave each other a little pep talk in the car, then went to make their pitch.

They were invited in to the modest two-bedroom home of Judy and Clayton Ellers. Looking around, it was hard to see where they thought they could put a baby if they got one. The second bedroom spilled over with so much junk it looked like the house had been constructed on top of an old landfill and they kept that part intact and built the house around it.

After declining an offer of sweet tea, Sam and Rachel sat on a threadbare couch while Judy and Clayton took matching armchairs and both lit up the same brand of cigarette.

"Like we said," Sam said, reminding them of the short pitch he'd given on the porch that got them invited inside. "We heard about what happened to you with Goldie, I mean, Mr. Washau, and it made us sick to our stomachs."

"Truly," Rachel added in her thickest drawl.

"And as we all know, God has put us on this earth to procreate and to make more life in His image."

"Praise be," Judy said.

"And as we also know, sometimes that old devil gets up in our business and conspires to leave us childless. And don't you know, that old devil laughs at us in our pain."

"He laughs, he does," Rachel said.

"But then, angels like yourselves, offer up your home and your hearts to a child in need, and let me tell you, Judy, Clay, there is nothing more true to the word of God than that."

"You're angels," Rachel said.

Clayton leaned forward in his chair and tapped off the ash from his cigarette into an empty beer can. "We appreciate your kind words, but what can y'all do about it? You said you had an offer of some notion?"

"We do indeed. You see, Clay, on our recent mission to the wild jungles of El Salvador and Honduras and other points south, we had chance to visit with a local padre who takes in lost souls like you and Judy are wanting to do. Only he takes them in by the dozens."

"Like eggs," Rachel said with a smile. Judy smiled back, but Sam gave her a warning look: *too much.*

"This padre, Montalban is his name, he's got more than he can handle. He's got very little money and fewer resources. When we saw your plight on the news, it came like a beam of light straight from the Lord and into our hearts—we can connect these fine people with love in their hearts with these poor children in need of that love. Across oceans and across cultures we can build a bridge and build families."

"They got little ones there?" asked Judy. "Little baby ones?"

Rachel nodded. "Sure do. Cute as a ribbon on a new dress."

"And we can right the wrong that's been done to you," Sam added.

Judy and Clayton shared a look through the smoke. They were skeptical, understandably.

"We just went through not only heartache," Clayton said. "But a deep hit to our finances, you understand?"

"We do. Of course."

And here's where Sam came armed with information. In the days since the scandal broke, lawyers and the state had been working to claw back some of that money. They hadn't been too successful, but somewhat. After Goldie's assets were drained, some hidden accounts uncovered, and a few properties sold off, each family got roughly half of what they'd put in.

Sam leaned up and set his elbows on his knees. His eyes burned a bit in the smoke, but he wanted to go in for the kill. And you could only reach the throat if you're close enough to see their eyes.

"I think what that man was doing to do was highway robbery. We can get you one of God's precious creatures up here to the States, paperwork processed, travel arranged and legalities handled, and we would only ask twenty thousand dollars. That includes a generous donation to Father Montalban so he can continue the Lord's good work."

Judy gave her husband a raised eyebrow look that said *hell, that's half of what Goldie charged us*. Exactly. And money Sam and Rachel knew sat right now in an account coming fresh off a check cut to them only last week.

Stepping off the porch, Sam gave Clayton's hand a vigorous shake. Judy and Rachel hugged like old school friends.

"Clay, you're saving a child from a life of misery, and I suspect he might be saving you too."

"You think it can be a boy?"

Sam put a hand on his shoulder. "I will guarantee it."

Clayton's face lit up and his eyes practically played a highlight reel of his son's future football achievements.

Clayton pulled Sam in close, whispering for an audience of one. He somehow knew he wasn't supposed to be saying the words sitting on his tongue.

"Will you do me a favor?"

Sam nodded.

"Try to maybe get us one who ain't so dark brown as the others? I mean, y'know, so he's comfortable around here. So he fits in a little better."

And there it was.

Sam tried not to let the shock play across his face. He hid behind his smile, one of his best defenses. "Hear you loud and clear, Clay. Your boy will be the talk of the town and the king of the prom. Don't you worry. With you and Judy on his side, the little guy will get to live the American dream."

Now it was Clayton's turn to pump Sam's arm for all it was worth.

Sam and Rachel drove away while waving out the window and calling out to stay in touch and they'd hear from them soon. A cashier's check would be sent out the next day to a P.O. box in Starkville they'd rented three days ago.

"One down," Sam said. "Not a bad start."

"Not bad? It was perfect. You were perfect."

She leaned over and kissed him as he drove. He swerved and laughed as she broke the clinch and settled back into her seat, smiling.

"You did pretty well yourself."

"I still have to find my accent. It's easy to go too big."

"Babe, you're doing fine. Now who's next on the list?"

Sam ticked up the A/C a notch and they headed East. After a mile of road had passed under them, Rachel turned in her seat and, smiling, said, "Montalban?"

Sam smiled at his own cleverness. "Hey, we're selling a fantasy, right? Why not use the name of the ultimate fantasy-maker?"

"As I recall not all of those fantasies went according to plan."

"Not for them. But for the man in charge? Every time, baby."

CHAPTER 4

A week later they have four couples signed up, checks in hand. Two had said no and Sam and Rachel turned one down. They arrived at a trailer home, rusted and sagging to one side. The single woman living there clearly didn't have enough money to raise a child, let alone the cash to hand over to Sam and Rachel. How she came up with the first forty grand was a mystery to them.

If they took another twenty off this woman she'd never recover. Their early success gave them some cushion, so they decided it was best to leave that one alone and move on. They were grifters, not sadists.

Only four to go.

Some members of the Shepherds were more well-hidden than the others. These last few seemed to not want to be found. Sam and Rachel kept their ears open and asked casual questions when they stopped to eat or fill up on gas. Some folks had powerful opinions on the Shepherds. Some claimed they handled snakes, one said they bled goats when they all got together out in tents back in the woods to worship.

"Least they don't burn no crosses no more," said Manny, a gas station owner whose dark black skin looked like worn leather from the seat of a well-ridden Harley. He sat and watched, but did not help Sam pump the gas.

"I thought those were just stories," Sam said.

"Nah. That there is the truth. Them golden lamb people come from bad stock. White sheets. Know how to tie a rope, y'understand?"

"Yes, sir. I think I do."

"Jesus come down and see what they're doin' in his name, he'd spit, then shit, then go on back up to heaven."

"So you're not one of the flock, then?" Sam asked with a grin.

Manny waved away the ridiculous notion. "What y'all want with them folks anyway?"

Rachel sipped at the straw dunked in a glass bottle of Coke. "We want to show them the error of their ways."

Manny laughed like dragging sandpaper across rough wood. "Good luck with that."

The next name on the list were the Whitmans, Barb and Ed. They'd found out Ed's nickname was Whip and that he spent a lot of his time away in Georgia where the aluminum siding company he worked for had moved their factory. Apparently he was rooted to this stretch of Mississippi, though, so he kept he and Barb there.

"I get why she wants a baby, then," Rachel said.

"Why?"

"Being alone like that? She wants some company."

"I guess."

"He's probably having an affair, too."

"You sure do seem to know a lot about human nature this afternoon."

"All day, every day, baby." She smiled and leaned over to steal a kiss while he drove. "And we're getting wealthy because of it."

She was right. Eighty grand so far and the potential for eighty more. This would make a nice score, all the more so due to how it all came together so quickly.

"Is this it?" Sam pointed to a dirt road turnoff. All around them stretched flat, brown weeds and clumps of trees off in the distance like the ground was a scalp with receding hair. Sam wasn't quite sure what Whip saw in this place that he wouldn't relocate to be closer to his job, but he stopped wondering about people's odd motivations years ago. The only thing that mattered was to get those motivations moving in the direction he wanted.

They bumped down the long dirt road and came upon a house easily a hundred years old. Wraparound porch, faded glory to go along with the faded paint. At one time this had likely been a fine place probably surrounded by fertile land. Today it looked tired and the land unkempt.

The steps up onto the porch creaked and the boards were worn into little u-shaped pockets from the decades of shoes trodding toward the front door. Several panes of glass on the ornate but out-of-date door were missing, filled in with crudely cut cardboard. In the window beside the door a small sign leaned against the glass with an illustration of a revolver pointed at them and the words in red: Never Mind The Dog, Beware Of The Owner.

Sam and Rachel traded a look and he pulled back on the screen door to knock. The hinges screeched like a cat with its tail under a rocking chair. He knocked hard three times.

They could hear footsteps and then the door opened and a short, pudgy, woman stood there with a smile filling her entire pie-plate face.

"How can I help y'all? Car trouble?"

Sam wished he had a hat to take off for her. "You must be Barb."

Her smile grew even wider. "Why yes, I am."

Sam could sense Rachel out of the corner of his eye giving him a look that said *I told you she was lonely.*

It took very little explaining before they were invited inside and served lemonade, a plate of cookies and offered a homemade apple crumble.

"Oh, no thank you, Barb. I wouldn't want you to go to any trouble."

"It's a family recipe. Don't even have to look at it anymore. Got it all right here." She tapped her temple.

Rachel held up her lemonade. "This is fine, thank you."

Inside, the house was well maintained, clean to a fault and nicely decorated, if outdated by a few decades. This was a woman who had been nesting, maybe for years even before the last scam.

They got back to discussing Goldie Washau. It seemed to be the only topic that could clear the smile from her face.

"He came to us good people and he used our desire for a family. I swear he's got Satan himself inside the man."

"Or at least sitting on his shoulder," Sam said before biting into a cookie.

"That's absolutely right."

"Barb, I can tell from your lovely home that you don't have any children at all, is that right?"

"That's right. We haven't been so blessed, just yet. I know some people in the flock gave him money to grow their families, but we just wanted to start one of our own."

"And I believe you will. We're excited to help you do that."

Barb flushed and set down her glass. The idea of a baby excited her.

"I will tell you, I cried for a week when I found out there was no baby coming. I laid right down and cried."

"And Ed took it pretty hard too, I bet?"

"Oh, well…Whip, he's…he's a strong one. Not one for emotions." She held out a hand to Rachel, like a plea for her to understand. "But as soon as he has a little one of his own, I know his heart is gonna melt like butter."

"Don't they all?" Rachel said.

"Well, the good news is," Sam said. "It's all going to happen very fast. Father Montalban is eager to get these children placed with loving families and the paperwork is all set to go. The only thing missing is payment and we can have your little angel in your arms in two weeks' time."

Tears brimmed at the corners of Barb's eyes.

"So, the thing is…"

She was reluctant to tell them something. Sam knew he was close to closing this one. Whatever this last hiccup, he could overcome it.

"What is it, Barb? You can tell us."

Rachel leaned over and laid a hand on Barb's chubby one. Sam knew the ploy of a little human contact, on the right mark, worked like setting the hook on a big catch.

"You see, Whip…he…he doesn't know I gave the money for the first one."

Sam and Rachel traded a look, nearly breaking character.

Barb went on. "It was sort of a surprise. And Whip's not around much these days. He's going to love the baby no matter what, I just…didn't tell him yet."

"And what a glorious surprise it will be," Sam said. "I hope you don't think I'm blaspheming when I dare to say it reminds me of another little surprise that came to a woman named Mary and her husband Joseph."

25

Barb blushed and hid her smile behind those fat little hands.

The sound of tires on the dirt road outside made them all lift their heads. Barb checked the clock on the wall.

"Oh, dear," she said. Once again the smile had faded. "It's Whip."

CHAPTER 5

"Barbara!"

It wasn't a *Hi honey, I'm home* sort of call. More like someone trying to scare a raccoon away from the trash cans. Sam and Rachel stole a look between them that said: *get ready.*

Whip Whitman pounded through the door. Six-foot-four and easily two hundred fifty pounds, he was broad, thick, and moved like a boulder falling down a hill. He tossed a small suitcase to the floor where it rolled once and came to a stop against the console table just inside the door, causing the carefully placed flower vase and picture frame to wobble and threaten to topple over.

Barb put a hand to her throat, clutching at pearls that weren't there.

"What the hell is this I hear about—"

Whip saw the two visitors. He stopped, drew a few deep breaths through his open mouth, then turned back to Barb. "Who the hell are they?"

"Whip, language, please."

"I don't give a rat's fat ass about language in my own house. Who the shit are these people?"

Sam put on his best charlatan smile.

"You must be Whip." He stood and offered a hand. Whip looked at it like it was shit on a stick. "I'm Gregory and my associate here is Leah and we were just commiserating with your lovely wife here about the troubles caused to you by Goldie Washau. We want to help you is all. Really, help God help you. We are merely vessels."

"Did you have anything to do with stealing my forty grand?"

"No, no, sir. As I said, we're as disappointed in Goldie as you are."

Whip turned back to his wife. "Barb, what the hell is going on here?"

Her voice came out weak. "They're going to help us get a baby, Whip."

"Now hold on a goddamn minute…"

"Language, Whip."

"Shut the fuck up about my language. I hear word through the church that people are getting ripped off by some snake oil salesman hocking babies for sale. Then I come to find out my own goddamn wife is one of the suckers." Whip flung his hands around, gesturing at the absurdity of it all. "To the tune of forty thousand dollars."

"I was going to tell you, Whip. We were going to have a baby."

"Well now I don't got a baby and I lost forty grand. When were you gonna tell me that, you dumb bitch?"

Rachel put a hand on Sam's arm, a signal both for them get the hell out of there and to hold herself back from kicking this asshole's skull in.

Sam helped Rachel to her feet. "Clearly this is a bad time for us to be here."

Whip kept his eyes boring into his wife's soft face while he aimed a finger at Sam and Rachel. "Now I come home to find two more instruments of the devil in my own damn house, speaking with forked tongues and telling you who the hell knows what because apparently you believe whatever some sweet talkin' stranger will tell you. How much did these two want from you?"

Sam raised a hand to try to cut Barb off from speaking, but she knew better than to make her husband wait for an answer.

"Only twenty thousand. Half of the last time."

Sam closed his eyes and exhaled. Rachel tightened her grip on his arm.

Whip turned to Sam, ignoring the other woman in the room.

"That true? You trying to bilk my wife out of twenty grand, you greasy son of a bitch?"

Rachel spoke up. "We're trying to make things right so you can have the family God intended for you."

"Demons," Whip shouted. "Goddamn devils and demons right in my own house. Ain't no place safe anymore."

He reached out with long arms thick as tree branches and grabbed Sam by the lapels before he could react.

Barb screamed, "Whip!" but didn't move from her seat.

Whip pulled Sam close to him until he could smell the man's aftershave. His breath poured over Sam's face like the heat from an open furnace.

"Goddamn devils come in my house and try to steal from me? You picked the wrong man to fuck with, instrument of Satan."

With a powerful tug to the left, he threw Sam to the floor. On his way down, Sam's legs knocked over a pile of old *Reader's Digests* off the coffee table along with the plate of cookies Barb had brought out. Barb began to cry, but still didn't move.

Rachel had no such trouble.

Like a linebacker she charged, knocking into Whip and throwing him off balance but not hard enough to knock him off his feet. She reached down and put a hand under Sam's arm and lifted. Sam scrambled up, losing his fake southern accent along the way.

"Go, just go. I'm behind you."

Rachel moved quickly toward the door. Sam stepped on a *Reader's Digest* and it turned out to be slicker than a banana peel. He took two steps in place, his feet sliding on the magazine. Whip's hand snapped around his right ankle like a bear trap snapping shut.

"Lord, help me get these devils out of my house." Whip said it more like a threat than a prayer.

Sam tugged at the vice grip holding his leg. "I'm trying to leave, you dumbass."

"Whip, please," Barb whined.

Whip pulled Sam down to the floor again and used his grip on

Sam to climb back to his feet. He spun quickly and turned back to Sam with a long iron rod from the fireplace set in his hand, the hooked end pointed at Sam. The look in Whip's eyes was like nothing Sam had ever seen. He could imagine this man and his fellow Shepherds in the throes of the spirit, speaking in tongues, flinging themselves around in spasms. He saw hellfire in those eyes.

"John, three-eight," Whip said in a low growl that seemed to come from below the surface of the earth. "He who does what is sinful is of the devil, because the devil has been sinning from the beginning." He stepped closer to Sam, raising the iron over his head. "The reason the Son of God appeared was to destroy the devils work."

Sam tried to scramble backward, but the pile of magazines made an oil slick under him and he could get no grip. A shadow passed over him and for a second he thought it was the light going out for good with a solid blow to the skull from that iron, but it passed over more like a bird in flight. A fat bird.

Whip grunted and Sam could see Whip's suitcase bounce off him and crash to the floor, latches popping and spewing his extra-large clothing; dirty socks and boxer shorts, yellow-pitted T-shirts and plaid shirts with pearl buttons.

Sam looked up to see Rachel panting, her face a snarl as she watched the handiwork of her throw knock the iron from Whip's hand. She waved Sam forward and turned to hold open the door. With some effort, Sam stood. Behind him, Whip moved with surprising grace for a man so big. Rachel ran out the door and down the steps with Barb's sobs following her out into the yard. Sam made for the open door. He heard Whip's crashing steps behind him. He reached the console table and raked at it with a hand, tumbling the narrow table, the vase and the frame down behind him.

Whip stepped over, through and on top of the obstacles like they were made of paper. Sam was out of reach, but Whip put a hand on the door and slammed it shut. Sam's body had made it nearly out the door with only his right leg trailing after when the door closed. Several of the remaining glass panels in the door shattered with the impact of the heavy wooden door on Sam's leg. There was another high-pitched snap like a branch snapping in icy weather.

Sam felt the sharp sting of pain race up his leg to his brain. He cried out.

The door bounced off and drifted open. Again, Whip's hand clamped on Sam's ankle. He twisted and the shin bone that had been merely cracked, snapped clean in two. Sam felt the tear of skin over the break and the flow of blood down his leg.

Without planning he kicked with his good leg and caught Whip in the face. The blow stunned Whip enough so he loosened his grip on the broken leg and fell on his stomach half in and half out of the door.

Sam hopped on one leg down the steps and across the lawn to the car where Rachel waited. A double dose of adrenalin propelled him forward despite the dizzying pain coming from his compound fracture.

Rachel had the back door open and he tumbled in, handing off the keys to her as he did.

Rachel got the car started and spun the tires on the dirt of the front yard as Whip thudded down the porch steps. They left him behind in a cloud of dirt and dried weeds. When they spun back onto blacktop and felt safe in their getaway, Rachel turned to look over the back seat.

"Are you okay?"

With the euphoric dose of adrenalin wearing off, Sam opened his mouth wide and howled in pain until his lungs were empty.

CHAPTER 6

Whip staggered into the house, wiped his face with his thick paw and flung a palmful of sweat to the rug.

"Where's a pen?" He swung his neck side to side, turning his head but not seeing anything. "Where's a crap-a-doodle pen, Barb?"

Barb finally unsnapped her hand from in front of her mouth, fairly sure she wouldn't scream now that the two people were gone—and with them, the chance for a baby again. She opened the narrow drawer on the round side table next to the couch and took out a pen and notepaper set in lavender. Whip snapped it from her hand so fast she thought she might have lost a finger.

Breathing heavy, he wrote in big block print like a third grader.

"What's that for, Whip?"

"It's a license plate number." He clicked the pen shut, turned and looked at his wife the way a predator looks at wounded prey. "You know, Barbara, the Bible says I'm well within my rights to strike you."

She slunk back a little deeper into the couch cushions.

"A wife who disobeys can be punished. No. *Should* be punished."

"Whip, I—"

"I could. But I won't. I know deep down you're too damn stupid to have known what those folks were up too. Or Goldie for that matter. You weren't thinking. Or, the scarier notion, you were thinking and that's all the brain power you could muster was to let yourself be duped by the devil's own minions."

He took several deep breaths to calm himself.

"Fact is, a whole lot of the Shepherds found themselves under the spell of this demon and his forked tongue. But now that particular demon is in jail and I can't get at him to send him back to hell." He held up the tiny scrap of lavender paper in his giant fist. "But these two demons? I can damn well find them and extract my pound of flesh."

Rachel used every last ounce of energy to get Sam up the back stairs and into their hotel room without being seen by anyone. She never complained, though, since she knew Sam was going through much worse.

He lay on the bed biting a hand towel and squeezing his eyes shut.

"We need to get you to a hospital," she said.

He mumbled behind the towel. "No."

"Sam, this isn't the sort of thing that's going to heal on its own."

He whipped the towel out of his mouth and slapped it against the bedspread in frustration.

"I know."

"Will you at least let me look at it?"

He tried to adjust himself to more of a sitting position, but she could see the hot bolt of pain run through him.

"Go ahead."

His jeans were soaked through with blood. She sat on the bed next to him and eased his shoe off as gently as she could. He bit down on grunts of pain as best *he* could. The sock underneath was drenched. She peeled it away and it dripped a line of dots onto the bed and the carpet. She flung it aside and it landed with a splat in the wastebasket, a splatter of blood decorating the wall by the air conditioning unit.

"I'm going to try to roll up your jeans now, okay?"

He nodded with fast pumps of his neck. His eyes were clamped shut.

Moving in slow motion, Rachel rolled the cuff of his jeans once, then twice. It became clear there was no way to do this without rubbing against the wound. No way to raise the pant leg high enough without making Sam pass out from the pain.

"I need to cut them off."

"Jesus."

"We don't have scissors."

"Can you tear it?"

"It's denim. And it's wet."

Sam rolled side to side like he was trying to get away from the pain surging through his body.

"If we go to the hospital," he said. "We go on record. We have

32

fake IDs and fake everything *except* medical insurance."

"So we pay cash."

He barked out a laugh like a car backfire.

"We have at least eighty thousand that will have already cleared the bank. Plus what we cleared in Sacramento. There's that bank literally two blocks away next to the tire shop. I'll go hit the bank right now, get ten grand out and then I'm taking you to the ER."

"But if we—"

"Sam. It's what we're doing. I decided. That's that. We've got the IDs and I'll pay in cash and nobody will know we've ever been there."

"God dammit, I hope they don't have to cut off my leg."

Rachel almost laughed. She knew he was in pain, but his fear made it more stark exactly how much pain.

"They won't. They'll reset the bone, put you in a cast and that's that. Then we get the hell out of Mississippi."

"Deal."

"Okay. I'll be back as soon as I can."

She leaned over and kissed him. His face was sweaty, his lips tense. She straightened and looked at her hands. Covered in blood.

"Better go wash my hands first."

CHAPTER 7

Earl Kinney rolled by slow in his police cruiser doing just what the name suggested: cruising. He scanned the parking lot of the hotel with a lazy eye doing his bit to keep Whip happy, but really using it as an excuse to get out of the office and be seen around town. If people saw a police presence they felt safe, protected. Didn't matter if the cop behind the wheel couldn't give a dead rat's ass if these people lived or died. Or that he would drop everything on his policeman's plate (which, admittedly, wasn't much) when the deacon of his church, The Shepherds of The Golden Lamb, gave a command.

Earl didn't really think he'd actually find the car Whip was looking for, but he cruised up and down the highway and in and out of parking lots for the better part of three hours now so he could say in all honesty to Whip that he'd done his due diligence.

Then there it was.

At first he reached for the radio handset on his dash, but then remembered this was not police business. He called Whip on his cell.

"Light gray Ford, you said?"

Whip was also in his truck, out looking.

"You find it?"

"Think so."

"Think so or know so?"

Earl double-checked the plate number. Yep. That was the one. He keyed the plate into his dashboard command center. Quickly it spit back that the car was registered as a rental. No name attached so Earl had no idea who the guy was who caused Whip to have such a fit, but he knew his location.

"We're on our way," Whip said.

Earl knew that meant he'd enlisted a few other Shepherds in his hunt. Twice a year the flock—well, the men anyway—took to the woods to hunt deer. The men Whip could call on a moment's notice were obedient to him the same way Earl was, and they all owned guns and knew how to shoot.

Earl could do stuff like find a car for Whip, but when he and the boys got here, Earl would have to set them straight on what happened next. That's because Earl was in charge and the law was the law. He could already hear Whip in his head arguing about God's law coming before the laws of man, but Earl knew his job depended on those man-made details.

He parked the cruiser and kept an eye on the car until the posse arrived.

Whip brought three men with him. Some of the younger members of the flock. Eager, but dumb. Ready to spout off something they read online, but not so quick to quote scripture. More than once Whip had cautioned them to read the good book instead of the Facebook.

Still, they took orders well and owned a near-arsenal of weapons. "Which room is he in?"

Whip licked his lips as he looked across the road to the hotel.

"I don't know," Earl said. "I found his car, not his life story."

"Well, how do we know what door to bust down?"

"We're not busting any door down, Whip. You want to talk to him we got to go knock on his door like civilized people."

Whip was obviously displeased. "How do we find out which door to knock on, then?"

"We'll ask the manager."

Whip started walking away toward the lobby. Earl nearly tripped getting out of the car to join him and try to skip ahead so he could make it first through the office door.

The men cradling hunting rifles didn't faze the manager. No big deal around these parts. The man in uniform at the front of this V-shaped gang of armed men did.

As soon as he saw Earl's badge on his chest the desk manager behaved like three animals back-to-back. His eyes went wide and he ducked down behind the counter until only his eyes were showing like a meerkat on the African plains. When it became clear everyone had seen him and there was no hiding, his feet shuffled in place and his back end shimmied like a cat ready to pounce. Finally he turned and bolted like a rabbit for the back door.

"He's running," Whip said. It acted like a starter's pistol to his trio of helpers.

They vaulted up and over the counter one by one. Earl drew his pistol, confused about what was happening. Whip barked orders, but did not chase.

"Don't let him get away."

"Is that the guy?" Earl asked.

"Hell, no. My guy has a busted leg."

"So why the hell is he running?"

The manager banged out the back door, hooked a quick right and pounded on the nearest door marked Maintenance. He hammered the door like a coked-up woodpecker.

"Get, man. Cops!"

He didn't wait around to see if his message had been received. The manager took off along the backside of the hotel and cut into the woods, vanishing in only a few seconds.

The trio of Shepherds hit the back door right as the Maintenance door flew open. Two men sprinted out, one going left and one going right. Both wore air filter masks. They brought with them a sharp chemical tang in the air.

Unsure of what to do, the three Shepherds started to follow one man, doubled back and tried to chase the other, ended up colliding into each other like actors in a silent movie.

Earl arrived at the back door. He knew that smell. Meth kitchen. He saw the backs of the two cooks moving away in opposite directions. He reached for the radio on his belt.

"Charlie, this is Earl. Come back."

Whip joined him at the back door.

"Who you calling?"

"I'm calling this in, Whip. They got a goddamn meth lab here."

Earl's radio crackled. "What's up, Earl?"

"Need backup out to the Grandview Hotel. Got us a meth lab, three of 'em took off on foot."

"No shit?"

"No shit."

One of the young Shepherds stared into the open door of the maintenance room.

"I'll be damned."

Earl cautioned him. "Hey, step away from there. Those chemicals are bad news."

As if he'd willed it to happen, there came a crack and pop, then a rush of flames. It wasn't an explosion exactly, but it made everyone take a step back.

"Dammit all." Earl keyed his radio again. "Charlie, make it a fire call too. Double time."

"Got it," Charlie answered.

Earl pointed an authoritative finger at one of the young men. "Go back to the office and find the fire extinguisher."

"What about my man?" Whip asked.

"It's gonna have to wait."

Rachel stepped onto the blacktop of the Grandview parking lot and saw commotion. She kept an eye on the door to her room with Sam. All the action seemed to be happening around back, which was good. With ten thousand in cash in a bag hanging from her arm, an injured man in the room up ahead and a list of offenses longer than both her arms, Rachel knew getting caught by the police would be very, very bad.

She opened the door to the room and didn't even set the cash down.

"Can you get up? We have to go."

"What was that noise?"

"I don't know, but there's a cop car and a very familiar truck parked outside."

"Shit."

"Shit is right."

They were experts at leaving fast. Leaving it all behind was part of the gig. They didn't know if they'd ever be back to this room, but for now all that mattered was getting away. And getting Sam some help.

Bracing Sam as he struggled to stay upright, Rachel pulled open the door and searched left and right for anything she didn't want to see. Satisfied, she walked Sam to the car. She laid him in the backseat and backed out, listening to the app on her phone direct her to the nearest hospital.

As she pulled out of the parking lot, she could hear sirens approaching.

CHAPTER 8

Rachel parked in the roundabout outside the ER. She left Sam there and walked forward until the automatic doors slid open.

"I need a wheelchair."

She turned and walked back to Sam, trusting the staff would come running. Sam sat in the passenger seat trying his best to bite back the pain. It was a losing battle.

A chubby orderly came out pushing a wheelchair. Walking a little slow, Rachel thought. Trailing after him, hand on her stethoscope to keep it from banging against her sternum, was a young, tired-looking doctor.

"What's the problem?"

"He broke his leg. Badly."

The doctor bent down to peer into the car to see Sam's leg.

"Lot of blood. Is it compound?"

Rachel looked to the orderly for help, but he shrugged. "I...I don't..."

The doctor turned to Rachel. "Is the bone sticking out?"

"Oh. Yes. I think so. He wouldn't let me roll up his pant leg."

"Yeah, that would suck." She stood and turned to the orderly. "Try to help him in." She spoke to Sam as if he were hard of hearing. "If the pain is too much, we can try you on a gurney, but I don't know if it's going to be any better."

"It's fine," he said. "Let's do it."

Sam scooted to the edge of the seat and let the orderly slip a beefy hand under his armpit. He moved from the car seat to the wheelchair in one teeth-grinding motion. The orderly stopped to scratch at the patchy beard growing from his cheeks like mold on old cheese.

"Bay six," the doctor said. To Rachel she said, "Admitting is to the left. You have to move this car first, though. Ambulances only."

They left Rachel alone.

She parked the car on a side street two blocks away, better to keep out of the ticketed garage for both a quick escape and in case anyone spotted the car. She came back in to talk to the serious, dark-haired girl at the admitting desk. She placed two fake driver's licenses down and felt the weight of the brick of cash in her hip pocket. It took some explaining and some deeply suspicious stares from the dark-haired girl, but some payment was better than no payment so she filled out the forms and told Rachel to have a seat.

Whip pounded the hood of his truck.

Earl came back to where the Shepherds were waiting with Whip for an update.

"You done earning your merit badge for the day?" Whip said. "Can we get on with it?"

"I'm doing my job, Whip. This is a big-time bust." Earl meant to say it with the authority of his badge, but it came out whiny and defensive.

"Cooking meth? There's more meth kitchens around here than there are McDonalds. This'll have about as much impact as spit in the ocean."

Earl was tired, in no mood for Whip's shit. "It's still *my job*."

"Well, I'm on a mission from God. So I think that wins."

"Did you just quote *The Blues Brothers* to me?"

"Son, I don't know what the hell you're on about. All I want to know is where that car went while you were out there chasing meth-heads who look like wet dogs."

"Once I stop off and fill out the paperwork on this, I'll get back out and keep looking."

Whip waved his hands at Earl and yanked open the door to his truck. "Oh, you're goddamn useless. C'mon, boys."

The three Shepherds carried their guns to the car they all came in together.

"Whip, don't do anything stupid now."

"How could I?" Whip said as he cranked the engine. "You went and used up all the stupid there was."

He drove away in a cloud of parking lot dust.

Two and a half hours later Sam lay in a hospital room with three metal rings running down his leg from his knee to his ankle and four new screws in his shin. A long incision ran down the side of his leg closest to the bone. The metal rings were held in place by long metal pins. It looked more architectural than medical.

The doctor, a different one than the ER doctor who first examined Sam, explained to Rachel that they couldn't seal up the incision inside a plaster cast otherwise it wouldn't heal properly. This way, once the bone started to set the pins would be removed and the incision would be healed enough that they could encase his leg and he'd look like any other guy with a broken leg. Until then, they had to keep an eye on it and that meant at least forty-eight hours in the hospital and that meant thousands of dollars. Maybe their whole take from this ill-fated con-gone-wrong.

Worth it for Sam's health, though.

Rachel patted his hand. He still slept off the anesthesia and he looked much more restful than Rachel felt. She sat down in the armchair beside his bed, but she knew she wouldn't be sleeping any time soon. After thirty seconds in the chair, she reevaluated that opinion. Exhaustion took over like flood waters rising.

This whole thing went belly up real fast. Worse than almost any other time in their career.

But okay, two days here in the hospital and then he gets his cast and they get the hell out of Dodge. They could do that. Easy. The worst part would be the hospital food.

CHAPTER 9

The Shepherds gathered at the altar. The small wood plank and tarpaper shack they called a church sat well back from any paved road. This was a place build in secrecy, for secrecy. A sanctuary from the world who didn't understand them, didn't understand the true word of God. Since it was built some eighty-odd years ago, the woods surrounding it had been trying to reclaim this rectangle of land. Kudzu grew up from the bowels of Hell itself to tangle around every inch of the property. Bi-monthly cutbacks had to be scheduled. The roof was a patchwork of tiles, tarps, wood planks, thick tar and prayers to keep the water out when it rained. The gap beneath the structure had been home, over the years, to raccoons, opossums, rats, rabbits, skunks and a nest of rattlers.

Whip looked at the three men with him and pounded his fist on the pulpit.

"Where the hell are they?"

Earl wasn't among the men and none of the blank faces looking back at Whip held any answers. A middle-aged man with long-gone hair spoke up.

"We don't know, Whip. They lit out of town."

"How hard could it be, Dave, to find a pair of strangers around here? We don't get a whole lot of visitors, in case you didn't notice."

"I don't know what else we can do."

"I can't be the only one concerned that a pair of demons came to our town and preyed on our wives. And I'm not even the only one who lost money. Jake, your wife gave them money, didn't she?"

"Twenty thousand dollars' worth," Jake said. He left out the part where he signed the check and shook Sam's hand same as his wife did.

"Well, there you go," Whip said. "And we're just gonna let them go?"

A younger man, fat around the middle, entered the open door of the church. The floorboards creaked when he stepped in. They creaked for everyone, but extra loudly for him. The men turned to look and he gave a sheepish look, scratched at his patchy beard with one hand and held out a six pack of beer with the other.

"Thought you boys might could use a—"

"Not now, Ezekiel."

The chubby boy lowered his outstretched arm.

An older man, Clement, took a few steps toward him, arms out to accept the beer.

"We done told you, Ezekiel, we ain't takin' any new members right now."

"Besides," Dave said. "This here is a closed-door meeting."

Ezekiel pointed over his shoulder. "But the door was open."

Clement took the beer from the boy and patted him on the shoulder. "Now's not a good time, okay?"

"When do you think I could take my baptism and join? Last time you said it would be—"

Dave raised his voice. "Not *now*, Ezekiel."

Ezekiel turned to leave, shot down again.

Whip pounded on the pulpit with renewed vigor to get everyone's attention back after the interruption. "How hard could it be to find a man with a broken leg and a succubus by his side? The devil has his trickster ways, but I believe we can outsmart ol' scratch this time."

"And then beat his ass," Jake said.

"Bring down the righteous fist of God." Whip made a fist and laid it on the pulpit as if it were something to behold.

"I saw a fella with a busted leg."

Everyone turned to the doorway again where Ezekiel stood half in and half out.

"Where?" Whip asked.

"At the hospital. Where I work."

A few of the men traded looks. Other than his name and the fact that his momma was a drunk and at one time had been a truck stop whore, they didn't know basic information about the young man trying to become a Shepherd of the Golden Lamb. They'd dismissed him. Until now.

Whip eyeballed his congregation. "Didn't you check the hospital?"

"Yeah," Dave said. "No matching car in the lot."

"Did you ask at the desk?"

Dave looked at his feet. "Well...no. But you said they'd be idiots not to go somewhere out of town. You said it was dumb to even check the hospital."

"I don't think I said that at all."

Dave looked at Clement who quickly darted his eyes away, not wanting to get into a direct conflict with Whip. Dave bit his lip and stayed quiet.

Whip turned away with a shake of his head. He said to Ezekiel, "Was there a woman with him?"

"Yes, sir. I helped a guy out of a car and a woman with him was running around barking orders."

Whip beckoned him back inside. "How long ago was this?"

"This afternoon." Ezekiel creaked floorboards up the aisle.

"They was from out of town?"

"Didn't really hear him but she didn't sound like she was from 'round here."

"What kind of car was they driving?"

Ezekiel stopped and thought. "It was gray. Or silver."

"A Ford?"

"Could'a been."

Whip uncurled his fist and extended his hand to shake. "Ezekiel."

Ezekiel took two creaking steps forward to take Whip's hand. "Welcome to the flock."

CHAPTER 10

Sam opened his eyes and took a moment to figure out where he was. Definitely institutional. Right, a hospital. He saw Rachel, eyes closed, head slumped to the side. *Was she hurt? No, wait. She's in a chair. I'm in a bed. Oh, yes, I'm hurt.*

Sam glanced down at his leg and quickly looked away. His gasp woke Rachel.

"Hey, there. You're up."

"What the hell did they do to my leg?"

Rachel gave him a slightly patronizing look, acknowledging he was still a little out of it. She reached for the button to ring for a nurse, but stopped herself. She could handle Sam better than anyone on Earth and they both knew it.

"They couldn't do a cast since they had to keep the incision available for treatment. The metal rings are to keep it place without a cast, and the pins are to keep the metal rod in your shin bone. Any other questions?"

Sam slowly rose to the surface back into full consciousness. He let out a deep sigh and sank back into his pillows.

"Okay. I remember now." He saw her set down a book on the side table. He looked closer and saw it was a Bible. "Really?"

She shrugged. "You were not much for conversation the past few hours so I figured I'd read up a bit on what these Shepherds are all so gung-ho about."

"And?"

"Not much of a story. A whole lotta names, some of them really weird. Overall, kind of confusing. I can see how it can get misinterpreted a lot."

"You let me know if you're going to run off and become a nun. Then again," he raised his eyebrows. "Maybe that'd be hot. You do look good in black."

"I'd say go ahead and ask for more pain killers but it sounds like maybe you've had enough."

"It's a dull throb right now. I can deal with it."

"How about coffee then? I can get you that without a prescription."

"Okay, yeah."

"Glad to see you back."

She leaned over and kissed him on the forehead. When she stood straight, she wiped at her lips. "Remind me to request a sponge bath for you."

"Sorry."

She gave a small wave as she walked out to find coffee.

Ezekiel walked from his parked car to Whip's truck. Jake, Dave and Clement sat on the back bench seat behind Whip.

"So what now?" Ezekiel asked.

Whip rolled his eyes. "You brought us here. You tell me."

Ezekiel stammered a bit, shooting glances over at the hospital entrance. "I don't...we can't really just go in there and bring him out. There's forms and shit to fill out."

"Can't you check him out, Mr. Big Shot?"

"I'm not even on the schedule today."

Whip closed his eyes in a prayer for patience. "Ezekiel, can you get us inside there or not?"

"I can get maybe one inside. But then what?"

"Let us worry about that." Whip cut his eyes to the rearview mirror. "Any volunteers?"

The three men framed hip to hip all averted their eyes. Again, Whip had to ask Jesus for strength.

"Jake, you'd know him if you saw him, right?"

"I guess so."

"Then you go with Ezekiel and make sure it's him."

"Okay. Then what?"

"You carrying?"

"Not a pistol. Got my pocketknife."

"Good enough. Now what, boys, is the devil best at?"

Like kids in Sunday school they all waited on the other one to answer. When none came forward, Dave ventured a timid, "Trickery?"

"That's right. And here he's taken the human form. Now, Jake, what I want you to do is make sure this is the fella, then you make your mark on him." Whip moved his thumb through the air in the sign of a cross. "You put that in this demon's flesh and watch him bleed. You'll know sure enough if he's evil through and through."

45

Jake nodded. "Whereabouts?"

"It don't matter."

"Doesn't need to be, like, on the forehead or nothing? Like a preacher giving a baptism or something?"

"Carve it in his arm, in his ass, I don't care." Whip turned to Ezekiel. "What time is visiting hours?"

"Goes until five."

With an angry sigh he said, "It's after five now. What time do they start up in the morning?"

"Nine a.m."

"Okay then. When Jake finds out this is our man, then, Ezekiel, you fix it so he moves rooms in the morning. Get him away from that woman. You get him moved and tell me where he is so I can find him and I'll take it from there. Me and God together. We'll bring the fight right to that ol' devil."

Ezekiel shrugged his shoulders. "I'm just an orderly. I can't transfer a room. There's forms and shit."

"You got until tomorrow morning to figure it out. One thing Shepherds ain't, is naysayers. We say yes to God in our hearts and we say yes to our elders making a suggestion. You get me?"

"Yes, sir."

"That's more like it. Now go on, you two."

Jake had to climb over Dave to get out. Whip sat and watched Ezekiel lead Jake in through the front door. He closed his eyes and tilted his head skyward.

"Lord, speak to me. Give me a plan here. I bought us a little time until tomorrow morning, but then we need to know what to do. Guide my hand, Lord. Guide my hand against the evil in this world."

There came a long moment of silence. Dave and Clement in the backseat waited for the voice of God to come booming through the truck's cab. When it became clear Whip wasn't getting through to the deity, Clement said, "You ain't got no plan, Whip?"

They could hear the sound of Whip's teeth grinding even through his closed-lip grimace.

"I'm waiting for the Lord to tell me what to do. Clem, you can't take a shit without your wife's permission so if I were you I'd keep my damn mouth shut."

Clement and Dave shared a look and the truck settled back into silent prayer.

CHAPTER 11

Ezekiel felt sweat drip down his back. This wasn't what he expected when he thought about being a member of the Shepherds of the Golden Lamb. He pictured prayer meetings and late-night poker games with the boys. Not this eye-for-an-eye mission they were on.

At least it was Biblical in that sense.

With Jake in tow, Ezekiel walked up to the reception desk. Judy had her wide backside parked in her rolling chair where it wouldn't rise from that threadbare seat for the entire eight hours of her shift. She ruled over the lobby of Grace Memorial Hospital from that throne with a skunk eye that could stop a train and a shrill voice that could cut glass.

"Hi, Judy." Ezekiel spoke quickly, rushing words on top of each other. "This here is my uncle and he wanted to look around where I work so I said I'd show him some stuff but don't worry we won't bother no one and I won't take him on the ICU or anything and we won't go to maternity and obviously he can't see no surgeries or nothing like that, but I'll just show him the break room and the mop closet maybe."

Judy's eyes narrowed at him, like she was trying to decide if he was normal stupid or really extra stupid.

"Zeke, I don't have time for this right now."

Ezekiel laughed, but he didn't know why. "Okay then. See you later."

He bulleted for the elevators and Jake had to rush to catch up. Inside the steel box when the doors closed Ezekiel exhaled what seemed like an entire hot air balloon's worth, filling the tiny box with sour breath.

Jake said, "I think it's best you don't say anything unless you really have to, okay?"

"Okay."

The bell dinged and they stopped on three.

Sam had let himself drift off again. Not much else to do when you couldn't walk. He heard low voices and thought for a moment how nice it was the nurses didn't want to wake him. He hoped they weren't here to take more blood. The busted leg was no fun, but needles were only a small step up.

The two hushed voices seemed to be in a disagreement. Sam slid his eyes open a sliver. One man, the tubby one, looked vaguely familiar. The other one, a middle-aged man, did too. He listened to their whispered argument.

The middle-aged one said, "Where do you think I should do it?"

The chubby one said, "I don't know. Anywhere."

"Like, his arm? Or does it need to be, like, over his heart or something?"

"How should I know?"

"Well, what did you think?"

"I think you should decide."

These weren't nurses. Sam opened his eyes all the way. They didn't notice. Sam did notice, however, the thin bladed knife in the middle-aged one's hand. It wasn't much, just a pocketknife. The kind not much good for anything other than carving your sweetheart's initials in some tree bark.

But still, a knife.

"What's going on?"

Both men froze still, caught in the act. They turned to Sam like if they moved slow he couldn't see them. He knew them now. The fat one was the orderly who helped him into a wheelchair when he arrived. A hospital employee. A good sign. The other one, Sam knew him from a visit to his house. And the twenty-thousand-dollar check the man signed over. This was one of his marks. But what did they have to do with each other? And why was he holding a pocket-knife?

The fat one said, "We're here to check on you."

Sam waited for more specifics. He got only silence.

"Check on what?" he finally asked.

The fat one's eyes darted around the room, finally landing on the control panel for his bed.

"The bed. The recline feature. It's broken."

"No, it's not."

"Yes, it is."

"No, it's not."

"Yes, it is."

Then, a woman's voice. "What's going on here?"

The men turned quickly this time. Rachel stood in the doorway, a paper cup of coffee in each hand and a quizzical look on her face. She, too, clocked the knife.

"Something's not right," Sam said.

The fat one was sweating. "Cut 'im," he shouted.

The one with the knife spun and slid the thin blade across Sam's arm making a straight line. Rachel moved forward and tossed hot coffee in the fat one's face. He screeched and collapsed. His friend turned and got the second cup right in the kisser. He reached for his scalded face with both hands, and with them came the pocketknife. The narrow blade plunged through his ear, making a thin opening in the cartilage. Both men were hollering and slipping on spilled coffee as they tried to gain their footing.

Sam had a hand clamped over the slice in his forearm. With his injured hand he pressed the nurse call button.

Rachel stepped over to the two strangers in her room and planted a firm heel of her shoe in each of their chins. They screamed even more. She held on to the railing of Sam's bed for leverage as she stomped the men twice more. The bed rocked with her effort.

"Babe, babe," Sam said. "Stop shaking the bed."

She looked at him and his grimace of pain. He pointed with a blood-soaked arm at his mechanical-looking leg contraption.

"Oh, shit, sorry."

The cavalry coming down the hall arrived on squeaky shoes. Two nurses rushed into the room and stopped in the doorway. Women used to seeing it all had to stop and take a moment to understand the scene in front of them. The two writhing men on the floor. The coffee puddle. The woman standing over the defeated men with blood on her shoes.

One nurse with straight black hair pulled back in a long ponytail leaned out into the hallway and called out, "Mac! Get in here."

Twenty minutes later Jake and Ezekiel were downstairs in custody and Jake was getting his broken nose set in the ER. Mac, the security guard on the third floor, had seemed genuinely excited to be able to use his plastic zip cuffs for once. He kept moving his hand over his pepper spray, but Rachel had sufficiently subdued the men so all the fight had gone out of them.

Doctor Post, the same woman who saw Sam when he checked in, leaned over the bed and put the final few stitches in Sam's arm. Twelve total. She said it was a clean cut, at least. No Frankenstein scars for him.

"So," Doctor Post said. "Do I want to know why those guys wanted to cut you?"

"We had a misunderstanding," Sam said.

"Same misunderstanding that led to this?" she said while pointing at his leg.

"I believe so."

"We're sorry," Rachel said. "We didn't expect them to come here."

"Lucky you have good aim with coffee." She turned to Rachel. "You pitch softball in high school or something?"

"No. Just lucky."

She turned back to tie off the last stitch. "Yeah, your partner

50

here seems to be the unlucky one this week."

"You can say that again," Sam said.

Doctor Post stood. "Well, Zeke certainly doesn't have a job here anymore. And the other man I recognize from around town. He's one of the Shepherds. Did you do something to piss them off?"

"I don't think we'll have any more trouble," Rachel said.

"I hope not. People come here to get better. If they keep getting more injuries while they're here, it's bad for our reputation." She peeled off the latex gloves. "At least you were already admitted."

"Thanks, Doctor," Sam said.

"The good news is your leg is looking great. No infection or anything. You heal fast."

"Good genes."

"Once we get a real cast on that leg you can get up and start moving around better. Then we can get you out of here. I see on your chart that you're paying cash."

"Yeah."

"I'll do my best to move things along and get you out quickly, okay?"

"That would be appreciated."

"All right. Get some rest. Those two won't bother you any-more. If you made anyone else mad, do us a favor and leave a list at the front desk."

She smiled as she walked out.

Rachel turned to Sam. "She's funny."

"Gallows humor. It's the only way doctors can function with-out getting depressed with all the sick people and death."

"Well, I'm not laughing at this."

They both studied the zig-zagging stitches on Sam's arm.

Sam asked, "Do you think those guys will spill to the cops about the scam?"

"I think they have a lot to lose if they do. My bigger worry is that they obviously didn't get to finish whatever they came here for. That means this isn't over yet."

"I guess you'd better get some more coffee. We might want to stay up."

CHAPTER 12

Whip watched as Ezekiel and Jake were led out of the hospital in handcuffs.

"You don't think those two idiots are dumb enough to talk about what they were doing in there, do you?" Dave asked. He and Clement had spread out across the back-seat bench of Whip's truck.

Whip shook his head. "I don't know how much sense the good Lord gave that fat kid. Jake knows to keep his mouth shut." Then, under his breath, "Damn cops."

One tenet the Shepherds preached as a founding idea to their world view was that the only law was God's law. Those who wore a badge were only pretending to have authority, and were undermining the rule of God.

But they could use Rudy so he was okay.

"My fear now," Whip said, "is that they'll get spooked and try to light out and get far away from here."

"Even if we miss them," Clement said. "Won't God strike them down eventually?"

"Clem, have I not told you in loud enough tones that I am the hammer of God in this situation? He is flowing through me. I'm only here to carry out God's will. And his will is that this punk and his woman deserve a beat down, Old Testament style."

"Well how do we get in there and get after him?"

"The Lord will show us a way."

With a timing as deft as any great magician, the air filled with the sound of a siren. It began as a low wail, then grew in volume and urgency. The ambulance came to a tire-chirping stop and the back doors flew open.

Whip turned to his two sidekicks. "What did I tell you? The

Lord will provide."

He jerked the door open and left Dave and Clement to scramble past the front seat to get out and follow.

The trio walked into a melee of shouting voices and people in scrubs giving orders. A station wagon had pulled in shortly after the ambulance and a woman got out sobbing and yelling about her poor, poor husband.

"Ma'am, you can't park here. This is the emergency vehicle lane."

She sobbed out a few more, *My husband, my husband* before another man put an arm around her and led her back to the truck. A stretcher slid from the back of the ambulance and a paramedic stayed with it closely pumping his fist around an air bag to breathe for the man laying catatonic on the stretcher.

Whip led Dave and Clement through the scrum and into the lobby. The sobbing woman had everyone on edge and a doctor called for people to clear the way as they rolled the unconscious man through. Even the people waiting with other injuries took a moment to gawk at the man in much worse shape than they were. But even so, a woman with an ice pack to her temple said out loud to no one, "Aw, c'mon, I was here first."

Whip reached the elevator bank and hurried Dave and Clement to join him. The doors shut and it fell refreshingly quiet.

Dave asked, "Do you know where they are?"

Whip stared at the buttons, one through five. "I do not." He pressed two.

"Do me a favor," Sam said. "Let's not come back to Mississippi for a while. Maybe ever."

Rachel smiled and nodded in agreement. "Where to next, then?"

"I'm thinking the opposite. Like Minnesota. Or Maine."

"Sticking with M, huh?"

"Nothing more opposite than a state that seems like it might be the same but then is different in every way."

"Hard to argue that." Rachel put her feet up on the edge of Sam's bed. "I'm sorry this one has gone so shitty for you."

Sam waved off her sympathy. "Hey, that's the game. As long as it isn't the cops, I can take a few rednecks and a few stitches."

Rachel looked at his fresh arm wound. "Do you think he was trying to kill you with that little whittling knife?"

"I don't know. Looks like he was trying to sign his name."

She looked at the single straight line. "Must start with an L."

"Levon? That's a good southern name, right?"

"Leroy?"

"We may never know."

Sam sighed as the smile relaxed from his face. "You don't want to hear this, but I need to go to the bathroom."

Rachel straightened up. "You want me to call the nurse?"

"No, I can make it on my own. Well, not entirely on my own. You need to help some."

"I'm not helping you with that."

"Just get me in there, I can take care of the rest."

Rachel dropped the rails down on one side of the bed and Sam scooted himself up to a sitting position. She stood by to take as much weight as he needed to put on her. He swung his leg and the metal contraption over the edge of the bed. He sucked air between his teeth.

"You okay?"

"Yeah," he said. "I might need to order up some of those pain-killers when I get back."

"Lean on me. I you need to stop, just say so."

"I need to go, that's the problem."

"Quit joking around and focus."

Using her like a crutch, Sam stood and limped his way into the bathroom.

Whip stopped at the nurse's station on the second floor.

"Excuse me. I'm looking for my brother. He came in here with a real busted up leg?"

The nurse at the desk crinkled her brow at him. "What's his name?"

"Well now, he might not be using his right name because you see," he glanced over each shoulder then dropped his voice to a low whisper. "He's got some outstanding alimony payments. 'Bout three years' worth if I'm honest. He don't want Darlene to be able to find him, so…"

He gave a shrug of his shoulders and waited to see if she would be kind enough to help him. She tapped at her computer.

"No broken legs on this floor."

"Thank you, kindly. I'll try upstairs."

"When you get off the elevator, turn left. To the right is maternity and I don't think he'd be in there."

"No, ma'am, I think you're right."

Whip nodded and have her a smile. He walked away and pulled Dave and Clement in his wake.

CHAPTER 13

Sam adjusted himself in bed. Being idle wasn't his thing. Bedridden was even worse. Even talking about painful things sounded better than sitting still in silence trying to think about the pain in his leg.

"So how much is this all costing us?"

"A lot." Rachel never lied to Sam, and wasn't about to start now. "But we'll manage. Good news is, before it all went to shit, this was quite lucrative play for us."

"Yeah," Sam mused, remembering it like a long ago weekend of romance. "It was a cool score. Bad target, though. Damn fundamentalists."

"I don't even know what to call them."

"Nut jobs?"

"That'll do."

* * *

Whip got off the elevator on three. Didn't even look back to see if his two sidekicks were with him. Whip was in hunt mode. The same mental headspace when he sat still in a blind for six hours waiting on a buck he just *knew* was there. A mixture of patience and a lust for the kill that made him an excellent hunter.

Would he kill Sam and the woman if he found them? He honestly wasn't sure yet himself. He'd set out on a path of righteous vengeance and prayed the Lord would guide his hand when the time came.

He veered away from the maternity side of the floor, the sound of crying babies like a warning siren. Whip stepped forward to the nurse's desk and played the same gambit as before about the fake brother.

Behind Whip, Clement and Dave slid left and right trying to keep up and moving like the tail of a snake. Neither one knew what would come if they found this guy's room. Neither one would admit it to the other, but when they saw Jake and Zeke being carted out in handcuffs, they both started to doubt the Lord's plan in all this. Perhaps Whip misinterpreted the signs. Maybe the busted leg was payback enough.

Clement whispered to Dave, "What do you think?"

"I ain't so sure."

"Whip sure is."

"Yeah, I can see that."

The nurse behind the counter pointed down the hall and Whip smiled.

Clement said, "Looks like we're gonna find out."

"Looks that way."

Whip turned to them with a grin on his mouth more sinner than saint. He jerked his neck to the right and started walking with a purpose like Jesus about to walk on water.

* * *

An hour earlier Barb had answered the phone hoping to hear Whip. Instead she got Earl, one of the Shepherds and all she knew about him really is that he was a cop. Shepherds called the house all the time and they all wanted to talk to Whip about church stuff. The things he kept her out of. Cut her off from the inside scoop, and from any decision making at all.

"That's for the men to decide," he'd say. Then he'd quote scripture so it would make it impossible to argue with him.

"He's not home, Earl."

"Do you know if he went to the hospital?"

She clutched at her heart. "The hospital? Whatever for?"

"No, no. Just to see someone. He's fine. I just…well, we brought in two fellas who caused a ruckus over to the hospital. Fellow Shepherds, y'know?"

"And you think it has something to do with Earl?"

"I also come to find out the man and woman who tried rob you—"

"Nobody robbed me."

"Okay, scam you then. Well, they ended up at the hospital and I know Whip was stinging mad about it and, well, when Jake got brought in I just thought…"

Barb sighed. "Is he in a mess of trouble?"

"I'm trying to avoid that if I can. You know Whip's temper sometimes."

She did know. All too well.

"I'm not sure if he's there or not but there's one way to find out."

"You're right. I'll swing by and—"

"You'll come get me first. If he needs talking to, I'm the only one who can do it."

"That won't be necessary, Barb."

"I hope it won't, but if it is, you'll be glad to have me along. I don't mean nothing by it, but he don't respect that badge of yours none. Sometimes I'm the only one who can talk him out of bad intentions."

Earl sighed into the phone. "Okay then. I'll come by."

Barb hung up and went to change into a new outfit. She couldn't remember the last time she'd gone into town.

CHAPTER 14

Rachel released him from the kiss. Alone in a room together, it was only a matter of time before they were nuzzled up next to each other, kissing and usually more.

"Better be careful now," Sam said. "The doctor said no vigorous activity."

"Vigorous? Well, someone thinks highly of their skills in bed, don't they?"

She smiled at him and pulled him into another kiss. Moments like this, eyes closed and enjoying each other, Rachel marveled at their life together. If they could make it through a mess like Mississippi and come out as strong as ever in their relationship, they could do anything. They worked the grift so well because most days it felt like they were two people with one heartbeat. They knew what the other was thinking, and sure, lots of couples claim that. Rachel and Sam lived it. And in times of adversity? When the money dried up, or when she'd had the miscarriage? Or more to the moment at hand, when some psycho hillbilly started breaking legs and cutting arms, it never broke them. Only made them stronger.

Rachel heard the door open. No knock, no nurse announcing herself. Good thing their intimacy hadn't progressed any further. She had been prepared to make Sam work it out even with his broken leg.

Breaking the kiss she looked up. Not nurses. Definitely not doctors. These two barely had one high school diploma between them, she'd bet.

"Can I help you?"

The older one tapped the other on the shoulder and pointed at Sam. "Busted leg." He leaned back out the open door and said to someone in the hall, "It's them."

The door opened wide and in walked Whip with a shit-eating grin on his face like he was first in line at the all-you-can-eat shit buffet.

Rachel went rigid, put a hand on Sam's. She could feel him tense as he lay there, helpless. One heartbeat.

"Well, well," Whip said. "Well, well, well."

"You must have been looking for us for a while and all you got to say for finding us is well, well, well?"

"I try not to let the devil tempt my tongue into profanity. But maybe this once." He aimed a pistol-like finger at them. "I fucking got you."

Rachel tightened her grip on Sam. "Okay, so now what?"

Silence took over the room. These three hadn't thought that far ahead.

"You come with us."

"And how do you suggest we do that, genius?" Rachel gestured to Sam laid out in bed, the contraption on his leg, the wheelchair.

The older one piped up. "Let's roll him out of here."

"Yeah," Whip said. "I'll be your chauffeur. Now get in the chair."

"And then what?" Rachel said. Stall them. Wait for a nurse. Don't let them get you to a location of their choosing. No telling what this fat-ass Jesus freak would do.

"You let us worry about that. Whatever the good Lord has in store for you, he'll let me know soon enough."

"And here I thought you were in charge."

"I am but a vessel."

Damn. Appealing to his ego didn't rattle him the way she wanted. Rachel knew Sam had the same thoughts she did. Don't make a fuss. Don't bring the cops into this. There was no way to bring law enforcement into this without Rachel and Sam ending up in jail. And a stay in jail anywhere in the U.S. would travel up a pipeline that eventually led back to Little Vincent in Philly. So go along with them, wait for your opportunity. Trust that we're smarter than them.

"You think you're gonna roll us right out of here, is that it?" Rachel said. "You can't even check out a library book without a card. Taking a whole person away from the people sworn to take care of him might be a bit harder."

Whip grew visibly frustrated. He made eye contact with Sam. "You let your woman do all the talking for you?"

"She seems to be doing pretty damn well at it."

"Get in the damn chair or we'll *put* you in it. I don't think your leg is gonna feel too good when we do, bedside manner not being a strong suit."

The two sidekicks made an attempt to look hard, but it failed. Still, three against two. And really, Sam didn't have much to contribute when it came to physical resistance. So go along. Wait for the chance. And for God's sake, don't ever come back to Mississippi.

Barb let Earl do the talking. The head nurse at the reception desk knew him, probably from late night ER visits with criminals or victims. Barb hated to think about all the violence in the world. Satan incarnate.

"Got a question about one of your patients," Earl said.

Barb left him to it and looked around the waiting area. Not too crowded. Nothing too serious looking. On the floor by a chair near the corner were a dozen droplets of dried blood and she had to look away.

The automatic doors to the ER opened and two men rushed in hollering something awful.

"He needs a doc."

They were dressed for hunting: camouflage head to toe, bright orange vest over their chests, heavy mud-caked boots, twigs and small leaves stuck in their beards. The shouting man had a shoulder under his buddy and Barb had to do a double take to make sure she really saw what she thought. The friend had an arrow sticking from high in his chest, above his heart but not by much. A dark stain of blood soaked into his high visibility vest and the man looked weak from blood loss. Barb swooned a bit herself. She grabbed onto Earl's arm for support.

"I gotcha," he said. "Let's get on out of here. I know where we're going."

With a hand up to shield her eyes, Barb let herself be led toward the elevators.

CHAPTER 15

Whip steered the wheelchair toward the elevator.

"Looks like you found him."

The bright, chubby-faced nurse smiled at the group as they moved past. Whip returned her look with a pasted-on smile. "Sure did. Just taking him on a little walkabout. Well, a roll-about."

Whip chuckled like a mall Santa while patting Sam's shoulder with a firm grip and a hard slap. Sam gave a pained smile and Rachel kept her eyes on the floor. Clement pressed the elevator call button.

The nurse gave a little wave. "You just be sure to have him back by dinner time."

Whip patted his belly. "Mmm-mmm. Wouldn't want to miss that."

The two side-by-side elevators dinged at the same time. The door on the left opened first and Whip hustled the group inside. Dave was the last one in as the right-hand door slid open and officer Earl stepped out with Barb on his arm, her eyes down to avoid seeing anything else to put her in mind of the violence that plagued the world.

* * *

Sam tried to identify the light, instrumental music in the elevator. He wanted to know what easy listening crap would be the sound-track to his death. He had no idea how they were going to get out of this and he felt useless knowing that whatever the outcome, he would be almost no help at all with these physical limitations. He tried to catch Rachel's eye but she kept staring at the floor. He knew she was thinking. Nothing in that woman would ever give up. Nothing in her would let these redneck Bible thumpers win. He also knew that sometimes, the bad guys win.

It's what kept them in the money all these years.

Was this some sort of cosmic payback for all the years of grift-ing? Maybe. It's the downside of not really buying into an afterlife—if there was going to be justice served, it was going to be here on earth.

"Okay," Whip said. "When we get out, we head straight for my truck. Dave, you and Clem will have to ride in the bed. Ain't enough room for all of you in the cab. Plus his bad leg's gonna have to lay out flat on the bench in back."

Dave and Clement looked disappointed.

"We'll get out to the church and see what the Lord guides my hand to do with y'all." He lowered a stare right at Sam. "In Hebrews ten-thirty it says, 'For we know him who said It is mine to avenge, I will repay. The Lord will judge his people.'"

Rachel spoke up. "Doesn't Proverbs say 'Hatred stirs up con-flict, but love conquers all wrongs'?"

Sam nearly did a double take. He had no idea she knew any Bible verses, then he remembered her light reading while he was unconscious.

Whip brought his rattlesnake-mean store toward her. "Proverbs also says: 'Do not say, I'll pay you back for this wrong. Wait for the Lord, and he will avenge you.'" The door dinged again as they reached the lobby. "So it ain't me who's judging you, little lady. It's the Lord."

The chaotic noise of the ER and the lobby flooded the elevator. An elderly woman with a walker stepped aside to let them out. Whip pushed Sam ahead of the group and aimed for the door. Dave and Clement dragged behind like beaten dogs. Rachel's eyes were up now and scanning the room.

They had to weave through people waiting to be seen. A shrill voice called over the PA system for, "Number eighty-three. Campbell. Is there a Campbell here?"

Sam saw the sliding glass doors looming closer and knew if they made it through that barrier, their chances of coming back at all were slim. He tried like hell to reach into Rachel's mind and see if she had any plan. There were times when they were on a job and it seemed like they could communicate telepathically. If ever there were a time for those powers to work, this was it.

Rachel clocked the people waiting. A man as thin as a scarecrow and old as a Model T. A woman with an ice pack on her forehead and a slow moan leaking out of her mouth. A nurse with a clipboard taking notes. A mother trying to wrangle her five kids to calm down, impossible to tell which one of them was waiting to see the doctor.

The double doors slid open, then shut behind an orderly wheeling out a woman with a newborn and a very nervous-looking new father.

Something. Anything.

And there it was. Enough to buy time, anyway.

Rachel darted left. Clement jerked his head up at the movement, but he didn't follow. Whip didn't notice since he was leading the pack.

Rachel made her way across a row of chairs and zeroed in on a man with an arrow sticking from his chest. He and his friend were both clad in camouflage and looking word out and ragged. Their bad day was about to get worse.

"Hey," Dave said, noticing that she'd broken from the group.

He followed her past the row of chairs.

Rachel put a hand on the arrow. The wounded man's eyes went wide with panic and pain. She gave him what she hoped to be an empathetic look and yanked hard. The arrow jerked free and his scream made everyone in the ER turn to look.

Rachel spun and held the arrow in her fist like a butcher's knife in a horror film. Dave had reached her and he got the tip of the arrow as a greeting. She pushed it through his shirt, between two ribs and deep into his chest. Dave's screams joined the other man's in a high harmony.

Whip spun around, wheeling Sam to face Rachel as he did so. Rachel saw a slight grin on Sam's face.

She pulled again and the arrow came free from Dave's chest. She advanced on Clement. He held up his hands and backed away, tripping over the woman with the ice pack and making her moans go up in pitch.

The ER erupted in chaos. The cammo-clad men were shouting for a doctor, the woman with five kids herded them toward the door. The nurses were trying to figure out what the hell was going on and Whip stared a laser beam through the madness at Rachel who held a bloody arrow in her hand.

"There is a devil among us," Whip said to the crowd. "And Satan takes the form of a woman this day."

The mother and her brood split the gap between Rachel and Whip and she took advantage of the cover. Rachel ran alongside the group and slid next to Sam, grabbing the handles of his wheelchair and aiming back toward the elevators.

A frightened-looking security guard came out of hiding from somewhere and made a weak attempt to calm the crowd. "Everyone remain calm."

He was ignored.

Both Dave and the man who no longer had an arrow in him were on the floor, bleeding. Whip turned to follow Rachel as she pushed Sam along, but he ran into Clement who grabbed him by the shoulders.

"We gotta get out of here, Whip. She really does got the devil in her."

Whip tried to pry away, but the old man's grip was stronger than he expected.

"We gotta go. Now."

"Let me go, you old fool."

"Whip, this is Satan's work. We need a damn exorcist."

"Clem, come on now."

Whip torqued his body left and brought Clement with him, spinning right into the oncoming Taser the security guard held out in front of him like a flashlight in the dark. He wasn't aiming at Clement, or at anyone in particular, but Whip put Clem's right arm into the bright blue sparking jaws of the Taser.

As he shivered in place with the current, Clement wet himself. Whip held up the quivering Clement as he went slack and slid toward the floor. Through the pain of the cuffs tugging at his wrist, he watched Rachel reach the elevators.

Rachel watched Clement collapse to the ground after the electric shock released him from its grip. Whip stayed upright, but shook off the shock like a boxer who just took an uppercut to his glass jaw. The elevator bell sounded and brought her head back around.

As she pushed Sam inside, she said, "We'll get our stuff and get the hell out. I need my purse and your clothes. I think that's it. Can you think of anything else we left in the—"

"Hey."

She stopped mid-sentence, looked at Sam who smiled as big as Christmas morning.

"I love you," he said.

She smiled. "Me too, baby."

She leaned down and kissed him to the sounds of a smooth jazz rendition of Phil Collins. Smooth on top of smooth.

CHAPTER 16

"His brother, you say?"

Earl leaned over the nurse's station desk, reaching for the phone.

"Yeah," the nurse said. "He had two other guys with him. Not sure if they were family too. Not a whole lot of family resemblance, to tell the truth. Said they'd be back real soon."

Earl knew Gregory didn't have any family nearby. And from the description the nurse had given him, Whip was in the building. Or had been. Who the hell knows where he took Sam by now?

Barb lingered back away from the conversation. She heard Earl get on the phone with his station house and call for a car to be sent over to check out the missing man. A sound caught her ear. It went deep into her unconscious mind, to some ancient receptor. A child's cry. A baby in need of a mother. She looked up at the direction of the sound and saw the words Maternity Ward on a sign pointing her forward.

Like a sailor following the call of a siren, she moved along the hallway toward the sound.

"Already on their way?" Earl crinkled his brow in confusion as he spoke into the phone. "Did someone else call this in?"

The dispatcher on the other end of the phone, Marla, said, "No, not this. Some big dustup in the ER. Some lady went crazy with a knife or something. An old fella got Tased."

"Well, shit. I'm here anyway. Lemme go check it out. Thanks, Marla."

Earl set the phone down. The nurse looked at him and asked, "Is there a problem? Someone get hurt?"

"It's a hospital," he said. "Everyone's hurt."

He noticed Barb wasn't by his side anymore. Where the hell had she gone? Oh well, she was the least likely person in Mississippi to cause trouble, so Earl headed back to the elevators. He stood in front of the door on the right, but the door on the left opened. He slid inside as the door to the right slid open as well. Rachel pushed Sam out ahead of her.

Rachel grabbed her purse, his pants, sucked down the half cup of lukewarm coffee left behind.

"Ready?"

"Where are we going?" Sam asked.

"To the car. Away from here. Once we're a good ways away we can stop in a clinic or something and get them to look at your leg. But we have to get out of here."

"No argument from me."

She set her purse and the rest of their stuff in his lap and spun his chair around to face the door.

"I wasn't sure how we were gonna get out of that," Sam said.

"Lucky break, the guy with the arrow."

"Lucky for us. Not so much for him."

"We've made a whole career out of lucky breaks, haven't we?"

"Think we got one more in us?"

With a wicked grin, she eyed the door. "Hell, yes we do."

Sam turned the handle and they did a quick scan of the hall. No cops. No Whip. Sam pulled the door all the way open and they moved out.

"How do you feel about stairs?" Rachel asked.

"I feel pain, and I'm not even going down them yet."

"Yeah, that might be a little much."

"Maybe there's another elevator."

Rachel pushed Sam to the nurse's station. A new girl sat manning the desk, one they hadn't seen before. Perfect.

"Excuse me, is there another elevator that doesn't go right through the ER? That place can get crazy."

"Yeah," she said, pointing past maternity. "All the way down. It doesn't let out near the parking structure though."

"Oh, that's okay. Just getting a little fresh air anyway."

"Just hit G for ground. Don't hit M. That's the…" She stopped as if she's said too much. "That's the morgue."

Sam said, "Not where I plan to end up today."

"Fingers crossed," Rachel said with a smile.

She'd just started to push away from the counter when the head nurse rounded the corner.

"Oh, it's you two. Hold on, Earl was looking for you. Oh, I mean, a policeman was here looking for you."

Thinking quick, her specialty, Rachel said, "Yes, we know. We're headed down to speak with him now."

"I think he went to check on the mess in the ER. You wait here and I'll page him to come up. That way you don't have to be rolling him and his leg all over creation."

"That's okay," Sam said. "My leg feels fine today."

Rachel said, "Yeah, we told him we'd meet him downstairs. I don't want to make him come up and down like a yo-yo."

The head nurse twisted her face into one of concern. "I think I should get Earl on the phone. You folks wait right here."

Like the bell to end round one, the elevator dinged behind them. A thundering voice spilled out.

"You! Satan!"

Whip stumbled out, the electricity still making his legs wobbly. Rachel didn't wait, she shoved Sam forward. Her shoes squeaked on the linoleum floors.

Barb stood in front of a glass wall. Two rows of clear-sided baby cribs lined the room beyond. Three of them held babies, fresh as muffins from the oven. All three were swaddled in hospital blankets, two in blue and one in pink. A nurse fussed over the little girl and rolled an ink roller across her tiny foot, then pressed it to a sheet of paper, imprinting the newborn's footprint.

Barb knew tears would fall if she blinked. She didn't want to embarrass herself, and she didn't want to blink and miss even a fraction of a second of this sight. God's perfect creatures.

Blessings to three families. Well, good for them. Yes, good for them. She'd never felt such a heavy weight of sadness mixed with the joy of new life. Her chance was gone. She knew it. Those charlatans, first Goldie and now these others, had taken it from her. But taken what? They couldn't take what she didn't have. Money, sure, they took money. But they gave her hope, and then took that away. Ripped it crying from her arms.

But she took comfort in knowing there were these perfect, unspoiled angels in the world. Innocent lives who didn't yet know the cynicism of being taken advantage of. Didn't know the hand of a man across their cheek, or the insults and put-downs of a marriage. Didn't know what pain life had in store for them. They were pure for the only time in their lives. Preserved behind glass. She wished they could stay that way forever.

Footsteps behind her. Then a familiar voice, raised in familiar anger. She didn't need to turn around to recognize her husband.

"Thus saith the Lord," Whip said as he chased after the two charlatans, his voice like a preacher on a street corner in hell, trying to save unsaveable souls. "In this thou shalt know that I am the Lord: behold, I will smite with the rod that is in mine hand upon the waters which are in the river, and they shall be turned to blood."

Barb turned. The couple, the charlatans, were running toward her. Him in a wheelchair, her pushing furiously behind him but losing the footrace with Whip who ran after in a lurching gait like a man possessed. She'd heard him screaming Bible verses before. It never ended well.

The woman saw her. Leah was her name, Barb remembered. A good, Biblical name. She stopped the wheelchair with a skid, staring at Barb as if she was acting with Whip to stop them. Barb showed her only soft eyes and a smile.

The pause was enough and Whip came crashing into Leah from behind. The man in the chair, Gregory she remembered, slid forward, his leg banging into the wall and he let out a wail. Whip climbed on top of the woman, trying to turn her over.

"You are the instrument of the devil and I am the mighty fist of God."

She fought. Fought back in a way Barb knew she never could, but secretly wished for the strength to do some days.

A metal stand, the kind used for holding IV bags, stood in the hall by where they grappled. They were out front of a door marked Delivery. Barb caught her breath. Was a child being born right this minute?

Leah kicked out and brought the metal stand down with a crash. She slithered away and got a hand on the stand, spun it around and hit Whip with it on his shoulders. Barb felt an electric charge go through her body. Rachel kicked out and caught Whip's head with her shoe. Barb felt another jolt.

Gregory rolled himself back from the wall, watching helplessly from his chair as Leah fought to her feet and away from Whip. She stood, using the metal stand to pull herself up. Leah went to Gregory. Barb saw their eyes lock together. There was concern there, a little fear, but love most of all. Undeniable, unbreakable love. Barb felt a similar weight of sadness like when she looked at the babies. Sadness for something she'd never had, and never would.

The Delivery door opened and a nurse stepped out. She wore a mask over her mouth, streaks of blood down the front of her navy-blue scrubs. She held a light blue bin out in front of her. *The placenta*, thought Barb. The baby had been delivered. This was the afterbirth.

"What in the hell is going on out here?" the nurse said, clearly angry about the noise. "We're trying to deliver a damn baby in here."

Leah grabbed hold of Gregory's chair and pushed. She caught Barb's eye as they began to roll past, asking her with only a look if she would let them go. Barb again gave her the softest eyes and a smile. They had love, as pure as a newborn.

"What the hell?" the nurse said.

The nurse backed away from Whip who had found his feet. His face flushed red with anger, his hair wild. Spit dripped from his mouth as he called after Leah in a cracked and worn-out voice, "Stop the devil. Satan is in our midst. God has chosen me to stop the devil in human form."

Barb took two steps forward and slapped the bin from the nurse's hand with a firm downward chop. The lid tumbled open as it fell and the contents splashed on the floor. Whip lumbered forward in his chase. His foot came down on a slick and shiny sheen of afterbirth. His leg shot out to the side. His other foot came down in the widening puddle of placenta and went the opposite direction. His scream of pain came out strangled, nearly drowned out by the sound of his hip dislocating and his body falling back to the floor in a pool of wetness and blood.

By the time Barb turned back around, Leah and Gregory were gone.

CHAPTER 17

After three hours, the cold in the morgue had gotten to them. With the craziness in the ER, cops on the way, and the hospital on high alert, Sam and Rachel decided to wait it out a while.

"Think it's safe yet?" Rachel asked.

"I think so," Sam said. "I hope so."

He reached out and touched her hand. Feeling the cold, he rubbed some warmth into her skin.

So far the morgue hadn't seen any traffic. They were in a hallway outside the actual rooms with the bodies, but they were close enough for it to be creeping them out.

"What do you think?"

Sam shrugged. "I think I'm ready to be done with Mississippi."

"Shall we?"

Rachel pointed toward the elevator.

"Let's do it."

She rolled him aboard and they ascended to the main floor, rear entrance.

Outside all seemed calm. They decided to check the parking

structure for their rental car. If it was crawling with cops, they'd hail a cab, rent another car under one of their many assumed names, and get the hell out.

Rachel rolled Sam around the side of the hospital. Things seemed to have died down. One upside to a small police force. Rolling past the main entrance neither one of them turned their eyes to the doors. Heads down, keep moving. Sam did think about the men inside. Whip, with his damaged hip and whatever other injuries Rachel inflicted on him. The old guy who got Tased. The one who took an arrow to the chest. For a moment he forgot about his own pain and laughed.

"What's so funny?" Rachel asked.

"Just thinking about some shepherds I know."

They drove west, promising not to stop until they were long gone from here. Rachel drove and when she saw the sign announcing their departure from the state of Mississippi, and it's invitation to come back soon, she hung her hand out the window, raised a middle finger high into the air and let that sign know what they thought about the hospitality state.

A month later, Sam got his cast cut off. There was some explaining at the clinic when they finally stopped to have him checked out, but the cash they paid with answered most of the questions. He stretched and flexed his leg, laughing at the pale skin now exposed.

The cast came off right on time. They had another job heating up. They needed it, too. The money they'd made in Mississippi had run out, gone to pay for Sam's medical costs. Some of it was their own fault. A little something they did as a thank you, or maybe to alleviate some guilt. Or possibly just another middle finger to another hateful piece of Mississippi.

"Back to normal," Rachel said, looking at his leg.

"Good as new."

"I don't know, I think I like you with a few road miles on you."

"We have plenty of those."

"Who's we?"

She playfully punched his shoulder and smiled. He pulled her to him and wrapped her in a kiss.

"Ready for the next one?"

"Always, baby. Always."

Barb crossed the lawn on her way back from the mailbox. Whip would usually get the mail, he was good like that. Like a trained dog fetching the paper off the front porch. Or maybe he only wanted to see what came in before she did.

She flipped through the mailer for a local grocery advertising grapes for two dollars a bunch. A letter address to Whip care of the Shepherds of the Golden Lamb. A second letter had her name on it, and the logo of a bank in the return address. Strange, since all their accounts were exclusively in Whip's name. Barb had no access and no control over a penny they had.

Must be one of those credit card applications, she thought. But below the clear plastic window showing her own name and address it read statement enclosed.

The porch steps creaked as she climbed and before she even opened the front door she could hear Whip bellowing from all the way upstairs. She opened the door to a deep, throaty call of, "Barbara!"

"What is it, Whip?"

"I need you to come up here."

"What for? I just put lunch on the stove."

Whip had been in bed for the better part of his time since he got out of the hospital. His hip went so far out of his socket that he had to have a surgery to put it back. He'd also cracked two ribs and that woman had given him a hairline fracture on his orbital bone, right over his left eye. As a patient, Whip was a holy terror. Whiny, childish, spoiled and demanding. She gave him some slack seeing as he couldn't bathe himself, couldn't walk to the toilet and couldn't sleep more than a couple of hours without waking up and swallowing another of those pain pills.

"Barb, come up here."

"It can wait. I'll bring you lunch in ten minutes."

She turned over the letter in her hand. Underneath it was a small envelope, like the kind for a birthday card. This, too, was addressed to her. No return address at all.

"Barb, I...I need you."

She huffed an aggravated sigh only she could hear.

"What is it, Whip?"

"God dammit, Barb. I...well, I need you to clean me up."

She rolled her eyes. *Not again.*

"Whip, did you...?"

She tore open the bank envelope. It was a statement. An account in her name, and her name alone. She hadn't set it up. She checked the balance. Twenty thousand dollars exactly.

"Dammit, Barb. I shit myself. I couldn't get to the damn bathroom and you weren't around and...well, for Lord's sake I need you come clean me up."

Ignoring him, in shock at the document she held in her hands, Barb tore open the card. On the front was a drawing of a stork flying down from the clouds in a heavenly light, a bundle in its beak. She opened the card. Printed inside was: *And though she be but little, she is fierce.*

No signature. No handwriting at all.

She flipped it again. Postmarked Florida.

"Barb!"

She smiled to herself, tucked the envelopes in the pocket of her apron, and started climbing the stairs.

"Hold your horses, I'll be there in a jiff."

ERIC BEETNER has been described as "the James Brown of crime fiction—the hardest working man in noir." (Crime Fiction Lover) and "The 21st Century's answer to Jim Thompson" (LitReactor). He has written more than 20 novels including *Rumrunners*, *Leadfoot*, *The Devil Doesn't Want Me*, *The Year I Died 7 Times* and *Criminal Economics*. His award-winning short stories have appeared in over three dozen anthologies. He co-hosts the podcast Writer Types and the Noir at the Bar reading series in Los Angeles where he lives and works as a television editor.

STILL LIFE WITH SUITCASE

SCOTT EUBANKS

A GRIFTER'S SONG

STILL LIFE WITH SUITCASE
Scott Eubanks

Even as a little girl, Rachel dreamed of living in hotel rooms. Everything orderly and neat, someone to feed you, to clean up, to open doors for you. Every morning, a different skyline, the promise of something new, of being anonymous. The best part about being nobody, was that it was easy to pose as somebody. Somebody important. She had never been to a yacht party before.

Guests haunted the deck, champagne in hand, while a superb band played Django Reinhardt tunes. All of it swallowed up by the slick blackness of the Atlantic.

She took a convincing sip from her old fashioned and slipped a hand in her pocket to finger the edge of a single crisp business card. In black slacks, heels, and a blouse, she was relieved to not be the sexpot this time around. Earlier, when they withdrew the gangplank in West Palm Beach and the motors began to thrum, she had felt a measure of finality, of fate as the lights of the city compressed behind her into a thin, bright line.

Tonight, her name was Amelia.

The mark: Gary Bagley.

The Bagleys were on a circuit of the outer deck, schmoozing, discussing travel, hired help, art, and politics. In a suit cut for a much younger man, Gary looked like a retired accountant, which he was. He'd gotten in early at the company that made oxycontin—conning the American public into thinking that there was such thing as a non-addictive opioid.

On the deck, a pair of older women with the last names of robber barons rolled their eyes behind the Bagleys' backs. Gary and his wife Teresa were new money. In the company of the movers and shakers of West Palm Beach, they reeked of desperation.

Teresa wore a cream-colored dress that was one size too small. She approached the bar for another iced tea and said to Rachel, "Well, hello again." She walked like she'd never worn heels. At fifty-four, she had the best face and tits money could buy, but to Rachel she just looked hungry.

She was surprised that Gary, with his money, hadn't traded his wife in for a twenty-something hardbody. The kind that worked out their rich daddy issues with a rich sugar daddy. Maybe he only kept one on the side.

"We meet again," Rachel said, raising her old fashioned at an aging socialite with crimson hair. "She reminds me of my husband. Pathetic, right?"

"You'd feel better if you tried to mingle?" Teresa said, pointing at an impeccable thirty-something gentleman brooding at the railing, "That one's been staring at you all night." And he had. Looked like a Kennedy, too. A shame.

"The best way to get over someone," Mrs. Bagley whispered conspiratorially, "is get under someone else." She laughed and glanced around to make sure no one else had heard. For a moment, Rachel felt sorry for her.

Before the money, Teresa had worked at a veterinarian's office. Her old friends were long gone. Her new ones had given up on educating her about class. A lonely life. Mrs. Bagley gossiped with their housekeeper and was an avid fan of telenovelas.

Gary, impatient, hurried to the bar to retrieve his wife. He took her by the elbow.

Before he could pull her away, Teresa said, "Gary, this is the woman I was telling you about—the art historian."

Ignoring her, Gary motioned with his head. "The Randolphs are at the bow. They want to hear about that time you got lost in that Hong Kong fish market. People love that story."

Withdrawing her arm, she said pointedly, "Don't be rude." Pointing at Rachel, she added, "Amelia has consulted for the Metropolitan Museum of Art."

Mr. Bagley offered a hand and fixed Rachel in a calculating expression that clearly showed how little she mattered. "Pleased to meet you."

"Your wife and I have mutual friends," Rachel said. "The Postlewaites."

He flinched. The Postlewaites had been social royalty in South Florida since the Spanish sailed back to Madrid with their egos bruised. Old money, they had continually undermined the Bagleys on principle for years. Gary was convinced that their lack of social standing in West Palm Beach had nothing to do with his crude wife or his own lack of grace, it was the Postlewaites snubbing of them. Sadly, Mr. and Mrs. Postlewaite couldn't make tonight's party due to a three-month trip to Africa. Clearing his throat, Mr. Bagley said, "I'm sorry, what was your name?"

"Amelia Depardieu," Mrs. Bagley said. "Like the actor."

"And how do you know the Postlewaites?" he asked.

Rachel blushed and said, "They invited my husband and I to the party."

"He left her, if you can believe it," Mrs. Bagley said, gesturing at her curves, "For a redhead." Thirty-four years before, Mrs. Bagley's first husband had also left her for a younger woman—a redhead. What were the odds?

Flushing with embarrassment, Rachel baited the hook. "I consult for the family from time to time."

"What exactly do you do?" Gary said, impatient, glancing toward the bow.

"I specialize in the Dutch Golden Age. Vermeer, in particular," Rachel said, doing her best to seem as though she was downplaying it.

"And," he said.

"She independently verifies the Postelwaites' new paintings for them," Mrs. Bagley said, exasperated. "I was telling her earlier that we should have her over to the house to look over our collection."

"Good idea, Tess," he said, losing what little interest he had, trying to flag down the bartender for another old fashioned. "How much would something like that cost?"

Turning crimson, Teresa slapped his elbow with the back of her fingers. "We can afford it."

"It's okay," Rachel said, filing away how the mention of money embarrassed Mrs. Bagley. "Usually, it's between ten and twenty thousand. I'd need to see the collection first."

Mr. Bagley snorted. "For a couple hours' work?"

"Don't get into art if you don't like spending money. There are maybe thirty people in the world with my qualifications," Rachel said.

"What's involved?" Teresa asked.

"I examine the painting and try to verify the provenance. We schedule a technician to sample the pigments and fibers to ensure they're from the period. I compare it to other works. It's remarkably demanding work." She couldn't quite tell, but felt as though Mr. Bagley was feigning disinterest. To push him off balance, she added, "Your wife told me you have a Bernard in your entryway."

"Yes, among others, the *Woman in a Hotel Room*," Mrs. Bagley said, eager to salvage the conversation. "It's lovely. The light."

"Yes," Gary said. "The composition and perspective are really something." One of the many reasons Sam and Rachel had chosen the Bagleys was because they knew almost nothing about art.

"You're lucky to have one," Rachel said. "Bernard's work has seen a resurgence of interest lately. Mrs. Postlethwaite, especially, has been looking to purchase a representative work for quite some time. As a matter of fact, it's practically all she talks about. I'm certain they would be interested in purchasing yours. If, of course, you'd be willing to part with it."

Gary's eyes went round as he grasped her meaning. The

Postlewaites wanted something that only he possessed. Rachel didn't like the ugly emotions that welled up in his expression. For a brief moment, she had the same question she had every time they started a con.

Had they chosen the right mark?

From her pocket, she offered her business card between her pointer and middle finger to Gary and said, "Call any time. I'll be in town until the end of the week." As he took it, he didn't seem notice that her hand was shaped like a gun pointed at his chest.

The following afternoon, Gary Bagley waited outside a private gym on the mainland. It was his ritual, forty minutes on the elliptical and twenty in the hot tub. As he waited for the valet, he stared at the stucco strip mall on the opposite side of the lot. Between the lots, a culvert choked with reeds and snakes. It was unusually hot and humid for after sunset. Flying insects the color of spoiled milk tangled around the parking lot lights as they began to flick on. Palm trees rustled like flags with each gust of wind.

Near the south exit of the lot, Sam waited in an idling used Mercedes and adjusted his neck brace for the twelfth time. The next part would be tricky. The reason he'd been watching Mr. Bagley for weeks, why he'd parked in this exact space hours ago: life was about timing.

Across the lot, the valet arrived in a baby blue and orange Ford GT, a street race car that had a spoiler the size of a coffee table. Mr. Bagley took the keys, didn't tip, and climbed in. Ten years before, Mr. Bagley had been an avid car collector, but recently, he'd lost interest. As usual, he drove toward the southbound exit with comic slowness, the enormous engine snarling.

Sam realized that he was rubbing his healed leg, a participation trophy from when the last job went to shit. Biting onto his mouthpiece, he pressed the back of his head against the headrest.

When Gary stopped to make the turn, to don his driving gloves, Sam popped the Mercedes in reverse and swung out of the space, ramming the back of the GT. The sound of a gunshot as the trunk of the Mercedes crushed the bumper of the half-million-dollar sports car.

Sam loved his job.

He parked, stripped the brace, spit the mouthpiece into the passenger seat, and got out, breathing as rapidly as he could to get his color up, his eyes dilated. A couple getting into their SUV stared as he approached the driver's side of the GT. One could tell a lot about a person by the way they reacted to the unexpected.

"You okay, buddy?" Sam asked, wide-eyed, leaning forward. He jumped back just as the door sprang open, barely missing him.

Roaring out, Gary Bagley grabbed the front of Sam's polo and forced him backward. An ugly tirade spewed forth from his mouth, his face the color of stubbed toe. He thrust Sam against the trunk of a sedan, shaking him. Sam played his part, hollering, covering his face, letting Gary know he was definitely—no questions about it—in charge.

As Gary continued to loom over him, bellowing on about what a dipshit he was, Sam recalled why they took this job in the first place. Beyond the money, the mark had a notorious temper. Gary's assistant even had a monthly budget for paying off aggrieved pro-shop managers and maître d's. And as a rule, when you're angry, you're stupid.

Finally, Gary let him go. He paced in a circle, gasping, his hands on his lower back. "You're lucky I wasn't hurt, pal. My lawyers would sell off your organs."

"Look, man," Sam said, straightening his shirt, letting his voice crack a little. "I didn't see you." To keep him worked up, he added, "Did you have your lights on?"

Gary scowled, his eyes red-rimmed. "You'd better have the best fucking insurance in the world." He leered the way the bull does at the matador, filled with malice and confusion.

"I have insurance." Sam stammered and pointed at the sedan. "For something like this." Pointing at the GT, he shook his head. "For that, I don't know."

Gary examined the used Mercedes and sized Sam up at once. "Then it'll be a civil suit." With a reptilian look in his eye, always the accountant, he added, "You own a house? What's your name?"

Sam shook his head. "It's Leland...Spinnaker." Pointing his thumb at the strip mall, at a yellow sign that read, Pawn Takes King, he said, "I run the pawn shop over there."

Uninterested, Gary surveyed the damage to the GT. "They only made fifteen hundred of these." The unmistakable sound of grief in his voice worried Sam a little. This wasn't about cars.

"Is that a Mustang?" Sam asked, unsuccessfully trying to piss him off.

Gary crouched and laid his hand inside the biggest dent, at the edge of the torn carbon fiber. "You have a stupid name, Leland."

"Well, my mom thought it was nice," he said. Now Sam was just toying with him.

Running low on patience, Gary huffed. "Does your mom own a house?"

"Why do you keep asking about houses?" He wished Rachel could be here for this, for him playing the fool.

"Because your parents are going to have to sell theirs to pay my legal fees. All because you can't fucking look where you're going in that Kraut piece of shit."

"We don't know whose fault this is," Sam said, dialing on his phone. "Let's call the police to sort this out."

Standing up, Gary said, "I don't have time for this shit. Let's trade insurance information. I got to get home soon." To watch SportsCenter with a light beer and a bag of popcorn. The truth was, Gary was about as comfortable with the police as Sam. He'd had more than a few run ins with them: shouting matches with friends, being tossed out of a couple restaurants, and one property line dispute last spring that ended up in the ER. Another research nugget that they were counting on to play itself out.

Sam turned off his phone. He followed Gary to the passenger side of his car where he opened the glove box for his insurance card. Sam cleared his throat and said, "I don't want to get insurance involved."

Gary paused, blinking up at him. "This is a five-hundred-thousand-dollar car."

"It's a glorified fender bender," he said, talking fast. "What's that cost? Maybe ten percent? I could cover that in cash." He had Gary's full attention. No insurance. No lawyers. No protracted legal battle that would likely cost more than he could get.

Pointing at the pawn shop, Sam said, "I've got over seven million in inventory."

The bell over the door rang. Sam did his best to conceal the slight limp of his right leg as he ushered Gary inside of Pawn Takes King. A limp is something people tend to remember. Dark, cavernous, and cluttered, the showroom was roughly organized by tools, musical instruments, and electronics. The reek of mold and glass cleaner as thick as smoke. Sam circumvented the U-shaped display cases in the center and went to the counter at the far end of the room.

Gary crossed his arms. The look on his face, like he smelled a particularly nasty fart. He waited by the door, glancing over his shoulder through one of the front windows. Too good for this place or afraid, Sam couldn't tell.

The shop was as hot and damp as a plastic bag over their heads.

A line of sweat dripped down Sam's ribs. He turned on a green-hooded banker's lamp at each end of the back counter. On a bank of light switches by the back door, he flicked the one marked with red nail polish to illuminate the empty gun racks, a small painting, and various tchotchkes, including a set of glass sex toys, on display. To set Gary at ease, Sam sounded worried as he asked, "You mobbed up?"

Gary, hands in his pockets, stifled a pleased look. "Why do you think that?"

Because if Sam seemed afraid and uncertain, it would make Gary remember how in control he was. Sam took out a thick set of keys and said, "The fancy car, no police, you being so careful."

From across the room, Gary gave a noncommittal shrug and strode around the display cases. "Let's just say that I'm the worst person in West Palm Beach you could possibly fuck with," he said, letting just a little Marlon Brando creep into his voice.

The keys jingled as Sam opened a locked cabinet and removed a battered steel lock box. The owner of the shop, Geno, wouldn't give him the combination to the wall safe. Smart, on his part. The most difficult part of the setup had been securing the pawnshop. Two thousand for one night with a five thousand dollar "missing shit" deposit. To ensure the owner didn't make any home movies, Rachel had watched Geno shut the security system down and unplugged each of the five cameras.

The air conditioner, a huge unit that hung from the ceiling like an upside down steel mushroom, had been shut off at lunchtime just so Sam could turn it on full blast now. Filthy with a couple of loosened screws, it made as much noise as vacuuming up nails, more than enough to cover their conversation in case Geno considered a sideline in blackmail.

Opening the steel case, Sam said, "How's this for collateral?"

Gary crossed the room, a scowl on his face. "I want cash. Fifty-thousand dollars."

"And I can get it," Sam said, flinching like he expected to be struck. "But it'll take me a couple days." He unfolded a microfiber cloth across the glass and pretended to pick lint from its edge. From the steel case, he opened three clamshell boxes. Reverently, he laid out a Rolex Yacht-Master, a Rolex Submariner, and a Breguet Perpetual Calendar/Moonphase. The tag on each showed they were each priced above twenty-thousand dollars. "You hold onto these until I get the cash," Sam said.

With a grimace, Gary leaned over them. Picking up the Breguet and squinted at the numerous dials. He tossed it onto the cloth and muttered, "How do I know these aren't fake?"

They were, Chinese fashion watches purchased online. Sam shrugged and said, "You know where I work, my name." He let his voice crack, his eyes fall to the watches. "You're also the last person in West Palm Beach I want to fuck with."

"Give me your driver's license, Leland," he said with a skeptical sneer. Sam pulled it out of his wallet. He polished the thumbprint on the face of the Breguet while Gary examined the fake ID. Pocketing it, Gary sighed and said, "Box up the watches. You got a card?" Sam handed over a business card with the number for the burner phone. Without looking up, Gary tipped his head toward the little painting next to the glass sex toys. "Throw in the painting, too."

Sam's eyes widened as he stammered, "I can't." The painting was half sky with a hump of trees and tangled branches. Darkened with age, the colors muted, it showed a cottage among the trees and two people on the road.

"You will," Gary growled, leaning across the counter. "For wasting my fuckin' evening, you'll throw in the painting."

Blocking the painting, Sam shook his head. "It doesn't belong to me." He gestured at the rest of the shop and pleaded, "Take anything you want, but I can't loan you the painting."

Gary slapped his cellphone on the counter and snarled, "All I gotta do is make a call, Leland."

"It doesn't belong to me," Sam said.

"You rat fuck," Gary shouted. "You come up with the money and I'll give it back. What the hell am I going to do with watches?"

"What are you going to do with a painting?"

Gary slapped Sam hard enough to nearly knock him down. Christ, he was fast for an old guy. Straightening, Sam's mask slipped a little as he glared. For a moment, he was tempted to stomp-kick Gary's left knee, the one he'd spent a fortune on—enough to send an entire raft of refugees to state college for a year. Rachel and him could skip town and be somewhere less humid. But they couldn't. They'd spent most of what they had on this job. Sam had to force himself not to touch his burning cheek, the drip at his hairline. Sweat or blood, he couldn't tell.

Gary, reading his expression, hesitated, took a step toward the door. Sam corrected, holding his face, slouching, and whimpering, but it had been too slow. A crack of himself had shown through. "Why'd you hit me?" he whined, averting his eyes.

"I don't like to be told no," Gary said. "I know that you don't want me to have the painting, so it improves the odds of me getting my money."

"My business partner will kill me," he said. His hand came away from his face with a line of blood. One of the green jewels on Gary's class ring had cut him.

"Not my problem," Gary stepped around the counter and lifted the painting off the wall. With his nose a few inches from the paint, he patted his shirt pocket for his reading glasses. There was something familiar about the lines, the color palette.

"You don't understand, he's dangerous," Sam said, blocking Gary, his voice nearing a wail. He wondered if he was overdoing it.

"So am I," Gary said, pushing past him. He pointed at the watches. "Put those in a bag."

"Please…I'm begging you," he said.

"*You* crashed into *me*," Gary said. "For that, I would normally take everything you have." His eyes pierced into Sam for a long moment. Finally, Sam sighed and placed the watches in a bag. Handing them over, he frowned and said, "It was just a fender bender, man."

Gary grabbed the front of Sam's shirt and said through his teeth, "I'll call in two days." He stormed to the front door, opened it, and added, "Next time, take the bus, shithead."

That evening, Sam and Rachel arrived at an apartment building in Miami. It was depressing. Cracked stucco, wilting shrubs, too many power lines, and a communal dumpster overflowing in the parking lot. Rachel unpacked takeout from the back seat while Sam took a substantial wrapped gift out of the trunk. They were dressed like suburbanites, khakis and a button-up, a blouse and slacks, matching watches and fun shoes. Only the scabbed over scratch on Sam's cheek spoiled the image.

"I hope you're right about this," Sam mumbled to her as they crossed the lot. They had considered a number of ways to approach Lisa Bernard, but settled on the simplest. The rarest commodity of all, the truth, or as much of it as they could afford.

At apartment five, the second floor of three, the doorbell was broken. Sam put his palm to Rachel's jaw and kissed her deeply.

"What was that for?" she asked, her heart racing as she glanced at the peephole for telltale shadows.

"Luck," he said, his expression unreadable.

She smiled and knocked. When the job was over, they would take a trip to Mexico, where she could use his name in public without worrying, without spinning a half-dozen plates in her head all the time. But that, she reminded herself, was how you began to go dull.

The peephole darkened and a woman cracked the door open. She was in her early forties, dark rings beneath her eyes, black done-up hair fraying apart with strands across her face. "Can I help you?" Her accent was fairly clean. She was still in her scrubs from Miami General where she worked as an ER nurse. She'd been home less than twenty minutes and was just about to order a pizza or whip up a boxed stroganoff.

"Hi, Mrs. Bernard," Rachel said, holding up the bags of take-out. "We're here about your brother."

Lisa's expression remained fixed but she stopped breathing. Her pupils dilated as she reached for the cross she used to wear. "I'm sorry," she said, closing the door, "but you've made a mistake."

Sam, careful not to drop the present balanced on his shoulder, wedged his foot in the door. "There's no mistake," he said. "Before he passed away, your brother was called 'The Artist'."

The color left her face as she said, "You two from Philly." Her accent, like she'd never left. Behind her, the apartment was dim, two floors, like an ant farm with a window at each end.

Sam shook his head. Rachel gave a reassuring smile and said, "We brought dinner. We just want to talk."

"I have nothing to say," she said, the muscle in her jaw flexing as she looked down. "You have three seconds to leave before I call—"

"What did they bring?" a man with a heavy French accent called from the hallway behind her.

Before Lisa could reply, Rachel hollered, "It's Le Provencal." She showed Lisa the name on the side of the takeout bags.

"We wanted to take you out to a nice dinner first," said Sam, "but given your situation, we figured we'd bring dinner to you."

The man appeared in the hall in a wheelchair. Lisa's grandfather, Papi, sat up straight to peer around her. He asked in a deep voice, "And what is it?"

They'd basically ordered the five most expensive items on the menu. Reading from the receipt, Rachel said, "*Coquilles Saint Jacques* and *Côtelettes D'Agneau* and—"

"Please stop," the man said, pressing a hand to his heart, "You speak French the way a dog wipes its ass." To his granddaughter, he whispered urgently. "The smell of it is driving me crazy. Please, let them in. I will never again eat so well."

It was obvious that Lisa wanted to disagree, but she sighed, opened the door, and beckoned them inside. She wasn't stupid. If they'd wanted to hurt her, there were hundreds of ways, none involving French cuisine.

The apartment hadn't been updated since the late 1970s. It was clean but cluttered. There was a diminutive kitchen to the left with a window overlooking the parking lot. A gilt mirror hung above a tiny table with two chairs. To the right, a bedroom/living room with a sliding glass door and balcony. From the twin bed on a metal frame, the weekly pill box organizers, and other medical equipment, it was apparently Papi's bedroom. Through the wall, a couple was in the middle of an argument.

Sitting on a pink yard sale loveseat, a boy of about eight with dark hair and large brown eyes studied a comic book. Lisa called to him, but he didn't look up. To Papi, she said, "Where's his hearing aid?"

Papi, who took out dishes from the lower cabinets, shrugged and said, "He likes the silence sometimes." She quickly located a bulky hearing aid in a bowl on the counter, strode across the living room, and startled the boy by holding it out to him. Sam gave Rachel a wary look. The boy took it and hooked it around his right ear.

"Henry," Lisa said. "Go read in your room. I'll send dinner up in a few minutes." In the apartment below, a TV was on, a police procedural from the sound of it. The walls and floors seemed to be as thin as wet toilet paper.

The boy stared at Sam and Rachel. Sam offered the present to Lisa and said, "We saw on Facebook that your son's birthday was two weeks ago." It had been wrapped in the store, blue and white paper with an orange bow.

"We understand how strange this must seem," Rachel said, unpacking the takeout boxes on the counter. "So we figured we'd bring a gift. A bribe, actually." It felt strange to come right out and say what they were doing. Lisa didn't move. Instead, she eyed the box as though a cobra might rise out of it. Sam smirked and removed the lid. Inside was a brand new PlayStation and a handful of games. The boy gasped.

"Also," Sam said, "this would give us a chance to talk without any interruptions."

Crossing her arms, Lisa said, "You have thirty minutes."

They ate in the no man's land between the kitchen and living room. Sam pulled the chairs together and set up a card table. Papi insisted on cloth napkins and a candle. The food, despite being lukewarm, was fantastic. The boy unconsciously cocked his good ear toward whoever was speaking. Rachel didn't ask about why he only had one working hearing aid. It was obvious. They were broke. Papi had a kidney transplant thirteen years earlier and the medication alone cost fifteen hundred a month.

"That was magnificent," Papi said, his eyes on the popcorn

ceiling, one hand on his belly. "My son trained to be a chef, but he became an artist instead. He made the most sublime beef bourguignon."

After they ate, Rachel helped set up the PlayStation. While Papi and his great grandson played a racing game in the living room, Lisa brewed a pot of coffee and met them on the balcony. Someone had a serious plant collection. Among the wicker chairs, it felt like they were in the middle of a jungle.

"I don't know anything about my brother," Lisa said, closing the slider behind her.

"We have it on good authority that the Artist was a fixer in Philly," Sam said. "Do you remember the name of his boss?"

She nodded and glanced over her shoulder at her boy. At first, she said it too softly and tried again. "Vincent."

Despite the heat, something cold climbed up Rachel's spine. They'd tried and failed to con Little Vincent in Philly, which put a price on their heads. Ever since, Sam and Rachel had been hunted. What if they were wrong, she thought, and Lisa wasn't completely divorced from Philly? All she had to do was make one call and they'd be dead.

"Then you do know something," Rachel replied.

Giving her a dark look, Lisa said, "Everyone knows about Little Vincent. And if he wasn't a thousand miles away, I wouldn't even say his name."

"We also heard that when your brother passed away," Rachel said, "you were the sole beneficiary of his estate."

Lisa laughed dryly. "No money. Just some paperwork and a box of crap. It's sad how little is left when you're gone."

"We're not asking about money," Sam said. "We're here about his personal effects?"

"Why? You're not cops," she said, looking them over. "And you're definitely not mobbed up. What do you want with my brother's things?"

Rachel liked her.

"You're right," Sam said, giving Rachel an uncertain look.

Sighing as though imparting a deep truth, he added, "We're independent operators."

"What's that supposed to mean?"

"We don't have an axe to grind with you or your brother," Rachel said.

"That only leaves Little—" She clamped her mouth shut, her eyes wide. "You're crazy."

"Your brother had something we want," Rachel said. "An insurance policy against his boss."

"We're here to buy it off you," Sam said. "Right now, you give us Etienne's things, and we'll pay you..." He looked at Rachel.

"Twelve-thousand, four-hundred and thirty-eight dollars," Rachel recited. She had read a magazine article about how the more precise the offer price, the more the other party believed you had inside information. They would counter a lot closer to your initial offer. They couldn't afford much more than that anyway. It was the last of the honey pot they'd stashed outside of New Orleans. Their last job pulled in a little money, but with Sam's medical expenses for his leg, it was a wash.

"You're not just asking me for Etienne's things," Lisa said, exhaling a long breath. "You're asking me to open up that part of my life again." Pointing into her apartment, she added, "Today, me and my family are safe. But if I give you his things, if I open that box again, my family would no longer be safe."

"We're not thinking of using it," Sam said.

"Of course you are, and it would be foolish to believe it won't prompt a reaction. Whatever your intentions, if I give you Etienne's things, the chances that two men with guns knock on that door go up." Her jaw tight, her eyes fixed on them. "I don't have much left and no amount of money would ever be enough to replace my son."

Sam leaned back in his chair and grinned. "What if we weren't offering money? What if we could return something more valuable than money, something that belongs to you, something you've lost?"

* * *

Later that evening, Rachel hung up the hotel phone and rolled back under the white down comforter. The room was spare, modern, and gray with wood accents. As cold as a meat locker. With her head on Sam's bare chest, she whispered, "The Bagleys have invited Amelia Depardieu to their estate tomorrow morning to look over their collection. Gary's convinced it could be the stolen Rembrandt." Worth millions today, Rembrandt's *Landscape with Cottages* was stolen from the Montreal Museum of Fine Arts in 1972. It had been called the Skylight Caper because three men entered the museum through a skylight that was under repair. They trussed up the guards and made off with eighteen paintings, none of which had been recovered.

"He'd better," Sam said. "The fake cost enough." Through connections, they'd found an art forger in New Mexico—a retired painting professor—who had a sideline in Dutch masters.

Rachel caught the annoyance in his voice and said, "Are you still dwelling of what Gary did to you?" She kissed his chest. "And not thinking of what I just did to you?"

He didn't answer. Instead, he pressed his palm against his cheek and went over every detail in the parking lot and pawn shop once more. Something could've gone wrong. It was more than nerves, a bad feeling. Maybe it was just the fact that they'd staked everything they had on the biggest payday they'd ever conceived of.

The cut on his cheekbone was clean and as long as a pinky nail. Nearly touching the vertical scar outside his eye socket, it looked almost like an upside down seven. That afternoon, when he had returned to the hotel, his shirt ruined, a line of blood dried on his cheek, they had ordered room service. He sat sullenly at the edge of the bed, flicking his lighter open and closed, as rhythmic as a clock, while Rachel cleaned the cut with a linen napkin and chilled Grey Goose.

As she lay there smelling the scent of him, worry percolated up through her ribcage. "Say the word," she said, sitting up, "and we'll leave town, babe." The air conditioner thrummed. She could never sleep in the heat.

After a few seconds, he said, "No, it's been set perfectly."

"Then what's wrong?"

"Nothing's perfect," he said with a shrug. "How many times has it gone this well in the setup?"

"A couple," she said. Hesitating, she added, "The St. Louis job started perfectly."

"Exactly." He rolled away from her.

She pressed herself against his back, her arms around his shoulders, and remembered Finch, the hungry look he wore when they decided to change the plan. The bravado. They'd gotten greedy, tried to shoot the moon. It was the last time they'd seen their friend alive. "What's bothering you? Is it the touch?"

Sam shook his head. "It could've gone sideways in a hundred different ways. A bystander to the accident, the Mercedes pushing Gary into oncoming traffic, and what if he didn't see the painting on the wall? What's bothering me is that it all went according to plan."

She understood. They liked their wrinkles up front. It wasn't superstition as much as it was an appreciation of probability. Something was bound to go wrong. Each step beyond the initial touch exposed them more.

"We can always walk away," she said, trailing her hand down his thigh. It didn't matter that they didn't have much money left. They could start over if they had to, somewhere else. No more hotels. "It's a good con, the fiddle trick," she said. A simple two-person con, more than a dozen old school cheats took credit for coming up with it. Like all good cons, it's based on the national sin of choice in America: greed.

Go to a fancy restaurant with an old fiddle in a case. Eat the most expensive thing on the menu and pretend that you forgot your wallet at home. Leave the fiddle with the owner as collateral and explain that it belonged to your grandfather, that it's probably worth a couple hundred dollars and you were going to sell it at the music store across town. After you leave for your wallet, the other hustler approaches the owner and requests to see the fiddle. Upon examination, hustler two proclaims it to be a rare violin from Russia or Prague. It once belonged to Shostakovich or was made by a student of Stradivarius, or whatever. Hustler two offers to buy the violin for six thousand dollars and leaves their card. At this point, the mark knows you are returning for the fiddle. He knows you will call the police if he sells your violin out from under you. So, what if the mark bought your grandfather's fiddle for a couple hundred dollars. When you return, maybe you talk him up to a thousand. The mark will still make five thousand in profit. Not a bad day's work. So, the mark cleans out the cash from the register to pay you because, of course, you don't trust him to write a check. Especially not for a fiddle worth about fifty bucks.

Of course, Sam and Rachel had made a few alterations. Instead of a fiddle, they decided to use a fake Rembrandt, but the real prize would be getting an insurance policy against Little Vincent. The payoff would just be frosting on the cake.

Sam nodded. "Gary will probably call me tomorrow, feel me out. See what I know about the painting—how cheap he can get it off me."

"And I will negotiate a fair price for my services." She grinned, rolling away with an armload of comforter bunched beneath her.

"I'll turn up the heat on Gary," he said, snuggling in behind her, his lips against her ear. "If this goes right, we can stop running and start over." He gripped the delicate fold of her bare hip, pulling her ass against him. He was hard again.

"And I'll verify the Rembrandt with an estimate," she whispered, reaching between her legs to guide him inside her.

The following morning, Rachel crossed the cobbled drive of the Bagley estate. In the style of an Italian villa, all stucco, ceramic roof tiles, and arched windows, it went on and on, obscuring the pale expanse of the Atlantic.

Before she could knock, an elderly Latino gentleman with white hair like a composer's opened one of the great doors. He beckoned her into a three-story foyer of gleaming marble. Across from her, a pair of staircases curved down from the second floor. On a round table at the center of the foyer, a riot of white and blue orchids. Rachel gasped, part acting, part genuine, when she caught sight of the wall behind her. From waist high to the ceiling far above, at least a hundred paintings in gilt frames. Museum-quality lighting for each.

A little dog barked, high pitched and enraged. Its claws scrabbled on the tile as it sprinted around the corner. Rachel backed up a step as it closed in.

"Sooty," Teresa Bagley yelled from the archway. "Knock it off."

The dog changed course, looping back to Teresa, who picked it up. It was a shih tzu, a fat tangle of fur with a smushed face and googly eyes. It alternated panting and growling at Rachel.

"It's hard to believe. Until three years ago, Gary and I didn't own a single piece of art," Teresa said, handing the dog to the butler who carried it away. "Unless you count a few Thomas Kincade prints." She laughed a little too loud. She was dressed comfortably, a skirt, loose top, and ornate sandals.

"Wow," Rachel said. "It's quite a collection." She walked the full length of the wall, her heels echoing. In front of the Henri Bernard, she bent down and wore a concerned expression. It was one of his most famous works, *Woman Dressing in a Hotel*. In it, a young woman slipped into a skirt by the window of her hotel room. On the bed, an open suitcase. At first glance, the tableau was serene, but the longer she looked at it, the more unsettled Rachel seemed to become. Frowning, she waited for Teresa to ask what was wrong and recalled what had led them to Florida in the first place. An insurance policy.

A couple years back, the Artist was a virtuoso of cleaning up crime scenes, talking mistresses into abortions, paying off judges, and disappearing all manner of people deemed inconvenient by local organized crime. He was so good at his job that even Little

Vincent didn't cross him. Rumor was, the Artist had a piece of blackmail so good on Little Vincent that it must have been like having insurance against God himself. For years, the Artist flaunted the rules: disobeyed orders, stole mistresses away from made guys, and ran his own rackets in neighborhoods that were already spoken for.

Faced with losing his territory, Little Vincent had no choice but to hire an outsider to put a bomb under the driver's seat of his car. Days after the explosion, while the Philly PD were still bagging smears of DNA off streetlamps, an entire crew turned over the Artist's penthouse and his businesses all over the city. They never found what they were looking for.

Last fall, Sam did a favor for the Artist's lawyer, who quietly revealed to him that the Artist's real name was Etienne Bernard, son of the painter, Henri Bernard. His younger sister, Lisa, was the sole recipient of all of her brother's worldly possessions, which, upon his death, were promptly mailed to her. Sam was certain that whatever the Artist had over Little Vincent had been sent to his sister in Miami. If they could get it, they could finally stop running or at least get even. This would've been a whole lot easier if Lisa just took the money.

"Is everything okay?" Teresa asked.

"I'm not sure," Rachel said, scrutinizing the Bernard painting.

The butler returned with two glasses and a pitcher of sweet tea. Teresa poured one and handed it to Rachel. She pointed at a large canvas near the front door. It was splashed with color and cartoon skulls. "That's our most recent addition."

Wracking her brain, Rachel came up with the name. "A Takishi...Murakami," she said, her voice a cocktail of disbelief and awe.

"It's *Takashi*," Teresa corrected.

Shit. Rachel didn't have to feign embarrassment. "I'm more of a Dutch masters kind of girl." In under a minute, she was already undermining her own credibility. She knew as much about art as she did about seventeenth century Russian agriculture: jack shit. That is, until she put herself through a crash course on the Dutch masters.

"Don't worry," Teresa said, pouring herself a glass of tea. "Gary still calls it Chai-roscuro. People think he's ordering a drink instead of talking about shading."

They shared a laugh. Rachel peered at a few adjacent works until she saw the one she had studied ahead of time, Edward Hopper's *Chop Suey*. In it, two women sat near the window of a Chinese restaurant. Their clothes and hair were odd and beautiful. "You're very lucky to have a Hopper," she said.

"Luck can easily be substituted for money," Teresa said, her mouth full of sweet tea, her expression turning to vinegar. "What do you know about this piece?"

Rachel flushed with relief. For most of these paintings, she didn't know a thing, but she'd studied a few key pieces that she knew to be Gary and Teresa's favorites. "It's representative. It's always included in retrospectives of Hopper's work. It's psychologically complex and cinematic."

"How so," Teresa asked, taking a last sip of her tea and chewing an ice cube.

Pointing at the woman in green, she said, "The expression on her face. She's not paying attention to the woman across from her. She's somewhere else. This effect is highlighted by the way the light from the window strikes her. Like theater lights." She had to remind herself to breathe, knowing that if she failed in this, if Teresa didn't think she was credible, the house of cards they were assembling would never stand.

"Very good," Teresa said with a grin. "For a Dutch masters kind of girl." Setting her drink on the orchid table, she approached it and added, "But how can you tell if it's real?"

With a straight face, Rachel said, "You do have a certificate of authenticity, correct?"

"It's just a piece of paper," Teresa said with a pout.

"There's provenance, the chain of custody," she said. "Can you trace this back to Hopper himself?"

"Let's say you can't get either one."

Rachel smiled. In under ten minutes, they were already angling toward the Rembrandt from the pawn shop. "You hire an authority to review the work."

"Could you research the Hopper for us?" she asked.

"I could get you in touch with a qualified authority on Hopper," she said. Deciding to show her hand, she added, "Besides, I seem to remember that Christie's sold *Chop Suey* to a private seller last November."

"But it was an anonymous bidder," Teresa countered.

"I could ask a few friends who work there," Rachel said. "Off the record."

Holding up her hands, Teresa grinned. "You caught me. You're something else, Amelia." The butler scooped up the pitcher and the empty glass and vanished through a side door.

Teresa said, "I need your help to authenticate our art."

Her eyes scanning the walls, Rachel shook her head. "For this many, it would take months, maybe years, I'm afraid." With a disappointed shrug, she said, "Classes start next week. There's no way I could get someone to cover in time."

"Of course," Teresa said. "It would only be a few pieces, what we've bought that didn't come with little pieces of paper." A note of sarcasm slithered into her voice.

"I don't know," Rachel said, her eyes going big and hollow. She did her best to look shell-shocked and vulnerable. "This was supposed to be my ten-year anniversary trip."

Taking her hand, Teresa led her between the staircases to the edge of a great room with a glass wall. Outside, there was a patio, a marble-edged pool with columns, topiary, and beyond that, the bright ocean. At the rear of the yard, a stunning gazebo, like Buckingham Palace, with fake dormers and a cupola on top. "Stay here for the rest of the week," Teresa said. "Authenticate what you can by Sunday morning. We will double your fee."

Outside, a man climbed out of the pool and glanced at her as he toweled himself off. Of average height, he was built like a bully breed dog and covered in tattoos. The bridge of his nose was smashed down like it had been broken with a hammer. "Who is that?" she asked, feeling her stomach drop. A stab of recognition. For a terrifying moment, she thought he was from Philly.

"Gary's nephew," she said.

"He looks familiar." Rachel realized she was staring and fixed her eyes on the ocean.

"He's Bob Clover. He's famous," Teresa said. "A couple years ago, he was the Heavyweight Ultimate Fighting World Champion." A broken-glass pattern of scars peeked through his buzzed hair. "He got into a bar fight last year with five men. It was over a girl, of course." Teresa patted her arm, like she was talking about a quaint misunderstanding. Rachel remembered. It had made the national news. At a Miami nightclub, Bob Clover had forced a woman into his truck. Her brothers and their friends had to use a bat and a tire iron to subdue him. He was in a coma for weeks.

On the deck, Bob wrapped the towel around his trunks and came inside. As if noticing Rachel for the first time, he paused and grinned, his eyes crawling over her body like an overturned bucket of spiders. More than a few of his back teeth were missing.

Teresa put her hand on Rachel's back and pushed her closer. "Bob, this is Amelia. She's going to stay here for the week to look at the art." Rachel resisted the urge to contradict her. She hadn't agreed to stay.

Bob snorted, his black dog eyes twinkling. "Plenty of naked women to look at here." He had a mechanical laugh.

Against her better judgment, Rachel held out her hand. "I've never met anyone famous before," she said. He took it in his own which was like a catcher's mitt, a hand that had inflicted terrible damage, a hand that could kill. The strength of him terrified her.

Misreading the interaction, Teresa gave Rachel a meaningful look. "You and Bob can share the north wing of the house for the rest of the week."

There it was, Rachel thought. The wrinkle.

***

An hour later, Rachel and Teresa were having brunch in the gazebo when Gary came home from golfing. With pit stains and beer breath, he kissed the top of Teresa's head and sat. His assistant, Ingrid, followed him out. "Should I schedule Peter for next Wednesday?"

Gary waved her off. "It was lip service. I hate that guy." To Teresa, he said, "Peter was at the country club again."

"Money for the wetlands?" she asked, feeding Sooty a piece of glazed salmon from her plate.

He nodded.

Ingrid waited at the top step. She was beautiful with blonde bangs and a swimmer's body. She was the kind of assistant no wife would ever want. As she turned to go inside, Teresa spoke up. "Why don't you join us, Ingrid?"

"No thank you, Mrs. Bagley." Her voice, perfectly girlish and meek.

Teresa gave Gary a meaningful look and he shrugged. "I'm not asking," she said. "You look half-starved."

Ingrid sat. One of the waitstaff filled two plates with broccoli salad and salmon and placed them before Gary and Ingrid. They ate in awkward silence for a few moments. Ingrid glanced at Rachel, who gave her a polite smile.

Sam and Rachel had gotten to her early. An aspiring world traveler, Ingrid maintained a travel blog, but had only left the country twice to visit Toronto and Jamaica. Convincing her to lie to her employer had been appallingly easy. Fortunately for them, she was also bought off for half what they'd budgeted.

When Gary had asked her to research Amelia Depardieu's background, she delivered a short report to the Bagleys that assured them that Rachel was the real deal. A qualified authority who had curated exhibits at the Metropolitan Museum of Art, who taught at Columbia, and published numerous papers on the Dutch Golden Age. The simple web presence they'd created would hold up if either Gary or Teresa got curious enough to look for themselves.

"You excited for your trip?" Teresa asked Ingrid, her voice cold.

She nodded, having just taken a bite. Chewing, she said, "I am." To Gary, her lids low, she added, "Sorry I'm leaving on such short notice." Her plane left in the morning. For her services, and to get her out of the way, Rachel had bought Ingrid an all-expenses paid Scandinavian cruise. Ingrid had told the Bagleys that she'd won the trip from a local country radio station.

"It's fine," Gary said, his expression indicating that it was not. Everyone at the table knew that Gary was fucking Ingrid, however, only Gary believed it to be a secret. Each Thursday at 3:00 pm, he brought takeout to her apartment on the mainland. As the food cooled on the counter, they had sex in the bedroom—always doggy style. He wanted to talk dirty, but Ingrid didn't know what to say, so she moaned theatrically to make up for it. Afterward, he would babble while they ate fried chicken or burgers. They never made any plans. He never made any promises, and he was back on the road by 4:00 pm.

Gary startled Rachel by acknowledging her. "Have you seen the paintings?"

Teresa rolled her eyes. "Of course she's seen them, dear."

"Has she seen the three we want her to authenticate?" he asked.

Before Teresa could answer, Rachel seized her chance and said, "I've seen two of them so far." They stared at her, and she played her part, the intellectual who was shy about being correct. Clearly, it bothered them that she'd seen through their ruse.

"How could you know?" Gary said, looking surprised and irritated all at once.

She couldn't. It was impossible to tell from a brief viewing.

"The Murakami," Teresa said as if she'd known all along.

Nodding, Rachel said, "Most of Murakami's works are limited edition prints. While an original painting isn't unheard of, they're notoriously difficult to acquire right now. Also—" she chuckled, "—you pointed it out to me."

One of the staff brought Gary a Bud Light Lime. Taking a discerning sip, he frowned and asked, "And the other?"

"The Henri Bernard, *Woman in a Hotel Room*," she said,

waiting for the inevitable question.

To her husband, Teresa explained, "When she first saw our collection, she stopped and stared at it." Turning to Rachel, she looked thoroughly baffled. "Out of all the pictures, why that one?"

"If you don't mind me asking, where did you acquire it?" Rachel asked.

"Germany," Teresa said. "An out-of-the-way gallery. One of our friends arranged for a private viewing. You didn't answer my question, Amelia."

"The perspective," Rachel said, as if that would explain everything. "It's slightly off. Bernard was a master of it, so at first I was wondering what was he trying to say by doing that."

"Isn't Bernard the one who hung himself?" Ingrid asked.

Rachel ignored Teresa's poisoned look and said, "Yes. He died poor and wasn't discovered until after he'd taken his own life." She folded her hands in her lap, her gaze falling. "I hope I'm wrong, and I don't know for sure, but there's a good chance that the Bernard is a fake," she said.

Gary bolted upright, his chair falling over. "I'll ring that little Kraut bastard's neck."

In a small voice, Rachel added, "I hope you didn't spend too much to acquire it." The plan had grown organically. Convince the Bagleys that their Bernard was a fake. Trade the painting to Bernard's daughter in return for whatever insurance her brother had against Little Vincent. But if they could con the Bagleys into thinking a real painting was a fake, wouldn't it be just as easy to convince them that a fake was real?

Gary laughed, pacing in a circle, his fists clenched. "Christ, we've spent more on houses we've never seen."

"It isn't for certain," Rachel said. The Bagleys looked grief-stricken. Gary took his beer to the edge of the pool, finished it off, and set it at the edge.

Rachel said, "I would strongly recommend further analysis, testing the pigments. If it is a fake, it's a very good one." To Teresa, she asked, "With your permission, I'd like to take a couple pictures of it. I can send it to a colleague who specializes in late-twentieth century French art."

Twisting a napkin in her lap, Teresa nodded.

When it was clear that brunch was over, Rachel stood to go inside. She needed to get out before Teresa remembered her suggestion that she sleepover. She caught sight of movement on the second floor beyond the marble balcony. Between the drapes, Bob watched her. His expression gave her chills. It was devoid of anything.

In the foyer, Rachel took more than a dozen pictures of the *Woman in a Hotel Room*. The woman in the painting was topless with creamy skin, the light falling across her face, which was a quarter turn away.

Sam had bought the camera for her, a high-end DSLR. It snapped and made a stuttering sound with each picture. No one had followed her from the table to the rental car. Only Sooty, who lingered beneath the archway, one bottom tooth stuck out from her lip. With some luck, Rachel would be able to escape before Teresa could broach the subject of a slumber party once more.

When she opened her bag to get the portrait lens, she flinched. Gary leaned against the doorway behind her. He had been there for a while by the look of it.

"So you're the real deal. An expert," he said, eying her bare legs. He spoke as if everything he said had a note of sarcasm to it. "Before Teresa called, I had you checked out. Called the museum, the university, even looked up a couple of the papers you published." All given to him by Ingrid. He waved his palm over his head. "They're beyond me, I'll admit."

She shrugged and secured the new lens. "I'm relieved."

"Why's that?"

"You'll trust that I know how to do my job."

He took his time to reply. "You sound like a woman who

hasn't been surprised in years."

Setting up, she took a close-up shot of the painting. "I haven't," she lied.

When she looked up, he was suddenly only a few feet away and grinning, which startled her. A key glinted in his hand. "I want to show you something."

She didn't like the scalpel-like gleam in his eye, the way his tone softened, but she lowered her camera and said, "Okay."

"Leave the camera," he said. She placed it in its case and left it on the orchid table. He led her up the stairs where he unlocked a door to a massive office. It gave her vertigo to see it. Like a movie set of an industrialist's study in the 1920s, all leather, wainscoting, wallpaper and mahogany. Even the faint smell of tobacco and books was on point. Heavy curtains were drawn, making the room feel smaller than it was. On a broad desk by the back windows, Gary turned on a desk lamp and touched the gilt frame of a painting that lay on its back.

Rachel did her best confused and a little impatient. "Is this the third painting?"

"What do you think, Ms. Depardieu?" he said, turning on a task lamp and swiveling it closer.

She stared at it for a long time, reminding herself that the best actors only needed their eyes. Slowly, she let it dawn on her, the realization that this was a Rembrandt, that it had been missing for more than forty years. "Oh my," she whispered, worried she was playing the reverence a little too hard. Careful not to touch it, she let out a shuddering breath as she studied it.

"Where did you find this?" she asked.

"Private seller." He was a halfway decent liar. No, she reminded herself. He was better than that. "You specialize in this, right?"

Using the task lamp to inspect the brushstrokes, she nodded. After a few moments, she asked, "Is it real?"

"That's what we're paying you for," he said.

* * *

The following afternoon, Sam relaxed. His head cradled against the leather of an antique barber's chair. The apartment smelled like fresh cut cantaloupe. Sunlight warmed his left cheek as Colin, a member of the local civic theater, worked on his face. Colin was tall and black with a graying beard, his bare feet tapping on the floorboards. One of his neighbors played the trumpet, an infectious tune.

Gary had called earlier, much sooner than they expected, which was encouraging. He wanted to "get it over with." They were scheduled to meet in a park to trade the cash for the watches.

"What's with your leg?" Colin asked, his deep voice filling up the room.

"Why do you ask?" Sam removed his hand from the scar on his shin. He'd been pressing his thumb into it, a tic he'd developed.

"Dog bite?"

Sam shook his head. "Car door. The bone broke the skin."

Colin whistled and shook his head. "Damn, looks like you just got back on your feet."

Sam smiled not liking how obvious it was. The tissue still red and tender, smooth as melted candle wax. He'd been laid up for months and had lost about fifteen pounds of muscle. Worse yet, they had spent what little they got on medication and physical therapy.

"Don't move or it'll smear," Colin said.

"Can I see it?"

"No," Colin said. "I'm gonna charge you extra if you keep moving around."

"What's your role of a lifetime?" Sam asked, moving his mouth as little as possible. Somewhere behind him, a pet iguana scampered across the floor.

Pausing, Colin said, "I played Willy Loman for two seasons in New York, off-off-Broadway. I would have done it for free, too. Each night was like eating a bag of caramels." Dabbing his brush, he added, "Now that I'm going gray, I'd give anything to play Lear."

"Shakespeare, right?" Sam said.

Everything about Colin's bearing suddenly changed to that of an older man with sore joints. Wide-eyed and breathless, he rasped, "When we are born, we cry that we are come to this great stage of fools."

"Wow," Sam said. "You'd nail any audition with that."

He made a dismissive noise. "I thought so, too." Holding out his arms, his chin raised, he added, "But they take one look at me and think Othello."

"I'd cast you," Sam said absently. "You ever been in anything I know?"

"I did some TV a couple years back," he said, pulling Sam's jaw to the right. "Thugs mostly."

"Jesus."

"It wasn't all bad," he said. "I got to meet Michelle Pfeiffer once." Before Sam could ask, Colin jabbed the end of his brush into the soft part under his jaw and seethed, "Gimme yo purse, blondie, or I'll cut you."

They shared a laugh. When he withdrew, Sam resisted touching his neck and said, "You ever get tired of playing a stereotype?"

"It paid the bills," Colin said, mixing a new color on his palette. "I played a crime scene technician for three episodes of CSI a couple years back." He delivered a few lines. He was intense, thoughtful, and utterly believable despite the environment.

"Can I see it now?" Sam asked.

Sighing, Colin held a mirror in front of him. In a sliver of sunlight from the living room window, he looked like he'd been beaten with a pipe. He was just barely recognizable, his left eye blackening, a gash along his lower jaw that swelled by his ear. Grinning, he couldn't shake the feeling that he was somehow tempting fate.

"What do you think, Leland?" Colin asked, wiping latex from his fingers. "Should I say on stage or work behind it?"

"How about some more work?" Sam asked.

* * *

An hour and a half later, Sam hunched at a bench that overlooked the edge of Pond Cypress Natural Area, a shaded cypress swamp with green water and birds making a racket. Just about every cubic foot of air must have contained an ounce of insects, droning so loud it almost sounded like static on a TV. The rank odor of mud and algae and rot clung to everything. On the bench next to him, a blue duffel bag filled with banded stacks of about three hundred dollars and fifteen dollars in paper cut to match the size of the bills. He wore a trucker hat pulled low and aviator sunglasses to conceal his face.

Gary arrived late in a black Escalade. Sam pretended not to notice the burly guy glaring from behind the wheel. For a moment, he wondered if they were in over their head. It made sense, though. After asking if Gary was mobbed up, of course he'd behave like a mobster. Good thing Gary didn't have a clue what mobsters were really like or Sam would wind up face down in the water, the gators rendering his corpse, joint by joint, like a roasted chicken.

Gary got out of the back seat and donned a pair of sunglasses that cost more than Sam's first car. In fairness, Sam stole his first car. In a cotton suit jacket, Gary strutted toward him, his face red from the heat.

Sam stood and held his hands up, "Where's the painting?"

"Sit down," Gary said. On the phone, he had insisted on meeting here. Away from the road, a fertilizer company a couple hundred yards away. About as private as you could get for West Palm Beach.

Sam sat, looking sullen and afraid. Instead of sitting, Gary stood over him and sucked on his cheek. "Here's what's going to happen, Leland." From his coat pocket, he withdrew the three watches and dropped them into Sam's lap. "You keep your money."

"You don't understand, man," Sam said, rising to his feet, "I need the painting." The watches thudded in the Bermuda grass.

Gary pushed him back down. "I'm not giving you anything."

"If I don't get it back, I'm a dead man," Sam said, letting his voice tremble. "My business partner isn't the kind of person you want to fuck with."

Gary shrugged, clearly loving every moment he got to be the tough guy. "Not my problem."

Sam couldn't wait to see how tough Gary really was.

Pausing, Gary said, "Take off your hat and glasses."

"Go to hell," Sam said.

Instead of getting angry, Gary pointed over his shoulder and said, "My nephew could do it for you. He was a world champion cage fighter."

Hesitating, Sam removed the hat and glasses, but kept his eyes on Gary's feet. He angrily flexed his jaw and winced from the pain.

Crouching, Gary examined his face. Clearly pleased, he said, "I want to find the guy who did this to you, buy him dinner and a box of Arturo Fuente cigars. Quit while you're ahead, Leland."

"Why do you even want it? It's just a stupid painting."

"My wife likes it." Gary shrugged. Leaning down, he picked up the watches, wiped a speck of dirt from the face of one, and set them on the bench. Sam shoved the bag of money into Gary's arms. Gary forced it back on him. "Keep your money," he said, breathing hard. "Use it to leave town."

"My partner will dump my body in the Everglades," Sam said, his eyes settling on the water.

"Either that or he could teach you how to fucking drive," Gary said. He stood and walked to his car.

Over his shoulder, Sam couldn't help smiling as he shouted, "He'll come for you next, Gary."

That evening, after Rachel stowed her bags in one of the Bagley's guest suites, she was escorted by the butler to the great room at the back of the estate where they ate French pudding with black salt.

Gary actually licked the ramekin clean and set it on the stone counter. "So, how long will it take to authenticate the Rembrandt?" He was already calling it the Rembrandt, which tasted even better to Rachel than the chocolate.

"It's hard to tell at this juncture," she said. "I've managed to locate a technician, a friend of a friend, who can sample the pigments and materials."

Teresa, who was feeding Sooty a little pudding from her spoon, raised a waxed eyebrow. "That was fast."

"It was luck more than anything," Rachel said with a self-conscious shrug.

"Excellent," Gary said, his eyes roaming for more pudding. "When can he get started?"

"Tomorrow," Rachel said, her eyes flicking to Teresa, "If that's okay with you." Instead of answering, Teresa watched Bob Clover descend the stairs. Suppressing a sigh, she checked a third tally mark in her head. Bob was three for three on not wearing a shirt.

"The sooner we're done with this, the better," Gary pronounced, getting a beer out of a refrigerator that looked more like a spaceship.

Getting off the couch, Teresa looked concerned. "You okay, Bobby?"

Bob pouted and said, "It happened again, Auntie. I was watching the gators and the sheriff gave me a ticket for it. They have it out for me, I swear." Teresa put her hands on his shoulders and whispered something. He nodded like an idiot.

In the kitchen, Gary made a disparaging noise and rolled his eyes. "It's against the law to feed the gators, boy."

Bob snapped a wounded look at Gary. "I wasn't feedin 'em. Everybody knows it's a fine."

Under his breath, Gary said, "Five hundred bucks every goddamned time." His phone rang with Frank Sinatra's "My Way." Rachel unobtrusively checked her watch. Among his many virtues, Sam had always been punctual. She wore a bored expression as she pretended to watch Teresa soothe Gary's nephew with promises of refilling his account.

"You better not be a telemarketer, pal," Gary answered. Rachel knew the script so well that she almost didn't have to listen.

"You have something that belongs to me," a man with a thick

French accent growled.

"National pride can't be given back," Gary said, smirking.

"My painting," the man said. "You stole it from my business associate."

Gary went still for a moment, his breath hitching. After a few seconds, he seemed to find his equilibrium. "I don't know what you're talking about, pal." He hurried through the great room and up the stairs.

"The painting from the pawn shop. You stole it from Leland Spinnaker after the two of you got into a…fender bender." In the protracted silence that followed, the man added, "Am I speaking to Gary Bagley?"

Gary snarled, "Leland must've made off with your painting. I never saw it."

The man laughed and hung up. Out of breath, Gary stopped at the top of the stairs and stared dumbly at his phone.

"Everything okay, dear?" Teresa asked.

"Yeah," Gary said. "It was a prank call."

Bob meandered into the kitchen where he began assembling the ingredients for the night's protein shake. He stared at Rachel's bare legs.

Just as Gary lowered his shoulders, his phone pinged. A text from a blocked number. A picture of Gary at the golf course earlier in the day. His mouth open, one arm raised to make a point, a beer in his other hand. A long way off, the photographer had used a zoom lens, but the message was unmistakable. It could've been a rifle.

Gary startled as his phone rang again. He hurried down the hallway toward his office. When he answered, the man on the phone said, "Leland had ample reason to tell me the truth. He told me that you took my painting."

"That asshole ruined my car," Gary said.

"Not my concern," the man said. "Leland has already paid for his stupidity."

"As far as I'm concerned," Gary said, "we're even."

* * *

In Lisa's apartment in Miami, Papi lowered the phone and coughed into his fist. They'd gone over this a dozen times. Papi was to scare Gary, keep him off balance, until Sam could close the deal.

"It is very dangerous to believe a man like you will ever be even with a man such as myself. You have three things to pay for: stealing from me, disrespecting me and, most grievous of all, you have wasted my time."

"So what!" Gary snarled. "You're going to have to do better than hire someone to take my picture, asshole."

They hadn't anticipated so much resistance. At a loss for what to say next, Sam rifled through his handwritten notecards. Papi held up a hand and grinned.

"Look around you, Mr. Bagley. At your house, your wife, your cars, your art collection—that is the price for stealing from me. You think you're such a big, fat fish in your little pond. But you are in the ocean, my friend, and if you don't give me what I want, I'm going to swallow you."

"Maybe I don't have your fucking painting," Gary said.

"Mr. Bagley, it no longer matters," Papi's voice dipped from civil to guttural, "because what I will do to you, *mère enculée*, it will be biblical."

"Now hold on," Gary said. "Maybe we could come to some kind of—"

Papi hung up. Out of breath, he grinned into his lap and looked twenty years younger. "How did I do?"

Sam clapped and said, "You're one tough gangster, Papi. You didn't even need the cards."

"I am a very natural liar. Ever since I was a boy." He handed the phone to Sam and wiped his palms on his sweats. "And I hate bourgeoisie assholes."

Sam nodded. "So I'll see you tomorrow?"

Frowning, Papi shook his head. "I may be busy sweeping women off their feet."

"What if I bring beef bourguignon?" Sam said, his voice flat. Henry sat near them on the floor, killing aliens on the TV.

Papi gave him a look of warning. "Don't toy with me, boy."

"I'll be here before lunch time," Sam said, patting him on the shoulder. "I have to go." He ruffled Henry's hair as he hurried to the front door.

"A bottle of wine wouldn't hurt," Papi hollered just as the front door closed.

While Teresa watched *The Bachelor* on the living room TV, Rachel savored the rest of her French pudding. By the time she had finished, Gary had returned downstairs. He was as pale as he could get with a South-Florida-golf-course tan, which was about hue of a baked chicken.

He jumped when Bob turned on the blender. Gary stared at the floor-to-ceiling windows, his expression clear. Anyone could be out there in the dark, beyond the lights, watching them.

Bob flicked the blender off and on to elicit the same reaction, but seemed disappointed when Gary retired to his study to watch Fox News.

"Oh shit," Teresa said. In her lap, Sooty was unconscious, her body like a wet mop. "Bob, can you get the insulin from the fridge?"

Taking his time, Bob took an ampule out of the door of the refrigerator and crossed the huge room. When he handed it to Teresa, she shook it and said, "My bag. Get my bag."

"Where is it?" he asked.

"The kitchen counter," she said, pointing at a brown leather purse patterned with golden dollar signs. Once Bob retrieved it, Teresa took out a disposable syringe, removed the safety cap, and filled it with insulin. Pinching skin between the dog's front shoulder blades, she gave Sooty the injection. She cooed to the dog as she came out of it.

Bob returned to making his shake and muttered something under his breath.

"I used to work in a vet's office," Teresa said, a note of pride in her voice.

"Oh," Rachel said. She'd feigned a confused interest in the exchange. Now, she lingered at the kitchen counter, paging through a binder of art history dissertations on Rembrandt. She had no idea what the writers were trying to say, but the word *locus* and *pedagogical* appeared multiple times. In her spare time, she'd rewritten some of the text in the margins and highlighted a couple sections in different colors just in case someone would snoop through her things.

For a time, no one spoke. On her electric massage chair, Sooty in her lap, Teresa seemed to have drifted into some kind of purgatory between sleep and wakefulness. Bob, who had been pretending to read a muscle magazine that promised better abs, closed it and stared at Rachel until she met his gaze.

"Wanna go for a swim?" he said.

She gave him a look that showed how unimpressed she was and yawned. "I'll pass."

"Then what are you waiting around for?" he asked, giving her a sly look.

Visibly surprised, she said, "I was just getting ready for tomorrow. The tech will be here early."

"You've been looking at the same pages over and over," he said in a low voice.

"It's called studying," she said, pointing at his magazine. "What about you? Does anyone actually read the articles?"

He rubbed his chin and pursed his lips. "I've been sitting here, trying to figure out how you shave your dick trap."

Rachel didn't react. Instead, she walked around the massive stone kitchen island to put her dish in the sink.

"Just leave it," Teresa said, switching off the TV. "Cecillia will take care of it in the morning."

Rachel ignored her. Her heart pounding, she rinsed her dishes. When she came back to the counter, no one noticed that a steak knife was missing from the block. Closing her binder, she said to

Bob, "I'll see you both in the morning."

Teresa looked between them, grinned, and said, "If you two want to go skinny dipping, no one in the house could see you."

Rachel laughed like it was the best joke she had heard all week and went upstairs. In her room, she locked the door, but it was the kind of lock with a hole in the middle of the handle, unlocked by anything long and skinny. Thankfully, the door itself was made of real wood.

She had been so rattled that she'd left her phone on the kitchen counter. Slipping out of her shoes, she padded back downstairs to the great room as silently as she could. In the hall, she couldn't quite place it, but something was wrong. The room had gone completely silent in maybe ninety seconds. No TV. No conversation.

Peeking around the corner, she saw Sooty alone on the couch. Maybe everyone had gone to bed. She retrieved her phone from the marble counter and caught sight of movement in the backyard. In the shadows, Bob sat on the steps of the Gazebo. Teresa, in a house dress, straddled him, moving up and down. Bathed in the blue light of the pool, they hurried to finish.

Frozen in surprise, it took Rachel a second to see that Bob was looking at her.

Retreating to her room, she wanted to take a shower. On the one hand, it seemed like poetic justice that Gary wasn't the only Bagley with an extracurricular activity, though Teresa certainly could've done better. But the way Bob had looked at her gave her the chills.

As quietly as she could, she dragged the bureau in front of the bedroom door. It wouldn't stop Bob, but it would slow him down. The room had a balcony. Even if he scaled the trellis, the balcony door locked.

She got ready for bed and changed into pajama shorts and one of Sam's Rolling Stones T-shirts. Lying down the huge four-poster bed, she pretended to read from the binder for fifteen minutes before turning the light out. In the dark, she donned jeans and sneakers. The posts for the bed were screwed in, so she unscrewed a four-foot long mahogany club and laid it on the floor. Then, she waited in the armchair in the corner, the steak knife in her hand.

Sometime after midnight, someone crept through the hallway. Slow footsteps creaking on the floor. Rachel held her breath and rehearsed what she had to do. The door handle would click, the springs contracting, followed by the *tink* of something being threaded into the handle to undo the lock. She'd have only a few seconds to pick up the bedpost, cross the room, and jab it screw-first through the gap. For a guy like Bob, she'd have to do a ton of damage before he'd give up. If he got past the bureau, she'd have to use the knife. It was as sharp as her grandmother's tongue and scallop-edged.

The footsteps stopped in front of her door. After a moment, someone continued down the hall. She let out a breath and loosened her grip on the knife. What the hell had she been thinking? She suddenly missed Sam so much that her chest felt hollow. It had only been one night and she was almost homesick for him.

The next morning, the technician arrived during breakfast. It was Colin from the local theater in a brown suit and orange bow tie. He set two tackle boxes in the foyer.

Teresa said, "Thank you for coming on such short notice."

He ignored her and glanced over her head. "Where can I get set up?" He asked with the perfect mixture of professionalism and disdain.

"This way," Gary said, leading him upstairs to his office where Bernard's *Woman in a Hotel Room*, Rembrandt's *Landscape with Cottages*, and the Murakami painting had been laid out on his massive desk. Rachel followed, a cup of coffee in her hand. Despite the bed being one of the most comfortable she'd ever known, she'd lain awake most of the night in her shoes.

Bob had gone to the gym earlier, which was a relief.

In the office, Colin was putting on a show of stunned awe for Gary. Setting his boxes on the floor, he approached Rachel and said in an urgent whisper, "How come you didn't tell me about this on the phone, Ms. Depardieu?"

"I wanted you to see it for yourself," she said wryly.

He cleaned his glasses and said loud enough for Gary to hear, "This could be one of the most extraordinary finds in decades." Near the window, Gary averted his gaze, but not before she caught the swell of pride—the thing they'd been aiming for these last few weeks: confidence. Gary had made up his mind.

As Colin straightened his glasses, she said, "It would be worth twenty million. Maybe more."

"I'm aware, Ms. Depardieu," he said. Colin had been unexpected cost, a last-minute addition. Sam had insisted on adding him after his makeup session. Rachel hadn't liked it at first, but now she understood. He was helping to tip the scales. For a moment, she wondered if they needed the other parts of the plan—the theatrics. But it might already be too late for that.

Colin opened his tackle boxes and set some brushes, tweezers, vials, and lights on the side table. All of it utterly convincing. He donned a pair of latex gloves and a device that looked almost like night vision goggles.

Rachel crossed the office and took Gary by the elbow. "Let's let Mr. Conlin to his work."

"You're going to do all three paintings, right?" Gary asked.

He nodded. "I'll take the samples to Miami myself. We should have results by this evening."

At their insistence, Rachel and Colin worked on the paintings all morning without being disturbed. They left the massive bay windows open, the ocean wind gusting between the drapes. The door to Gary's study stayed closed, except for the butler, who brought refreshments every half hour whether they ate them or not. Rachel was no fool. Teresa had sent him to spy on them, but all he could report was that they poured over the paintings for hours while listening to the complete works of Philip Glass. Colin had brought a portable speaker in one of his tackle boxes and explained that his character, Mr. Conlin, was a dedicated aficionado of minimalist composition.

Between interruptions, they quietly negotiated new terms for his employment. Sam had paid him three hundred dollars. As far as Rachel was concerned, it was the only real crime they were committing. She offered three thousand if he never breathed a word of this. He agreed with a wink. It was impossible not to like him.

They took a break for a lunch of yellowfin tuna steaks and kale salad in the gazebo out back. Afterward, Colin shook each of the Bagley's hands and touched the narrow steel case in his other hand. "I'll take these to Miami and call you with the results this evening."

The rest of the afternoon proceeded like erosion, each minute taking an age to wear away. Outside, the breeze ruffled the palms. Cars hissed by. Further down the beach, a dog barked. Gary went to the gym early and Teresa watched her *telenovela*. Bob worked on his tan in a lounge chair out back.

Rachel went to her room for a nap and locked the door. In the bathroom, she ran the fan and sat on the toilet lid to call Sam, who picked up on the second ring.

"I think we should revise the next step," she said.

Instead of answering right away, he took a breath. One of the many reasons she loved him was that he listened. While anyone else would list off what they'd already agreed on, she could almost feel the gears in Sam's head turning. "What's changed?" he asked.

"Mr. Conlin was so amazing," she said, keeping her voice low, "that Gary's ready to buy."

"That's good news," he said.

"I think the next step would be overkill." She decided to point out the obvious. "Also, it's risky."

"Is Gary ready to pay Leland off in the next twenty-four hours?" he asked.

Shit. She hadn't considered the timeline, which was tight for a dozen reasons. Primarily because the longer they waited, the odds of Gary engaging the critical thinking part of his brain increased. Even a perfect plan had edges. The mark could see them if you gave him enough time to think about it. The trick was to keep Gary hopping from one foot to the other, reacting to what's right in front of them. Gary might be ready to buy, but there was a high degree of likelihood that he would drag it out, demand meetings, stall for time, and haggle for weeks.

"No," she admitted. "He's greedy for the status of finding the stolen Rembrandt, but he'll still try for a bargain. He's no fool. He's covering his losses just in case there's an angle he doesn't see."

"So I should proceed as planned?" he asked. She could hear that he was smiling.

"Yes," she said, wondering where he was. She had no illusions. Ever since Gary had cut Sam's face, Sam had looked forward to the next part of the plan.

"I missed you last night," he said. "Any chance you might be able to get away for a few hours?"

She laughed. "You're impossible," she said. The next twenty-four hours would be crucial. They muttered a couple of sweet nothings and hung up. Setting the alarm on her phone, she got into bed. The room was cool, the sheets slick across her neck. She should've felt foolish for suggesting to change the plan when they were so close. Instead she felt something she hadn't in what seemed like a long time, the wild possibility of hope. Everything in life was about odds, and for the first time in a long time, there was small chance that they could stop running. Not just because of money, either, but actual leverage. The payout might be large enough to get them new identities and across the world with enough left to start over. But most importantly, they would never again have to worry about Little Vincent.

She allowed herself the luxury of imagining what it would be like to stay still for a time. Maybe rent a cabin in the Rocky Mountains or an apartment in Rio de Janeiro, a place they could make their own for a couple seasons. She could collect paperbacks on her nightstand the way she had when she was a little girl. She had difficulty imagining what Sam would do. He would be restless, dreaming up another con, flicking his lighter open and closed, telling her he was fine. It wasn't the first time that Rachel questioned why they were running.

That evening, Rachel ate with the Bagleys in the dining room where Ingrid had set up a conference phone as the centerpiece in case Mr. Conlin called early with the results of the carbon dating test. It was a cold room with white wainscoting, pale blue wallpaper, and elaborate woodwork on the ceiling. Someone had hung the three paintings on the far wall of the dining room. At Gary's insistence, the cook had made pork chops, greens, and red beans with rice.

As the food was set out, Bob slinked into the room and sat next to Rachel. He gnawed at his pork chop, his jaw muscles like golf balls. He smelled rank, like algae and rotten meat.

"I'm heading into town for a bit," Rachel said, surprising herself. She needed to get out of the house, at least for a little while. She could surprise Sam. Missing a couple hours this evening wouldn't jeopardize anything. "For a massage," she said. "I was thinking about what you said, Mrs. Bagley, about how I should treat myself a little."

"I'll give you a massage," Bob said between mouthfuls.

Ignoring him, Teresa said, "We don't need to be so formal. Please call me Teresa."

Before Rachel could reply, the conference phone rang and lit up green. "Shut up, all of you," Gary said, swallowing and lunging toward the phone. Mashing the button, he raised his voice. "Yes, Mr. Conlin?"

"Hello, Mr. Bagley. Is this a good time to call?" Colin said. His voice was too loud through the conference phone. Teresa frowned and set her fork down while Bob speared a second and third pork chop from a silver platter.

"Just tell us. Are they real?" Gary shouted.

"I've been going over the findings," he said. Paper rustled in the background. "While the age of the pigments cannot conclusively identify a painting, it can accurately identify the age of the paints used in its creation, which can, as you know, support a claim of authenticity."

"Yes, yes, we're aware of that," Teresa blurted, gesturing for him to move on.

"Before I give you the results, I have to ask," Colin said, "How much did you pay for the Bernard?" Gary stood at the end of the table wearing a worried expression.

"Two million," Teresa said, the corners of her mouth hooked downward.

"We were told it was worth at least four," Gary said.

"Bernard's *Woman in a Hotel Room* was created in 1988, during his most prolific period. I'm sorry to inform you of this, but the carbon date for the pigments is unequivocal. The paints used in its construction are less than ten years old."

Gary collapsed into his chair, his hands covering his face. Teresa picked up her knife and fork and cut her food into equally sized squares. "Serves us right," she whispered.

As if just catching on, Bob furrowed his brow and spoke, his mouth filled with meat. "Who cares if the painting is real or fake? Didn't you spend more on Gary's Bugatti?"

Gary dropped his arms to each side of his plate and, in one great jerk, flung the dishes against the wall. On his feet, he shouted, "It isn't about the money, you ape."

Rachel remained still, her face a mask of surprise and fear. Bob grinned and kept eating, his shoulders hunched.

"The Murakami falls within the expected dates of creation," Colin said.

The Bagleys shared a relieved look.

"The pigments from the Rembrandt, however," Colin said, pausing for effect, "were manufactured in the mid-seventeenth century, which is conclusive with the original."

"Excuse me?!?" Teresa said, her knife slipping from her hand and clattering on the plate. The Bagley's shared a look.

"It's real?" Gary said, a triumphant smile spreading.

"The odds are promising. Barring an X-ray and more thorough testing, I would conclude that the painting I saw this afternoon was the original *Landscape with Cottages* stolen from Montreal Museum of Art." Breathless, he added, "Congratulations, Mr. and Mrs. Bagley. This is an astonishing stroke of providence. You and your wife will be the toast of the art world for years to come."

Catching the triumphant look the Bagley's shared, Rachel almost felt bad. The intimacy of it. In a single exchange, Teresa forgave Gary, who went from contrite to cocky within seconds.

"Congratulations," Rachel murmured, setting her napkin on her plate. "I'll leave you to celebrate your—"

Shouting echoed through the house like a trapped bird. Still chewing, Bob rose and followed the noise to the rear of the estate. Rachel and Gary followed at a safe distance. The back door was open. The butler stood in the darkened backyard, at the edge of the pool, yellow-blue lights shining out from the water. He pointed at the deep end, his eyes fixed wide.

Bob leaned over the deep end, his eyes slitted. For a moment, Rachel was tempted to push him in. A few feet below the surface, a man in a gray suit was suspended in the water, facedown, limbs like seaweed. For a long time, the only sound was the boiling-pot sound of the hot tub.

"I was tidying up and…and—" the butler said.

"Goddammit," Gary said, his face flushed. The four of them lingered near the water, uncertain and perplexed. No one dove in.

"I can already hear my lawyer racking up fees," Gary said, sitting on one of the steps that led to the gazebo. Rachel was suddenly glad they had chosen him. Even though she knew better, she wanted to dive in, hook her arms under his armpits, and kick to the surface, but it wasn't something Amelia Depardieu would ever do.

"At least drag him out, Bob," Teresa said from the back door.

"He's dead," Bob said.

"When the police show up, we'll look guilty if we leave him there," she said. "If he's still in the water, it will look like we didn't try to save him."

Bob dove in, shattering the jewel-like perfection of the surface. He hauled the body to the surface, but instead of kicking to the shallow end, he swam to the ladder. One-armed, he lifted the body out. Water spilled from its joints, its perfectly symmetrical, forgettable features.

"It's a mannequin," Gary said, stating the obvious. Bob dropped it on the deck and retrieved a towel from the pool house. The mannequin smiled at their feet, a life-size ken-doll in a new suit. Something was written on the shirt. Teresa unbuttoned the jacket and peeled it back. On the white oxford shirt someone had written *mère enculée* in black marker.

"Mare enculy?" Teresa said. "What does that mean?"

"Its French," Gary said, looking as though he might fall over. "It means motherfucker."

Teresa frowned and said, "I suppose we don't need to call the police."

Gary nodded. From his expression, Rachel could almost see the waves of understanding break over him. Papi knew where he lived and had gotten close enough to harm him. Not only that, the crazy bastard had hauled a mannequin across his property under the cover of darkness, all to leave a warning.

Nice work, Sam, Rachel thought.

"Is something going on?" she said, letting her voice warble a little.

"It's nothing, honey," Teresa said. She closed the jacket over the words as though it would make the threat go away.

"Maybe we should call the police anyway," she said, her brow furrowed, her teeth clenched tighter.

"It's nothing," Gary said. "It's probably a joke."

"Who would think this is funny?" Rachel demanded, looking afraid.

Gary opened his mouth to yell, but Teresa cut him off, "Let's all get some sleep. You shouldn't miss your massage in the morning, Amelia."

The next morning, Rachel lay across Sam's chest, listening to his heart decelerate. She was breathing hard, sweat-slick sheets knotted around them. She had surprised him at the door and they'd wasted no time. Any regrets she'd had about leaving the Bagleys to stew had vanished when they made love in the shower, her hands clutching the handles, her legs wrapped around his lower back.

In bed, exhausted, luxuriating in every moment they had together, she knew she had to get dressed. She kissed his chest and said, "One more minute."

"Agreed." His voice was heavy and muffled as though he lingered at the edge of wakefulness.

She rolled onto her back, his bicep behind her head, and looked at the ceiling fan. "I'll be happy when this one is over," she admitted.

"Me too," he said. Then he added, "I'm thinking of asking Gary for two-point-five."

"You're crazy," she said, rolling out of bed to search for her underwear. She felt almost drunk. They had planned on asking for 1.5 million for the Rembrandt and settling on 1 million, chump change for the Bagleys. "You sound like Porter," she snapped, her expression darkening.

Sitting up, he watched her get dressed and said, "I'm a lucky man."

"Don't change the subject," she said. "Flattery doesn't work on me."

"Flattery works on everyone. The real painting could be worth up to twenty. Aren't we being too cautious?"

"Caution never got anyone killed," she said, threading her arms through her bra.

"Caution keeps most people from living," he said. His

eyebrows shot up. "Oh, I almost forgot. I got you a present." From the nightstand, he handed her a knife that was a little longer than her hand. It had holes in the handle. She had to pull back a plastic catch to remove the blade. The sheath had two nylon straps.

"It's a dive knife," he said. "I meant to give it to you the other day in case Bob tried anything. You could keep it in your purse until this is over."

"What are the straps for?" she asked, unsnapping one of the clips.

"Divers wear them on their leg."

She smirked and tried to put it on. After some adjustments, she had the knife strapped high up on her right thigh. It was more comfortable than she thought it would be. She struck a pose in her bra and underwear like she was on the cover of a sci-fi novel from the '70s. Sam laughed. Part of her felt foolish, but given the circumstances, having the knife made her feel a little less unsafe.

A chill passed through her. Goosebumps rose up on her arms. She stepped into her loose flower-print skirt and checked to see if the knife was visible.

"I can't tell," he said, pulling on a pair of boxers on the other side of the bed.

"It's too dark, too cold in here," she said with a smile. She donned a camisole and flicked on the lights. Sam held up a hand to shield his eyes from the brightness.

"It burns," he joked.

She pulled the drapes back to check the temperature on the air conditioner. No wonder she was cold. It was set to fifty-eight degrees. "It's freezing in here," she said, opening the window to let in some warmth. Sam came up behind her, his hands running down her body, reminding her of all the things they'd just done together, the things they still could do. For a moment, she was drawn back to the bed like gravity.

"I should go," she said, turning to face him with a grin. "Unfinished business."

He dropped to his knees, his hands trailing up the back of her thighs beneath her skirt. Cupping her ass, he gently kissed her leg and said, "*We* still have some unfinished business."

Laughing, she closed the drapes and said, "Not in front of the window." Twisting out of his grasp, she crossed the room.

"You should stay another hour," he said. She had already been gone over an hour and a half.

"Is it worth a million dollars?" she asked, unable to keep a straight face.

"Yes, but not two."

She'd already been gone too long. She gave him a lingering kiss and pushed him onto the bed. "See you tomorrow night."

Later that morning, Gary Bagley hurried into an Applebee's restaurant just off Okeechobee Blvd. Inside, a handful of staff prepped for the lunch rush. The air heavy with the odor of oil and solvent. Oldies on the sound system. A pair of old ladies shared a table by the bar. When the waitress tried to seat him, Gary said through gritted teeth, "I have a reservation."

She gestured at the empty restaurant and smiled. "You didn't need one," she said. She had dark hair and blue eyes and was either finishing up high school or starting college. These days, Gary couldn't really tell the difference.

"My friend and I like to sit at the same table each time," he said, annoyed that he had to explain it. Papi had been very particular about the time and reservation. They were supposed to meet and discuss the return of his painting in person and alone. "It's under Rembrandt."

"Oh, like the toothpaste," she said, delighted. "Table fourteen."

He followed her to a booth in the corner and leered at her ass in tight black pants. Pretty decent, he thought. Too good for a place like this. She could work at the country club, probably make better money. Maybe he could put in a word for her. She'd owe him, of course. Ingrid had waited tables at the country club. He used to send his food back just to see her come and go. Not once did she lose her cool. It's why he'd offered her the assistant job—her patience and discretion. And the great ass.

Ingrid had been cooler than usual lately. His friends at the gym, who listened to his weekly exploits with the bombshell twenty-five-year-old, told him it was only a matter of time until she got ambitious, until she started fancying herself as the next Mrs. Bagley. Now she was leaving for ten days on a cruise. He briefly wondered if she had found someone else to take care of her.

Gary didn't touch the menu as he watched the waitress pour his Coors Light at the bar. He felt like a worm on a hook. Was this some kind of trap?

As if on cue, two burly guys from the security company entered. They wore ball caps, polos, and khaki shorts. They didn't make eye contact with Gary and sat in the bar. Ex-marines who had done nine tours of duty between them, their manager had told Gary that they could handle just about anything. For a laughably small bonus, they were also discrete. Each man carried a telescoping baton made of black steel called an Asp. They ordered light beers and some food and pretended to argue about the Dolphins.

When the waitress brought his beer, he checked his watch. Papi was late. With each passing minute, he grew more frustrated. After fifteen minutes, he risked a glance at the security guys. They stopped talking. One of them shrugged.

It didn't make any sense, he thought. The only reason to meet in a restaurant was to ensure that there were witnesses, but the place was practically empty. He could think of fifty better places to meet. Hell, maybe a place with a decent brunch menu. Why be so tacky? His eyes widened. The bastard was ridiculing him, repeating what was being whispered across West Palm Beach: Gary Bagley had no class.

Glancing at his watch, he decided to give Papi one more minute. That's when he heard it, a phone ringing nearby. He searched around his booth and found a cell phone taped to the underside of the table. The security guys motioned for him to answer it, so he did.

"I see you cannot follow basic instructions," Papi said.

"You're late," Gary sputtered. "I'm here like we agreed."

"Not alone. Those two *connards* at the bar couldn't be more obvious."

"You threatened my family," Gary snapped. "The dummy in the pool scared my wife." He used a napkin to dab at his temple where a bead of sweat trembled.

Papi chuckled. "That was but a kiss on the cheek, Mr. Bagley."

"You've done your homework," Gary said. "You got to know that I'm one of the most influential people in West Palm Beach." What was it that the technician had said about the painting? That it would be *the most extraordinary find in decades*. Teresa and him would be the toast of the town. Those Postlethwaite assholes would have to accept them as equals if they had a goddamned Rembrandt in their foyer. He wet his mouth with some tea and said, "How much do you want for it?"

"The thief decides to pay for what he stole?" Papi spat. "How kind."

That triggered something in Gary's brain. A month before, Ingrid had given him an article on stolen art. Priceless works were nearly impossible to sell. Because of the money and the risk of exposure, so many works just rotted in basements and attics because the thieves couldn't stomach the thought of selling a hundred-million-dollar masterwork for forty grand to some local hoods. Gary smiled and asked, "But you're the one who stole it, right? You can't fence it. It's why you've held onto it all these years. How much could something like that be worth, an unsellable painting?"

"It is priceless," Papi roared. Lowering his voice, he added, "You continue to confuse us for peers, Mr. Bagley. Not only will you return my painting, you will pay an apology tax."

It was Gary's turn to laugh. "Fat chance of that, pal," he said. The waitress looked up from wiping down menus and mouthed something to him.

On the other end, there was a long pause. "You don't

understand your position. I have arranged for a firm reminder." Papi sounded out of breath as he added, "Your wife will be calling shortly."

He hung up.

Out the window, there was a smudge in the sky above downtown, a dark line. It took a moment for him to realize that it was smoke. His cell rang. It was Teresa.

"Gary, you need to come home," she said, her voice higher than normal.

"What's happened?"

"The gazebo is on fire," she said, her voice cracking. "The fire department is on their way. I have Cecillia outside hosing off the roof of the house. Come home."

"I'm leaving now," he stammered, his mouth dry. The smoke, he suddenly understood, was coming from his house. It was why Papi had arranged to meet here at this table, by this window. For a long moment, he just sat there unable to move. Gary felt like he was looking through a backwards pair of binoculars. The front door of the restaurant seemed like it was a hundred yards away. It was the first time that Gary felt the giddy rush of fear.

The phone from under the table rang. When he answered it, Papi said, "Not only are you going to return my painting, but for my patience, my time, and my reputation for not erasing you, you owe me an apology fee of two million—unmarked bills in two bags. I will contact you to arrange for a time and place to deliver my property."

In the Bagley's guest room, Rachel finished packing her bag. Through the bay window, she stared at the ocean, pale blue stretching to the horizon where a strip of bruised clouds threatened a storm. She took Sam's Zippo from the nightstand and kissed it. Under different circumstances, she mused, this could be paradise.

The fire department had put out the gazebo a few hours before, leaving a collapsed heap of smoking rubble that reminded her of a meteor strike. When the text from Sam had come, she'd been as careful as she could, announcing a shower to Teresa, and locking her bedroom door. She scaled down the trellis next to the balcony and crept through the bushes to the back of the yard where she sprayed a whole container of charcoal lighter fluid from the barbeque on the Gazebo.

When she touched the flame to the wood, it made a tearing paper sound as it spread across the wood. She hurried to the front of the house and waited in the bushes until she heard yelling out back, then entered through the front door, popped the lock on her bedroom door with a hairpin, and took a quick shower to wet her hair and remove any evidence or suspicion.

Putting the lighter in her purse, Rachel wore a red sundress patterned with white flowers. She wore the diving knife Sam had given her underneath, part good luck charm, part caution. They weren't finished yet.

She carried her bag downstairs. The Bernard painting had been taken down. It lay on the floor of the foyer, leaning against the little table of orchids, like a bag of trash waiting to be taken out. Teresa, looking haggard, was in the kitchen furiously working chocolate chips into a bowl of dough with a wooden spoon.

"Where's the cook?" Rachel asked.

"I sent her home," she said, setting the bowl on the counter and wiping her fingers on a towel. "The fire has my nerves worked up. I bake when I get stressed, or I used to." She looked around like she didn't belong in a place like this. Rachel almost felt sorry for her.

"It could've been worse," she said, deliberately not looking out the filthy back windows. The bushes had been trampled, cut away by saws and axes to make room for the hoses. The water in the pool had turned black from the flow of ash and soot sprayed into it.

Teresa nodded. "Did Gary pay you?" she asked.

"Not yet," Rachel said shyly.

Teresa went to her brown leather purse and withdrew a

checkbook. "It's been a real pleasure having you around, Amelia." She chuckled and filled out a check. "Things aren't usually like this around here. Is there any chance you could stay for another day or two? I think you and Bob—"

"I wish I could, but my flight leaves in two hours," she said.

Teresa handed her the check and surprised her by wrapping her in a tight embrace. "Thank you." She almost whispered it.

Rachel gave her a brief squeeze and pretended to dab a tear out of her eye. "I wish I could stay but I should get going."

Teresa followed her to the foot of the stairs where she left her carry-on bag. She let Teresa see her gaze linger on the Bernard before she spoke. "Such a shame," she said.

"It is," Teresa said.

"What are you going to go with it?" she asked.

"Gary wants to throw it out or burn it, but I was thinking of hanging it in the guest bath right across from the toilet." They both smiled politely.

"It's remarkable for a forgery," Rachel said, picking it up and peering at it. "I teach a class each fall on fake art. Something like this would be an exceptional resource."

Teresa rolled her eyes and grimaced, "Oh God. Each fall, you could tell a whole new class about those dummies in South Florida who couldn't tell the difference."

"Not at all," Rachel said, her voice even. "It belonged to an anonymous collector." Giving her a confidential smile, she added, "Most of the students wouldn't be able to tell if it was real."

Her comment had the desired effect. Teresa settled down. With an uncertain look at the painting, she said, "I don't see the harm in it."

Remembering that Mrs. Bagley could be made uncomfortable when someone mentioned money, Rachel set the painting down and took her checkbook out of her purse. "I insist on paying you for it. It won't be much, but how about a thousand dollars?" As she clicked her pen, Teresa held up a hand.

"That's not necessary," she said. "Please, I insist you take it as a bonus."

Rachel eyed her for a long moment and unclicked her pen. "Thank you, Mrs...I mean, Teresa."

Teresa grinned and said, "As long as you promise never to tell anyone our name, you can have the damned thing."

In Miami, Sam sat across from Papi, who set down his wine glass and said, "You feed me like a goose, my friend." They were on the balcony among the plants. Inside, the boy played video games.

"I'm fattening you up," said Sam. "You ready to make the call?"

He pouted. "I wish it wasn't the last. I've enjoyed these diversions."

"We'll be back sometime late tonight," Sam said.

Papi rubbed his hands together, "Excellent. Lisa will be home in a few hours." Picking up a cell phone from the table, he waited to dial until Sam inserted a muted earpiece into his ear. He pressed a finger onto the yellow legal pad in front of Papi. On it, the address for the meeting at 10:00 p.m.

"This should be short. Control the conversation," Sam said. "Give him the address and the time. If he keeps talking, hang up on him if you have to. It'll remind him of the last time you ended the call and his house almost caught fire."

Papi nodded and dialed. His normally jovial expression melted into a bitter scowl. It took a couple rings for Gary to answer. "Mr. Bagley," Papi said. "Have you been able to collect the fee we discussed?"

"Yes," Gary said. Sam didn't like how sure he sounded. Not blustering, just confident.

"Good," Papi said, putting on his reading glasses, which were on a pink lanyard. "We meet tonight at ten o'clock at the True East Marina, pier eleven. If those men from the restaurant drive within two miles of the marina, I will consider this a final betrayal of my goodwill."

"I understand," Gary said. "You'll be there, right?"

Papi gave Sam a precarious look. Sam nodded. "Of course," Papi said.

"Since I'm handing you two million in cash, you don't get to pick the location."

Papi cursed in French. "You're the one who stole my painting. Now I must bargain to be compensated?"

"You picked the last location," Gary said. "And it sucked."

"Where you brought two men," Papi said. "A violation of our agreement."

"You have the upper hand here, pal. You know where I live. I want this over with as soon as possible," Gary said, a hint of helpless anger in his tone. Sam's thoughts raced. Did the Bagleys figure it out or was this more bravado? Papi shrugged, his eyes wide. Sam nodded. Might as well hear him out.

"This smells like *merde*," he seethed. "Where do you propose to meet?"

Gary gave them the address to a rundown nine-hole golf course called Sotogrande. They would meet at 11:00 p.m. in the greenskeeper shed. Sam looked it up on his phone. It was about as remote as you could get without taking a canoe into the swamps.

"Just you, Mr. Bagley," Papi said. "My painting, and your fee in two bags."

"It isn't a fee, Papi," he replied. "For me to go along, I'm thinking it's more of a down payment."

"And why on earth would you think that?"

"Because I have the means to buy it," Gary said.

Papi waited a beat before saying, "How do you know it is the real thing? Has it occurred to you that it might be a cunning forgery?"

Gary laughed. "Yeah, but old cons don't burn down buildings to get their forgeries back. You know what I think? I think you robbed that museum in Canada and you've been sitting on this for the last couple decades. Obviously, you can't fence it."

"Even if I entertained the possibility of you purchasing the

Rembrandt, you would never be able to tell anyone," Papi said.

"The first thing I'd do is invite every mover and shaker in town to dinner at my house. I'd hang it in the great room just so I could watch their stupid faces gawk at it. Then, I'd have the local news pay me a visit."

"It would only be a matter of time until the FBI contacted you," Papi said.

"And I'd tell them that a guy named Papi sold it to me," Gary chuckled. "I doubt that's your real name anyway."

"The museum would also possibly sue you for custody."

"Litigation is the only full-contact sport of West Palm Beach," Gary said. "We'll go to court and it'll take years. For something as exotic as a suit from a Canadian museum, I'd wear it like a badge of honor."

"You return the painting and pay your fee, Mr. Bagley," Papi said, "then we can discuss any future arrangements."

"Deal, but I want to hear you say it," Gary said, his voice breaking. "You'll leave my family alone."

"You have my word." Papi spoke a little too quickly, but for an amateur, Sam thought, he was marvelous.

As the sun slinked behind the trees, Rachel parked her Honda in the hotel lot. One errand complete, she had stopped at a greasy burger joint and gotten a heart attack special—something she only allowed herself when a job was done—double-cheeseburger, fries, and a strawberry milkshake. It would make her too sluggish to be nervous.

Locking the car, paper bag in hand, she used her keycard to enter through the back door. On the stairwell, she considered the rest of her evening. Sam had texted earlier about the change of venue, some golf course named Sotogrande. He would arrive early to stake it out in case it was a trap. She made him promise to be careful.

She had a few extra hours on her hands to pack their stuff,

check out of the hotel, maybe catch a movie. They had agreed to meet at a rest stop an hour's drive north. It felt good to be done with her part, to be out from under a microscope.

The carpet in the hallway was hideous, huge orange and red flowers. The heavy salty smell from the bag made her stomach ache. The truth was, during a job she couldn't ever really eat. Five doors past the elevator, she became aware of a presence behind her, closing in. She spun, nearly dropping her food as a little boy raced past her, shoes thumping. His mother called out for him to slow down.

At her door, Rachel took her keycard from her purse and shrugged as the woman apologized. Don't do anything memorable, she reminded herself. It's why they picked this hotel. Near the airport, it was among a cluster of four with high nightly turnover. Inside the room, she flicked the locks. With the drapes closed, the room was dark and warm. Only the vague shapes of the furniture silhouetted like a distant mountain range. As she turned on the entryway light, Bob Clover said, "You're late."

Dropping her food, she clawed at the locks. Before she could scream, before her food splattered on the floor, he was on her, dragging her toward the bed, one arm under an armpit. She elbowed his chest. He dumped her on the bed, where she rolled aside. A strange animal noise erupted out of her throat.

A white flash was the first thing she saw, her eye malfunctioning under the piston-pressure of the blow.

"Be quiet," he said.

Her arms and legs turned to water. Suddenly, she felt like she was spinning inside a washing machine. One cheek on fire, the other against the duvet.

"You think you're so smart, don't you," Bob said, his voice pitched low. "I followed you this morning and saw you kissing the guy from the pawn shop. You've been working together since the beginning."

When she opened her mouth to speak, her tongue felt weighted, she tasted blood. Instead, she rolled onto her back and groped for the edge of the bed.

"Where's the painting?" he asked, his mouth a broad line.

She smiled. "Gone."

He clucked his tongue. She flinched at the snap of the bedside lamp being switched on. A dozen cable ties of varying length were arranged on the table, causing a tremor to run through her. "Without the painting, this could be bad for you," he said.

"How did you find out?" She hated how small her voice had become.

"Teresa asked me to follow you. I got pictures, but you left with the painting before I could show her," he grinned, his black dog's eyes looking her over. "Your boyfriend is going into an ambush."

With her head clearing up, she began to understand the look in Bob's eyes, how it translated to hours of humiliation and agony followed by a grisly end, but all she could think of was Sam. She had to stop him. She lunged for the edge of the bed, but Bob's hands were like snakes, almost too fast to see. He caught her by the hair and punched her in the hip. She yelped and kicked out, her fingers clawing down the inside of his arms.

There was still time to call Sam, tell him to go to the meeting spot. She reached for the knife strapped to her thigh, but Bob swatted her hand aside.

Scowling, he climbed onto the bed, straddling her, his hands crushing down on the sides of her neck. She didn't understand what was happening until black spots welled up in her vision. The supply of blood to her brain was being cut off. She squeezed Bob's wrist, but only managed to feel his pulse, which couldn't have been above eighty. Gasping, she kicked and struggled, but it was like watching someone else get smothered. Then blackness.

After dark, Sam crept along an isolated road that led from the highway to a cluster of houses on the shore of a small lake. He'd parked about a half mile from Sotogrande in a gravel turnout beneath a live oak and listened to the oceanic thrum of insects. It took a long time for his eyes to adjust to the only source of light, the quarterly moon, which was obscured every other minute by thick clouds. Instead of black, he wore a dark blue T-shirt, gray running pants, and dark gray sneakers to blend into the moonlit foliage.

He was two hours early for the pickup. The air was heavy, wet, and warm, reeking of earth and decomposing plant matter. He didn't like how Gary had changed the location but, looking back on it, something like this was inevitable. He wanted to get a sense of the area, the parking lots, the best places to hide, and at least three routes of escape, before things went down. It had saved his life more than once.

At the back of the driving range, he slipped behind a row of trees, not liking how his right foot dragged slightly more than his left over the gravel. He followed a rutted road to the fifth hole where he found the greenskeeper shed. It was a pole barn with a fenced-in area for golf carts, the buzz of the battery chargers louder than the bugs.

For a long time, he just listened. When he was sure he was alone, he walked the periphery of the golf course. A landscape of artificial hills and manicured trees. He paused beneath an oak tree about a hundred yards from a copse of trees that overlooked the parking lot. An excellent ambush point for someone with a gun.

After ten minutes, Sam took a step out of the shadows and spotted a brief flash of light. Retreating behind the trunk, he watched as a man crouching among the branches lit up a cigarette. By the shape of his face, thick jaw and slabbed nose, it could be one of the men from the Applebees. Shit, he thought, that's why Gary was so confident. He'd planned to bring his hired guys. Some people never learn. Glancing at his surroundings, he considered how many there could be. He waited for the clouds to shroud the moon to run back to the shed. He would slip behind the driving range and make it back to his car. He'd call Papi, who would call Gary, and hopefully bluff him into calling off his guys.

As he skirted the greenskeeper shed, Sam's stomach dropped

at the sight of the opened bay doors. Two clicks startled him, the click of the light inside and the hammer of a gun.

Rachel gasped awake to the sound of a motor, the shush of wheels over water, and wind rattling plastic bags. She was in the back of a Jeep on the floor. Above, stars wheeled between clouds. Low-hanging branches clawed past.

Her hands and feet were bound. Cable ties gouged into the sides of her wrists. Tugging at them, she found another cable tie shackled her hands to a bracket beneath the passenger seat. Her head ached like she'd been hit with a hatchet. As far as she could tell, she was still in one piece. The hot night air that billowed through the cab smelled like a terrarium.

Bob was taking her into the swamp. No doubt to rape and murder her, leave her body for the gators. She was supposed to be terrified, but instead she felt numb. A part of her was already working on the odds, the few angles she still had left. In a way, she'd always known that this life would end this way. Con artists didn't succumb to pneumonia in their nineties.

She tugged against the plastic restraint until she couldn't breathe. Using her teeth on the plastic, she tasted blood.

Bob glanced over his shoulder at her. She closed her eyes and went still, but wasn't sure if she was convincing. She still had one thing he wanted. The Bernard. By now, he had searched her car. She didn't bring it into the hotel room, proving she wasn't a complete idiot. That left about two million reasons why he wouldn't kill her outright, but after she told him where the painting was, it would be a foregone conclusion. She shivered in waves at the thought of what he would do to her to get her to talk. No matter what, she thought, she would make him take her back to town before giving him the painting. It was her best chance to escape.

A sound on a speaker by her head startled her. Clocks ticking. Then an alarm rattling, followed by chimes. When the beat came on, she recognized it as Pink Floyd's "Time" playing just below the volume of a chainsaw. More than anything, this pierced her numbness. Bob would only play his music if he was certain that no one would hear it. No one would hear her screams. Why he'd taken her from the hotel. All she could think of was Sam, how she would never forgive herself if he got hurt.

Bob downshifted. Weeds slapped against the fender as they pitched downward. Before she knew what was happening, they had stopped. Bob leaned over her with a knife and cut the cable tie binding her hands to the front seat. She kept her eyes closed, her body limp. He lifted her out like she was a doll. For some reason, she thought of Frankenstein, the black and white version, where he carried some dead woman.

Bob carried her a short distance and set her in a lounge chair. Rows of plastic straps pressed beneath her calves and upper arms. He cut the bindings on her bare feet. The sound of night insects and water couldn't obscure the unmistakable tearing sound of duct tape being unraveled. For the next minute, she felt the tape securing her ankles to the metal tubing of the chair.

When he was finished, he said, "You wouldn't shake like that if you were unconscious."

She opened her eyes and squinted in the harsh lights from the Jeep's light bar. They were at the edge of a lake. Cypress trees in every direction. Something moved in the reeds and splashed. She didn't like how close to the water she was.

The blade of his knife caught the light. He said, "I'm going to cut your hands free and tape them down. If you move, I'll break your arm."

She lifted her bound hands and smiled. "You're in charge," she said. He cut the cable tie on her wrist and pinned her right arm to the armrest of the chair. As he yanked a strip of duct tape, she added, "There's been a misunderstanding. Call Teresa. Let me talk to her."

Finished securing her right wrist, he pressed down on the sides of her neck and said, "If you keep talking, I'll knock you out again." His hands were like oven mitts, huge and surprisingly soft.

The next track came on the stereo: "The Great Gig in the Sky."

She shut her mouth and let him tie up her left arm. Resisting would only hurt her more. Force wouldn't get her out of this. Bob would start talking soon. He wouldn't kill her without knowing where the Bernard was, she told herself. There was too much at stake for that. He was trying to frighten her. She kept her mind busy working on plausible reasons Amelia and Leland would be seen kissing in the window of her hotel room without it being an obvious con.

On the other side of the lake, tiny red lights shone.

Bob returned to the Jeep and placed a couple energy drinks on the hood. He dropped a half dozen plastic shopping bags on the clay. Removing his shirt, he sprayed himself with a cloud of bug repellent. Approaching Rachel, he knelt at her side, his face obscured by shadow. "I'm only going to ask you a couple times," he said, his voice flat. "Where is the painting?"

She started crying, taking huge gulps of air. "It was all Leland's idea," she said. "He said that if I didn't help him, he'd kill me. He'd drive to my parent's place in Decatur and shoot them, too." She couldn't see his expression, couldn't read if what she said was landing, so she kept it simple. "I'll take you to the painting. It's in town."

He shot to his feet and strode across the bank to the shopping bags. Opening a package, he flung something pale and vaguely pink into the water. It splashed and bobbed on the surface. When he stood and faced her, Bob was twisting apart a chicken carcass. "Come and get it!" he yelled.

A tidal wave of panic crashed over her as she realized what the red lights were. Alligator eyes, reflecting the light, their blunt bodies straining through the muck, closing in on the smell of food.

Rachel stared in disbelief as Bob emptied most of the shopping bags, leaving a rudimentary breadcrumb trail of raw chicken that led from the water and onto the shore. She started when a gator thrashed in the water only twenty feet out. At least a dozen alligators clustered together in the water, splashing and hissing, turning the brown water frothy. They stayed back, shy of the light.

Bob sang along with Roger Waters as he knotted a rope around a chicken carcass. Swinging it like a grappling hook, he lobbed it into the water just in front of the gators. A couple vanished below the surface. One hand over the other, he reeled the carcass in. He was baiting them, she realized.

After the third cast and retrieval, a medium-sized alligator burst from the reeds, its jaws wide. But Bob jerked the carcass clear at the last moment. It waddled onto the shore and went still, a noise like a diesel engine in its throat, its scales dripping, looking at him through one eye.

Behind it, Rachel saw that the other reptiles were much closer to the shore, looking for an opening. More than half were missing, beneath the water. The smell of the raw chicken, the blood and the fat, driving them mad.

Bob moved like spilled mercury, seizing the gator's tail. When it thrashed to get loose, he stomp-kicked its back leg and hoisted its tail to roll it into the water. Something flung itself sideways in the shallows to avoid the falling gator.

Bob made two more passes with the carcass to lure a huge gator with one eye onto the bank. It swung its head and tail. Droplets of water hit Rachel's bare legs.

This seemed to snap her out of it. Her dress had hiked up her thighs, showing the tip of the dive knife sheath. Stretching her fingers, she couldn't reach it.

Bob deftly sidestepped the gator and dropped onto its back. Sitting up, he hooked his fingers under the its jaw and pulled its head up to practically a ninety-degree angle, which caused the lizard to go still. Rachel wondered if it could breathe that way. Bob was clearly enjoying himself. He might be out of the ring for life, but he had found another way to use his training. Springing off its back, he dragged it by the tail along the water.

"Money" came on in the Jeep, the sound of cash registers echoing across the water. Rachel bent forward to tear at the duct tape with her teeth. The angle was bad, but she managed to get a bit between her front incisors. Her neck muscles ached as she tore away a piece that was half the size of a postage stamp.

Flopping the huge beast back into the water, Bob mopped his brow and howled. Trudging to the Jeep, he guzzled an energy drink. Behind the light bar, she couldn't quite make him out.

Another gator slipped out of the reeds ten feet to her left and seized on half a chicken in its jaws, which it bolted down with a clack, as fast as a sneeze, a copperhead strike.

Unable to get a full breath, Rachel gnawed at the tape on her wrist. Something on her right rushed at her and she screamed. Bob backhanded her across the face so hard the lounge chair nearly tipped over. The blow short circuited her brain for a few seconds. Something felt like it had split open, the muscles in her face, her jaw. Bob loomed over her. She was surprised that she could still see out of her right eye.

"Tell me where the painting is," he said.

It took her a moment to find the air. "I'll show you," she spat, "in town."

She wailed as he seized the lounge chair by the armrests and hoisted it in front of him. Behind her the gator growled. Turning her head, she tried to see where it was, but Bob shook her so violently she bashed her head on the aluminum frame.

"I'll only ask one more time," he said, walking forward, his eyes focused on the ancient reptile. The sound it made, a hiss like a dull stone rasping across her exhumed skull. Cruel amusement flickered in Bob's black eyes just before he thrust her forward.

Something wet and cold jabbed into her shoulder blade through the plastic straps. Screaming, arching back, Rachel felt like her arms might snap from the restraints. The sharp smell of decay—rotting meat—stung her nostrils.

Bob's grin vanished as he tried to keep a hold of the lounge chair. She was fiercely jerked sideways, her right leg colliding with Bob's knee, sending him backpedaling. The ground seemed to rise up as she fell face down, her nose ground into the red mud. A series of tugs battered her body. She struggled to breathe, but her nostrils and mouth were packed with mud. A huge weight pressed down, like a car driving over her back, the mud squelching.

When the weight lifted, she managed to position her right arm under her. The tears she'd made in the tape with her teeth had been enough to free one arm. She gasped, clawing wet soil and roots from her tongue. She didn't know where the gator or Bob were, but she could still move. Maybe she was in shock, but she didn't feel anything but the slickness of the diving knife in her hand. She was careful not to cut her left wrist as she drew it across the tape.

Behind her, Bob dragged the gator to the water by its tail, narrowly avoiding another one that lunged out of the shallows. The plastic straps below her upper back were missing, torn to jagged strips by the gator. A section of aluminum frame near her neck pinched flat. Ignoring it, she focused on cutting herself free. The tape of her left hand split open and she hurried to work on her right foot.

"Hey," Bob shouted, closing in.

She ignored him, peeling the tape from her right foot. He slapped at the knife and howled. He'd misjudged the angle, the sharpness of the blade. It was the only reason it hadn't spun into the cypress trees.

"You hateful bitch," he shouted, clutching his bleeding palm and circling behind the chair. Rachel tried to cut her left foot free, but he tugged on the other end of the frame. She tumbled out of the chair, a flash of pain in her left ankle, the tape stretching, acting as an opened hinge. On her stomach, she was dragged backwards away from the light.

Bob dragged her into the bushes. It took her a moment to figure out what was happening. He was going to throw her into the lake further down the shore. It would take the gators a few moments to figure out where they were. The delay would be enough time for him to get clear of the water.

Still strapped to the lounge chair, she wouldn't drown, but she wouldn't be fast enough to escape. No way she could cut her ankle free while they were moving. He had at least a hundred pounds on her. Each time she got a hand or leg under her, he tugged on the frame, knocking her off balance. A root struck her left elbow, causing her to yelp.

This section the shore was swampy, crowded with reeds. His boots made sucking sounds as he walked backwards in the mud. The gators would follow. It was everything she could do to keep a hold of the knife and her face out of the muck.

Through a gap in the cypresses in shin-deep water, Bob paused to get both hands on the frame and fling her like a discus into the water. "Fuck the painting," he said.

The clouds parted. Weak moonlight fractured across the surface of the water. Rachel thought of Sam, what the Bagley's were likely to do to him if they caught him. She ignored the pain in her ankle as she rolled over, scaled the lounge chair, and punched the dive knife through the hole in the straps. Bob threw his hips back, his boots splashing, but the blade still pierced his right thigh, barely missing his crotch.

Roaring, he upended the chair, flinging her onto her back in the water. He panted for a second and felt the wound. Not deep, she knew. He crouched, bleeding, and dug out a fist-sized rock from the water. She scrambled on her back toward the shore. His voice, eerily calm as he said, "I'm going to fuck you with that—"

An explosion of water behind him materialized into a huge gator. A flash of white as it closed its jaws on his knee, ripping his leg out from under him. His upper body slammed into the shallows. On all fours, he rose up, an ugly, girlish scream came out of him as the bones in his leg shattered.

The one-eyed gator ripped him sideways, sending a sheet of spray slicing into the air. It dragged him into deeper water. Wild with panic, Bob rolled on his back and beat its head with the rock until a second gator seized his forearm in its jaws.

On the shore, Rachel watched, mesmerized by the shrieking tug o' war that took place in the lake. Over and over, the alligators took Bob under. Each time, the screaming diminished until he went quiet. After a while, the only sound was the churn and splash of the gators rolling, twisting off parts of him like taffy.

Rachel cut herself free from the lounge chair and followed the sound of music back to the Jeep. The key was in the ignition. Moments later, she was back on the causeway, the dive knife in the passenger seat, and Pink Floyd's "Money" blasting from the speakers. She didn't have her purse or any of her things, but if there was any chance to save Sam, she had to hurry. On the dash, Bob had left his cell. It was unlocked. She called Sam's burner three times. When he didn't answer, she said the name of the golf course: Sotogrande.

One of the security guys finished tying Sam to a dilapidated office chair with wheels. The rope was stiff, scratchy yellow plastic that bit into his forearms and neck. The shed reeked of fertilizer. Tools and buckets of chemicals lined the walls. Overhead fluorescent lights flickered.

The security guys were far from the best money could buy. Six and a half feet tall, bald, with expensive tattoos and glam muscles straining their tank tops. They each wore an oversized handgun, chrome with pearl-handled grips.

They had never been boy scouts either. The knots were crap, but Sam hoped he didn't get his makeup on it. One guy sat with him, while the other slapped mosquitos by the open bay doors. It was clear what their orders were. Sit tight until someone arrived.

"You two look like navy pussies," Sam said to break the ice. Jutting out his chin, he grinned at his babysitter, who leaned against the bucket of a tractor.

The guy near him bared his teeth. "Special Forces."

"More like Special Olympics," he said.

Point to them for not reacting. No way these two were Special Forces. They were too big, too memorable, too inefficient, nothing like the guys he had known as a boy. One of his friend's dads had been Special Forces during Vietnam. They had an annual reunion, a barbeque of silent, wary men with eyes that noted everything and chatty wives. Even though they had gone to seed by then, they had a look to them. Under six feet, under two hundred pounds, boring if you didn't know each of them could whistle while eating a box of wood screws.

Outside, headlights strafed the front of the shed and went out. Two sets of footsteps approached. Teresa entered first, a look of exhaustion and disappointment on her face. Behind her, Gary glowered at Sam.

"Papi's going to kill us all," Sam spat. Gary glared at his loafers. He struggled against his restraints and shouted, "Are you people crazy?"

"Where's Papi?" Teresa said, her skin yellow under the lights.

"He's late," Sam said, glancing around the room. "He'll have a couple of guys, too. Ex-Mossad, I think."

"Bullshit," Gary said.

Teresa leaned over Sam and ran her fingers along his swollen eye and busted nose. "Careful, lady," he said, "The bone just started to set."

When she dug her fingers into the skin of his face, screamed and threw his head back. She gritted her teeth, stripping away layers of latex and makeup. The wheels of the chair chimed as they struck the concrete. Finished, she stepped away, holding tattered strands of fake skin in her hands.

She glowered at him and said, "You look more like a clown." Wiping her hands off, she took out her phone, and said, "Your sweetie better return our Bernard." She dialed a number.

Sam breathed slow, in and out, pulling his heart rate back down. This was bad. Somehow, they knew. But he'd talked his way out of worse. He doubted that the hired guys could hit anything beyond fifty feet with their sidearms, but getting outside that range was going to be a problem. Also, he could always be wrong. One of them could be some kind of regional pistol champion.

Teresa hung up and dialed again. "It's not like him to not answer," she muttered.

"'Cause he has brain damage," Gary said, rolling his eyes,

pointing at the security guys. "We should've sent these two to grab her."

Everything inside Sam went still. Bob had taken Rachel. God knew what he would do to get the location of the painting out of her. A montage of horrific images, the kinds of things a guy like that would do to a woman, shuffled through his head. The ropes groaned as he strained against them. He grinned at Gary, his heart hammering. "You're just digging yourself a deeper hole."

"Shut up," Gary said, all wiseguy swagger again. He paced the floor, kicking things out of his way.

Sam had to get out of here, he thought, find Rachel and put as many miles between them and West Palm Beach as they could before sunrise. His chest burned and his back ached from being arched so long.

Teresa set an ugly leather purse covered with golden dollar signs on the workbench and ordered one of the security guys to bring Sam closer. The wheels screeched as he was positioned next to it. From her purse, Teresa took something out. Sam flinched when he saw what it was. A syringe.

"Before I married Gary," Teresa said, "I used to work in a veterinarian's office." On the edge of the table, she set two ampules. Crouching in front of Sam, she pointed at them and whispered, "Dogs get put to sleep for a number of reasons. Usually, they're old or sick, but sometimes, they're just dangerous." Grabbing his hair and jerking his head up, she added, "You're too dangerous. In a couple of days, the police will be called to an abandoned house. They'll find your body without a mark on it. The trace evidence of makeup on your face will throw them off."

Sam jerked against his bonds and glowered at each of them. "No one's getting out of this unscathed."

This is the only way out for you," Teresa said. "We can't go to the police, and we can't let you steal from us."

"Do you think we're fucking stupid?" Gary roared. He punched a stack of fertilizer bags.

"I thought you were greedy," Sam said. "And I'm right." As

subtle as he could, he worked his left hand against the ropes and the armrest.

Picking an ampule up, Teresa said, "This is enough morphine to put you to sleep." Lifting up the other, she added, "This is enough Fentanyl to paralyze the lungs of fifty people." Her hands were shaking as she withdrew an unmarked container of orange-tinted liquid from her purse. "And this will make you tell us everything."

Sam realized that they'd completely misjudged the Bagleys. All along, they'd assumed that Gary was the one in charge, that he hadn't remarried a twenty-something out of some kind of attachment or kindness. But that was wrong. Teresa was the one in control. Sam struggled as she put a rubber tourniquet around his left arm. She unscrewed the cap on the orange liquid and drew it into the syringe.

"What's that?" Sam asked, panting, his veneer of confidence gone.

"It'll be suspicious if you don't have any track marks," Teresa said with a shrug. "This is hot peppers soaked in water. Fortunately, it will burn." She plunged the needle into his inner elbow. It felt like a trickle of molten lead dripping down his arm. The ropes bit into his chest and neck as he twisted. He jerked so wildly that the chair tipped over and he bashed his head on the concrete. He became aware of a horrible keening sound, like a hurricane. His screams.

When he paused to gasp for breath, Gary said, "Where's the fucking painting, asshole?" The two security guys lifted him upright, setting the wheels on the floor. His eyelids fluttering, Sam could barely breathe from the pain. A line of blood from his scalp slid down his neck.

"I guess I won't have a mark on me," he said, forcing a smile.

Instead of answering, Teresa gave him another injection.

Rachel heard Sam's screams from behind the driving range. Light from the open bay doors shone across the fifth fairway. Checking

Bob's phone, she saw the text from Colin. She should've waited for him, she knew, maybe surprise the Bagleys, or maybe drive Bob's jeep through the wall, but she was no action hero.

Instead, she limped closer, covered in dried mud, her right eye had almost swollen shut.

Beyond the rectangle of light thrown across the grass, she considered her odds. Four against one. She had her knife but only one truly useful weapon: her voice. When she stepped into the light, she shuddered at what she saw. Teresa injecting something into Sam, who was pale and limp, tied to a chair, his head flopping like a suffocating fish.

"Stop!" she shouted, giving them what Sam called her winning-hand smile.

The security guys drew their sidearms. Gary grabbed an edger, while Teresa withdrew her needle and asked, "Amelia?"

So much for the element of surprise, Rachel thought.

"Where's Bob?" Teresa demanded.

"Dead," she said. "Papi shot him."

"Bullshit," Gary said. To the security guys, he said, "Grab that dumb slut."

Rachel glanced to her left, made an okay symbol with her hand, then pointed into the bay doors. "That a bad move," she said. The security guys paused and shared an uncertain look.

"How so?" Teresa asked.

"With your light on," Rachel said, raising her arms. "Any shooter with a Walmart deer rifle could set up and just pick you off one at a time." Raising her voice, she asked, "How much do you suppose four .30-30 shells would cost, honey?"

"About a buck," Sam answered, his voice raw and almost unrecognizable from all the screaming.

"Look at that," she said, clicking her tongue. "All that money of yours can't fend off one dollar's worth of bullets." From their expressions and posture, she could tell that Gary and one of the security guys were spooked. Their eyes scanned the dark the way little kids looked under their beds at night.

"Shoot her," Teresa said, calling her bluff. "Just shoot her." But the security guys were looking around, calculating the odds. Only an idiot would walk up to the shed unarmed and smiling. Not unless Rachel had an ace up her sleeve. Otherwise, it was suicide. The security guy with the ball cap muttered something to Teresa.

"I don't care. What do we pay you for?" she said. "Shoot her in the leg, then."

"Another bad idea," Rachel said, taking a few steps closer. Where the hell, she thought, was Colin?

Sam chuckled.

"They're liars," Teresa said, her voice cracking. "Bob's not really dead."

"Call him again," Rachel said.

Hesitating, Teresa dialed Bob's number. A few seconds went by. The phone in Rachel's hand lit up, accompanied by heavy metal music. Rachel answered it. "Cut Leland free, now."

Teresa dropped her phone, her body sagging against the workbench. Her features scrunched together as if they could contain her grief. "It's not possible," she said.

"Papi made me get rid of Bob's body," Rachel said. "In the swamp." She glanced at her phone, a text from Papi. Rachel allowed herself to breathe.

Gary took out his phone and seemed dumbfounded by the factory ringtone. "It's Papi," he said. After a long moment, he answered it. Even from the grass outside the shed, Rachel could hear Papi yelling.

Quickly, he handed the phone to Teresa, who said, "You don't tell me what to do, you frog. How do I know this isn't another scam?" When Papi replied, she laughed. "You know what? I'll just have to see for myself."

Pushing past Gary, she took the handgun from the security guy. She strode to the edge of the shed and pointed it at Rachel's chest. That same moment, a red dot of light appeared on her outstretched hand. Steadily, it slipped up her arm and crossed her sternum to stop on her heart.

Teresa's mouth hung open and she lowered the gun.

"A shot like that," Rachel said, "at this range would empty out your ribcage like a jack o' lantern." She wore her winning-hand smile as she added, "Cut him loose."

Less than an hour later, a gray Honda Civic and beat up pickup truck pulled over on a country road. Rachel got out of the Honda and shielded her eyes in the truck's headlights. Colin rolled down his window and shook his head.

"Part of me is horrified that I fell in with you people," he said.

Rachel handed a paper bag through the window. "Your cut," she said. She'd cashed the Bagley's check earlier that afternoon. Seventy percent of it was under the spare tire in the trunk of the Civic. The other thirty was beneath the passenger side door panel.

Colin unrolled the top of the bag in his lap and peered down at three thousand dollars. "And part of me is absolutely elated." He grinned and added, "If you're ever in the seedier parts of West Palm Beach, look me up."

She glanced back to where Sam waited. The image of him in that chair—Teresa with a needle full of god knew what poised near his neck—returned to her. She clenched her jaw and willed it away. They had been careless, kissing in front of the window, especially after all the precautions they'd taken.

Speaking of precautions, they'd left the Bagleys in the shed, the doors locked. On the phone, Papi had told Teresa that if anyone left the shed before the sun came up, he would burn their house down with all of their art in it.

"How did you keep the laser pointer so steady?" Rachel asked Colin.

He grinned and lifted a contraption that looked like a black question mark off the bench seat. "I taped it to a gimbal."

She laughed and said, "You ever get tired of making honest money, look us up."

Arching an eyebrow, he said, "I doubt that's possible."

Back on the highway going south, Rachel took the turns by memory. Despite her best attempts to clean herself off in the bathroom sink of a rest stop, the strong odor of mud filled the car. Sam hadn't talked much. His eyes closed, he leaned against the passenger door.

When they were back in town, they parked behind Pawn Takes King. Sam used a copy of the key they'd made to open the grate. With an old comforter balled under her left arm, Rachel punched in the code. Inside the shop, they didn't bother turning on the lights. Behind the counter, where the Rembrandt once was, the *Woman in a Hotel Room* hung. She carefully peeled the blue NOT FOR SALE Post-It note off it. They wrapped it in the comforter and locked up. In under five minutes, they were back on the highway, headed toward Miami.

At the apartment complex, Rachel carried the wrapped painting up the stairs. Sam, hollow-eyed and unsteady, gripped the rail and gave her a long look. "It's good karma, right?" he asked. "Giving it back?"

"Not much else we can do with it," she said. "Unless you want to pawn it." They shared a smile. While the legal owner of the Bernard could get millions for it, Rachel and Sam would get only a fraction of that. Not only would it take years to fence it, most buyers of stolen art were, in fact, law enforcement. Besides, they were after something more important.

Lisa opened her door before they could knock. From her reaction, Sam must've looked like a walking corpse. Behind him, Rachel carried the comforter into the kitchen. Although it was a little after three in the morning, Papi and Henry were still awake. Papi insisted on getting them each a cup of coffee.

"Is it true?" Lisa asked, her hooded eyes wary.

Instead of answering, Rachel set the comforter on the little table in the kitchen and took down the gilt mirror from its nail. She shared a look with Sam, who gave an imperceptible nod. Despite being nearly broke, they'd decided whatever insurance they could get against Little Vincent was worth it.

Rachel wondered if she was conning herself on this one, telling herself it was pragmatism when it was really exhaustion. They both wanted to be done with South Florida. Slowly, she unwrapped the Bernard and hung it on the wall.

Papi exclaimed and dropped his coffee.

Lisa covered her mouth, her eyes wide. Tears streaked her mascara. She stepped toward it lightly as though it gave off its own radiance.

"What is it?" Henry asked.

Papi made the sign of the cross and said, "My son, he made this."

"I remember him painting this," Lisa said. "Normally, kids weren't allowed in his studio, but I was home sick from school that day." Gently, she touched the canvas and met Rachel's gaze, tears on her cheeks. "It's of my mother," she said. "From their honeymoon. They went to Rockaway Beach in Oregon." She touched a single yellow brushstroke that ran along the bedspread and said, "People think this is a reflection of light, but it isn't. My dad let me mix it and paint it. He said no one would notice it, but I do. Each time I look at it, I only see the line I made, how it doesn't quite fit."

"She was beautiful, your mom," Rachel said. The back of her throat burned. How long had it been since she'd thought of her own mother? Papi wrapped an arm around the boy, his head on his shoulder, muttering over and over "My boy, my beautiful boy."

Sam said to Lisa, "We'll let you folks get some sleep."

As they stepped into the hallway, Lisa said, "Wait." She hurried upstairs. From the noise, one of her neighbors pounded on the wall. She returned and handed Rachel an old shoe box. "My brother's things," she said. When Rachel moved to open it, Lisa put a hand on hers, "Just keep it. That part of my life is over."

They didn't speak as they went back to the car. Sam drove, the horizon on their right transforming from black to blue. In the passenger seat, Rachel held the box in her lap the way one would hold a loved one's ashes. A part of her didn't want to open it, didn't want to be disappointed. Sam winced when she rested her hand on his. They had given up so much for what was inside. Rachel made a deal with herself: once they were beyond the city limits, she would open it.

An avid practitioner of the long con, **SCOTT EUBANKS'** essays and short stories have appeared in *Memoir*, *The Yellow Medicine Review*, *Zone 3 Magazine*, and *Lilac City Fairy Tales*. He has an MFA in creative writing from Eastern Washington University and lives in Spokane, Washington.

DOWN COMES THE NIGHT

FRANK ZAFIRO

A GRIFTER'S SONG

BOOKS BY FRANK ZAFIRO

River City Series
#1 *Under a Raging Moon*
#2 *Heroes Often Fail*
#3 *Beneath a Weeping Sky*
#4 *And Every Man Has To Die*
#5 *The Menance of the Years*
#6 *Place of Wrath and Tears* (*)
#7 *Dirty Little Town* (*)

Stefan Kopriva Mysteries
#1 *Waist Deep*
#2 *Lovely, Dark and Deep*
#3 *Friend of the Departed*

The SpoCompton Series
At Their Own Game
In the Cut

Other Novels
At This Point In My Life
The Last Horseman
Chisolm's Debt
The Trade Off
(with Bonnie Paulson)
Some Degree of Murder
(with Colin Conway)

The List Series
with Eric Beetner
#1 *The Backlist*
#2 *The Short List*
#3 *The Getaway List*

with Lawrence Kelter
The Last Collar
Fallen City

The Ania Series
with Jim Wilsky
Blood on Blood
Queen of Diamonds
Closing the Circle
Harbinger

Charlie-316 Series
With Colin Conway
Charlie-316
Never the Crime
Badge Heavy (*)
Code Four (*)

(*) Coming Soon

DOWN COMES THE NIGHT
Frank Zafiro

Even if you want to otherwise pretend
Even if you never give up the fight
Every day winds to its end
And down comes the night.
—Rebecca Battaglia

They decided to wait until Atlanta to open the box.

The trip up from Florida was quiet, both lost in their own thoughts. Sam sat in the passenger seat, staring at the countryside as the miles flew by. The dull ache in his bones kept him from bringing his full faculties to bear on what their next move should be.

Not that it mattered. They both knew the next move was simple. Open the box. See what was inside.

But they waited.

Rachel drove the entire way, silent and contemplative. When Sam found it hard to strategize beyond using whatever was in the box to back off Little Vincent so they could live their lives, he let his mind drift to what they'd been through. He'd taken more beatings in the last year than any decade of his adulthood, culminating in the shattered leg that still occasionally throbbed and pulsed at him from the floorboards. He still bore the scar on his face from another con that went bad, a vertical line next to his left eye. Both the limp and the scar were bad for business. A good grifter was memorable, but in an emotional sense, not a physical one. These new developments were going to affect how they plied their trade in the future.

But what filled his thoughts as they rolled up I-95 was what Rachel had endured. In that same time period, she'd also been kidnapped, beaten, and nearly killed. Plus, the miscarriage.

He wondered how heavily the last weighed on her. How much of her silence came from processing that loss? Sam looked out the window as the coastal scene flit by, remembering an important fact where that was concerned.

She didn't tell me about the baby. Not until it was too late.

Rolling down the highway today, he couldn't feel the ache that first came with that discovery. He felt slightly detached from it, as if it had happened to someone else. Regardless, he realized that he couldn't blame her for remaining silent. She must have wondered if having a child was something they could do and still remain who they were. The prospect must have been daunting, and in typical Rachel fashion, she tried to protect him from that.

Sam touched the bruises on his face. They were purple when he'd looked in the mirror at a rest stop, already beginning to heal. He had always been a fast healer, but now he wondered if that was fast enough.

He stared at the St. John's River as they passed through Jacksonville. The enormity of the waterway surprised him a little.

Yeah, but it ain't the ocean, is it?

He blinked, unable to decide if he'd stumbled upon something profound or if he was just overwhelmed by everything that had happened over the last several months. He followed the thought.

It ain't the ocean. Meaning...what? That there was always something bigger. In his world, there was always another job, another mark, a bigger score. Did it ever end?

Sam never used to think so. He never wanted to do, or be,

anything else. Trying to imagine a different life never got out of the gate with him.

But now?

He didn't know.

"It's beautiful," Rachel said.

Sam turned his head to look at her. The late afternoon light struck her through the windshield, crystallizing her features. He let his gaze drift over her bruises and cuts, wishing he could have a go at the man who gave them to her. But the quiet of the drive and the bubble existence created inside the car kept the rage at bay. He settled for the consolation that the man met a more fitting end than Sam could ever give him.

For Rachel's part, her expression wasn't entirely relaxed, but her usual edge was muted. As she glanced at the waterway, and then at Sam, a light smile creased her mouth.

"*You're* beautiful," Sam told her.

Her smile widened slightly. "You're crazy."

"Maybe a little," he conceded. "Doesn't mean I'm wrong."

"How're you feeling?" she asked, turning back to the road.

"The leg hurts some."

"I think it will for a while."

"Probably. How about you?"

Rachel shrugged. "Nothing that won't heal in a week or two."

"We should lay low for at least that long before we decide our next move. Maybe get a bungalow on a beach somewhere."

"That sounds nice."

Sam nodded. "Someplace quiet. Except for the waves."

"We'll AirBnB it. I'll do a search once we get to Atlanta." She paused, then added, "After."

Sam didn't reply. He knew what *after* meant, and that was all right with him.

She sat next to him on the motel bed, her legs crossed. The box was perched in front of her atop the ugly floral comforter. To

Sam, it seemed like she was hesitating, as if the moment deserved some sort of pomp and circumstance. They'd been running from Little Vincent for years, and this was what would end it. There should be a glass to raise, or some words to say.

He stared at the simple and feather light cardboard box. It had cost them a swindled painting worth seven figures. That price tag was on the legitimate market, sure, but even in the shadow economy of their world, it'd still bring six figures.

Not that the woman they gave it to would ever sell it. To her, it was priceless, in the same way the freedom inside the box was to Sam and Rachel.

Open it, Sam thought.

He opened his mouth to say it but Rachel was already tearing the tape away and lifting the lid.

Inside, all he saw was crumpled newspaper. He frowned. Was there a hint in the news stories, or...?

Rachel dug out the newspaper, carefully squeezing each piece before dropping it on the bed beside her. When she pulled out the final one, her eyes widened slightly.

"What?" Sam asked her.

She tipped the box so he could see inside.

Taped to the bottom was a nickel-colored key, unadorned except for the numbers seven-one-seven on the head.

There was nothing else.

They stared at the key in silence. Sam's leg throbbed, the pain gaining a sharpness after being motionless during the long drive. He tried to ignore the pain, but it intruded on his thoughts.

"No note?" he asked, though he already knew the answer.

Rachel shook her head. She'd already closely examined the newspaper packing. Aside from the fact that it came from *The Inquirer* in Philadelphia, there was nothing to learn from the balled up sports pages.

"It could be anything," Sam mused aloud. "There's no way

to know."

"Maybe." She traced the numbers etched on the head. "Seven-one-seven."

"A locker number?"

"Could be." Rachel turned the key over in her fingers, its generic shape revealing nothing beyond the three digits. "It could be to anything. A locker, like you said. Or a storage unit. With the shape, it could even be to an apartment. Or a desk drawer." She shook her head. "I can't tell."

"At least we know it's in Philadelphia."

"We don't even know that."

Sam pointed to the newspaper.

Rachel shrugged. "We know that he packed it up in Philly. *Maybe*. But the key could be to a locker in Atlantic City. Or who knows where?"

She was right, he knew. Still, the Artist had been an associate of Little Vincent's. Much of his world centered on the city and its underworld. Odds were, the key opened something somewhere in Philadelphia.

Like that helped.

"Let's think it through," Sam said. "We know he had something that kept Little Vincent in check for a long time, while he broke all the rules: running his own rackets, sleeping with whoever he wanted, whatever. Until..." He trailed off.

"Until they blew up his car and him with it," Rachel finished.

"But when they searched afterward, they didn't find whatever they were looking for. His leverage. Not at his house, not at his mistress's apartment, and not at the club he worked out of."

"You have to think they tore the place apart, each time."

Sam nodded. "If they came across something locked, they wouldn't need this key. They'd just crack it open."

"The Artist would know that, though, right?"

"You'd think so."

"That means he'd put whatever he had somewhere way off-site. Somewhere safe." She held up the key. "And make sure this got to his sister if anything happened to him."

"But why wouldn't he tell her what the key was for? She didn't even know what was in the box when she gave it to us. It was still sealed."

Rachel thought about it. She picked up her pre-paid cell phone and dialed a number. After a few rings, someone answered. In the quiet of the motel room, Sam could hear Papi's distinct French accent when he greeted Rachel. She smiled slightly and asked for Lisa. A few moments passed before he heard a tinny, muted "hello" from the earpiece of Rachel's phone.

"It's a key," Rachel said, without preamble. She was met with silence on the other end. "Any idea what it might be to?"

More silence. Then a few indistinguishable words, but Sam could hear the tone of regret in them.

"How about the numbers seven-one-seven?" Rachel asked. A short pause, then more regret. "Are you sure?"

Another pause, then Sam heard a distant "yes."

Rachel frowned, though he knew she must have expected the answer. "If you think of anything over the next few days, call this number."

She broke the connection and gave Sam a short shake of her head.

He looked back at the key, the beginnings of despair swirling in his chest. They were *so* close to being free. So close to an easier life, a wide-open world to work their magic, instead of constantly looking over both shoulders everywhere they went. He hadn't realized how persistent and heavy Little Vincent's shadow was until he'd felt it start to lift, but now it crashed back down on him.

"What are you thinking?" Rachel asked.

"I'm thinking let's sleep on it," he said.

He took the last of his pain medication, which helped him get to sleep, and kept him that way. When he finally woke, his mind was muddy. He got the sense it was nighttime. After a little while, he realized that he knew this because the window was open and cool air seeped in along with the sounds of the evening. Then he noticed the drone of the shower in the bathroom when it stopped suddenly.

He rubbed his eyes. He must have still been foggy, because it seemed only a moment later when Rachel sat on the bedside next to him. The damp, clean smell of her skin broke through the haze.

"We're thinking about this all wrong," she said.

"Honestly, babe, I'm not doing much thinking at the moment." He rubbed his eyes again. "These pills...I'm done with them."

"Good thing the bottle's empty, then."

"That's a good thing. I can't keep a straight thought in my head."

She kissed him lightly on the temple. "I've been thinking for both of us. And like I said, we've been thinking about this all wrong."

"What do you mean?"

"What have we been trying to do?"

He peered at her as if it were a trick question. One thing the two of them never did to each other was run any kind of con or game. That was for the outside world. "Figure out what the key goes to," he said, his voice a little thick.

"Right. Because the key opens some door somewhere that leads to what we really want."

"The leverage on Little Vincent."

"No." Rachel shook her head firmly. "That's only a means to an end. We want to be free of the man. The leverage is only a tool to accomplish that."

"All right, but so what? We don't even know what the leverage is yet, or how to use it."

"True. We've been in this hotel room for fourteen hours, spinning our wheels—"

"Fourteen hours?" He hadn't realized how long he'd slept.

"Fourteen hours," she repeated. "Spinning our wheels to figure out what the key goes to, much less what's behind whatever door it opens. Which, I admit, is what any normal person would do. But we should be thinking of this the same we think about everything else."

"Like grifters," Sam murmured.

"Exactly." Rachel's eyes bore into his. "And when you look at it that way, the game changes, doesn't it?"

He thought about it, the itch of an idea in his mind, just outside of scratching range. Then he smiled slightly. "You want to run another con on him, don't you?"

"Why not? It worked so well the first time," she dead-panned.

He shifted on the bed, grunting as a flare of pain erupted in his leg. "You're saying we don't need to have whatever is behind the mystery door, because...?"

"If he believes we have it, that's enough. We don't even need to know what it *is*."

Sam thought about it, variances flitting through his mind. He tried to grab onto them, but the thoughts were elusive. "We'd need someone as a go-between."

"Of course."

"Even then, he might not buy it."

"He will."

Sam took a deep breath and let it out slowly. Then he said, "It's an all-in move."

She shrugged. "It's worth the stretch. Otherwise, we spend the rest of our lives with his shadow falling across us every other day."

Sam closed his eyes. He needed to sleep again. Before he slipped off, he murmured, "Do it, baby."

The next morning, he tossed the empty pill bottle into a garbage can outside the motel. While Rachel got a message to Porter, he went to the drug store and bought some ibuprofen. When he came back, she flashed him a smile.

"What's the word?" he asked.

"He'll be here tomorrow."

Sam smiled back at her. "What will we do with our time until then?"

"If you're not too beat up," she said, "I have an idea or two."

Sam kissed the yellowing bruise on her forehead. "Even if I were on death's doorstep..." he whispered.

Rachel's mouth found his.

They located the bookstore coffee shop easily enough. It was spacious, but with lots of nooks and crannies inside. The music was precisely loud enough to mask conversations without interfering with the same. Sam sipped a cappuccino while Rachel flipped through a book on psychology.

"Will you look at these two sorry motherfuckers here," rumbled a familiar voice.

Porter stepped around the bookshelf into the corner they'd chosen. The thick-bodied man moved with an easy confidence that Sam had always admired. He held out his hand and Porter took it for a firm shake. "Sammy Sometimes," he said, his voice softer.

Sam smiled in spite of himself. As a young man, he'd once made the mistake of running a three-card Monte scam on the sidewalk near a shoe store that served as Porter's straight establishment. Sam's game only lasted about an hour before he found himself hauled into the nearby alley and getting an education. Porter interrupted the work his men were doing, and asked, "You always this stupid, son?"

"Sometimes," Sam had managed to say. He spit out some blood and stared up at Porter calmly.

Porter smiled then, just a little one. He told his boys to bring Sam inside and let him clean up. Then he put Sam to work.

Years later, he'd told Sam it was that calmness that made him do it. "The one thing a con man can *not* do is panic. Not ever. You've got to stay centered. That's where you do your best thinking."

Rachel interrupted Sam's reverie by embracing Porter. She could barely get her arms around the big man. "I've missed you," she said.

"Sure you have. Don't run no con on me, girl." His tone belied his words, though, and after Rachel kissed his cheek, Sam saw the warmth in his eyes.

The three of them sat down.

"You want a coffee?" Sam offered.

"You going to limp up there, all grimacing and shit, and play barista?" Porter shook his head, tapping his onyx ring on the table between them. "Nah, I'm fine."

"You look tired, is all."

"I just flew from Cleveland to Hot-lanta. Excuse me if I'm not daisy fresh for you."

Sam raised his hands. "Sorry." The big man had turned grouchy in a hurry.

"What is it?" Rachel asked him in a soft voice. She'd always had a way with Porter, ever since Sam showed up at his place with her, years ago. Almost immediately, anyone watching would have thought she was his protégé and not Sam. Their connection had overtones of a father-daughter kinship, or perhaps a big brother, little sister.

Porter sighed. "I'm tired, like he said."

"Long flight?"

"Not so bad." He grinned at her. "Maybe I'm just tired of the game. It grinds on a man."

"On a woman, too."

His grin broadened into a smile. "Girl, don't even try to tell me you don't have the world by the ass."

"Things could be better."

"Well, then let's get to it. You said this was big enough to get you out from under? Lay it on me, girl."

Rachel glanced around, then pulled a key from her pocket and placed it next to Porter's hand.

Porter stared down at it. Then he looked up at them. "Seven-one-seven?"

Rachel shrugged. "We don't know what it goes to. But we got it from the Artist's sister. You know about the Artist?"

"Formerly known as Prince?"

"No. The one who used to be with our friends in Philly."

His expression darkened. "I remember what happened to him."

"Then you remember *why* it happened."

"Of course. Motherfucker pushed and pushed until he finally pushed too far. Even guineas got a breaking point."

"Right. But with those guys, it's usually a lot sooner. Must be a reason he got away with it as long as he did. Like maybe he had something on Little Vincent."

Porter eyed Rachel. Sam could see his gears turning while he thought it through.

"And you've got it now?"

She motioned toward the key. "We've got that."

Porter sighed. "So the truth is, you don't have shit."

"We have the key," she emphasized. "As for the rest, it doesn't matter. Little Vincent knows what the Artist had."

Porter thought some more. Then he scratched the short beard on his face. "You're talking about running a risky game, girl."

"That's why we can't face-to-face."

"But you want me to?"

"You'll be safe."

"Easy for you to say."

"Porter, think how long that leverage kept the Artist alive. Do you really think Little Vincent is going to risk whatever it is getting out?"

"No, I don't. I think that's why he killed the man in the first place." He turned to Sam. "Are you really down with this plan?"

Sam leaned forward slightly. "We've thought it through. You're only a messenger."

"Messengers get axed all the time. There's a damn saying about it."

"Okay, messenger was the wrong word. Someone of your stature, you're an emissary."

"Don't try pumping my tires, Sammy."

"I'm not. Even if they don't know who you are, they'll be able tell simply by how you carry yourself."

"Oh, they know who I am. That's part of the problem."

Sam stopped, then leaned back. "Tell us."

"They've caught wind of me a few times. If all I did was stick to Cleveland, I'd never come up on their radar. But I work with independents like you, and with that comes having your name drop into the whisper stream."

"So you're just some leaf on the wind to them?"

"Somewhat. They've never been motivated enough to run me down, or have a conversation. Like I said, I'm Cleveland, they're Philly." He hesitated, then added, "But the rumor is out there that I've helped you. And they've had this guy, Rocco, asking questions everywhere. He's the one you ran into in St. Louis."

Sam remembered him. "He hasn't found you?"

"Not yet. And even if he does, you don't think I have enough game to back off some guinea muscle if he comes knocking?"

"I know you do."

"It won't even come to holding out on hard questions. I've got plenty of ways to say I don't know who the hell you are. You ain't my brother, I'll say. You ain't even *a* brother, I'll say. And how could I *ever* forget a stone-cold fox like the one you talking about, I'll say. Deny, deny, deny." Porter shook his head slowly. "But I go to NYC, and walk right into the lion's den, I lose that. I become part of the problem, see? And you know how these people solve their problems."

"You've got a guarantee."

"What's that?"

"The same as ours. The leverage. It guarantees our freedom and your safe passage."

Porter considered. "Except they've got to believe it. From what I hear, fools been dropping in every so often with news about you two."

"Snitches." Sam shook his head in disgust.

"The money they're offering, it brings them out."

"How much?" Rachel asked.

Porter's gaze shifted to her. "You won't believe me."

"Try me."

"One mill."

"Get out."

"I wouldn't lie about money. That kind of bounty on your heads brings a lot of people out, taking their run at it like it's a lottery ticket. The worst they'll get if they're wrong is thrown for a beating, and that's only if the dagos call bullshit right then and there, when they lay out their info. If it turns out to be bogus later on, who's going to take the time to run down some bad informant?"

"It's a goddamn cottage industry," Sam muttered.

"That it is. But the point is, they're a skeptical bunch now. I walk in with a key and some story, they may not believe the story, but they'll surely believe that I know you, and know where you are. Even a big man like me ain't walking out of that room, 'cept rolled up in a carpet."

Sam didn't reply. Porter was right.

"They'll believe you," Rachel said.

"How you figure?"

Rachel tapped the key. "Because he'll recognize the key."

Porter looked at her, saying nothing.

"He's seen it," Rachel insisted. "And he'll recognize it."

"How do you know that?"

"Oh, please. Something that important to him, he'll recognize it. The nickel color, plus the seven-one-seven. He'll know what it is."

"No, how you know he's ever seen it in the first place?"

"Think about it. What kind of guy was the Artist?"

"An asshole, what I hear."

"An asshole who flaunted everything. And got away with it because of whatever he had on Little Vincent. But for that to work, they had to have a conversation. They had to reach an understanding." She looked at both of them pointedly. "At a meeting like that, there's no way he doesn't pull out this key and show it to Little Vincent to make his point."

"That's a bit of a leap," Porter said, his tone doubtful.

"Wouldn't you?"

"Sure, but—"

"And you?" she asked Sam.

Sam nodded. "Of course. It's psychological. The physical object makes the concept of the leverage more concrete for the mark."

Porter shook his head. "You're pinning a lot on him knowing what that key goes to." He jabbed his finger. "That *specific* key."

"So when you contact him, feel him out before you meet. See if he recognizes the key or the number on it. If he does, you know you're safe. You sit down with him and give him our price."

"Which is?"

"He leaves us be. That's it. We stay west of the Mississippi, and he pulls the bounty."

"And my safe passage."

"Of course. As long as that happens, the leverage stays hidden and never sees the light of day. Anything happens to you, or anyone comes after us again...then we shine a light."

Porter sighed. "It's a big damn risk."

"Which we would compensate you for," Rachel answered immediately.

Porter waved her words away. "You can't pay me enough to buzz on out to some warm island country somewhere, so it ain't worth talking about. And if your plan doesn't work, I won't be around to spend whatever you're promising anyway."

Both Sam and Rachel remained silent, waiting for him to make his decision. If he refused, Sam was unsure if there was anyone else competent enough to do the job that they also trusted enough to do it.

Finally Porter let out a long sigh. "I owe you," he said, glancing at Sam when said it. "I'll do it."

Sam grinned at him. As far as he was concerned, the ledger had been more than balanced for years now, but he wasn't going to argue. Besides, maybe someone saving your life was a debt you never fully paid back.

Rachel stood and came around the short table to hug him. "You're a beautiful man."

"Yeah, yeah. Not as beautiful as this one—" he motioned

toward Sam, "—or you'd be living in my crib."

Rachel took his face in her hands and gave him a short kiss on the lips. "I love you too much to do that to you," she said.

That made Porter chuckle out loud. "There you go," he said, "running a game on me. You just can't help yourself, can you?"

Rachel hugged him again.

"Shut up," she said.

The three of them drove to Myrtle Beach and rented a small house for a week. When they went out for some supplies, Rachel made a copy of the key.

"I don't know why," she said, in answer to Sam's querulous look. "Porter has to have the original but...it feels right to have a copy."

Sam didn't reply, but he understood. In the life they led, following your instincts was every bit as important as having a plan.

That night, they opened a nice bottle of scotch and sat together on the deck, drinking slowly. The mood was somber and bittersweet. They spoke haltingly of old times, frequently lapsing into silence to listen to the waves crashing on the dark beach. Then someone would mention a name, or an event, and the low rumble of Porter's laughter made Sam feel better again.

The next morning, Porter was eager to get the thing underway. "I figure a day to travel, then two, maybe three to get in touch. Maybe less, if I find them quicker. Once we talk, he should decide fast, so you should hear from me inside of five days. Six, max."

"Sounds about right," Rachel said.

Porter gave them each a long, hard hug before he left. Embracing Rachel was normal, but when the big man pulled Sam into a tight clinch, it surprised him a little. "You take care of her, Sammy. Hear?"

"I always do."

Porter gave a last squeeze and released him. "Bullshit. From where I sit, she takes care of you more often than not."

Sam couldn't argue that. "Thanks for doing this," he said. He stared into the big man's eyes. "I mean it."

"Like I said, I owe you. Besides, you're family." His eyes shone, and his voice quavered slightly with emotion when he spoke.

Sam squeezed Porter's forearm. "So are you."

Porter nodded solemnly. "If it works, I don't imagine I'll be seeing much of you two again."

"Not for a while," Sam agreed.

"Well, it's been a good run." Porter turned abruptly and strode away.

The first two days were easiest. Even though the plan was in motion, both knew it was unlikely Porter had made contact yet. The two of them sat in the Adirondack chairs on the deck of their rental, watching the ocean and sipping drinks. Along with the booze, Sam's supply of ibuprofen took the edge off of the pain in his leg. They spoke only a little, lapsing into the secret, verbal code that is woven into the tapestry of every long-standing relationship. They made love in the middle of the day and listened to music while the ocean air wafted through the open window. If Porter's mission hadn't been looming over them, things would have seemed like a picture-perfect vacation.

As day three rolled around, the tension in the small beach house mounted. The hearty breakfasts of eggs, bacon, and hash browns became simply coffee and toast. The drinking on the deck was heavier that night, and Sam slept late the next day.

He woke to an empty bed. Rubbing his eyes, he stumbled out of the bedroom and through the empty kitchen. The only sign of Rachel was the half-full pot of hot coffee. Sam poured himself a cup and wandered out onto the patio.

Rachel sat, loosely bundled in a blanket, her hands wrapped around her own cup of coffee, cradling it. She looked up when he approached.

"You been up long?"

She shook her head. "Second cup."

He raised an eyebrow.

"Maybe the third. You the java police now?"

"Not at all." He lowered himself into chair next to her. He took an appreciative sip of the coffee, still surprised at how good it was. When they'd rented the place, he'd expected something more akin to motel coffee. "What's on your mind?"

Rachel moved her head almost imperceptibly. "A bad feeling I can't shake."

"How specific?"

"Not very. Just a general ache."

Sam thought about everything that could go wrong. It was a lot, he knew, but it all seemed to rest on whether or not Little Vincent believed in the key. If he believed *that*, the rest of the dominos should fall exactly as they'd planned.

"Porter seem different to you?" Rachel asked.

He considered. "A little, yeah."

"How so?"

Sam took another drink of his coffee before closing his eyes and recalling their recent time together. Porter had always been a gruff man, at least on the exterior. That was a job necessity, in Sam's estimation. But for those he cared about, the big man expressed genuine affection. He was more demonstrative with women in that regard, but a handshake or a shoulder slap between him and another man carried the same emotional weight. That had been true during this most recent interaction, too, but...

"He seemed sad, somehow," Sam finally said, putting his finger on it. "And tired."

"He said as much. On the tired part, at least."

"You're right. He did."

"I thought he seemed sad, too," Rachel said. "I don't remember him ever seeming that way before."

"Never?"

"Not like this. It felt so...final." Rachel stared out at the morning water.

"Babe."

"Huh?"

"Look at me."

She turned slowly and stared into his eyes. "Of course he was sad. We've had a long partnership, all of us. After he does this for us, we probably won't ever see him again. The man deserves to feel a little something, doesn't he?"

Rachel grinned slightly. "You almost sounded like him there for a second."

"Perils of the trade. But you know I'm right."

Rachel turned away, her smile fading. "I thought that, too. At first. But now I'm not so sure."

"Why?"

"I told you. I can't pin it down. Something just feels wrong."

"With Porter?"

"Maybe."

"Are you thinking he doesn't have this job in him? That this whole thing is going to be some kind of sacrifice?"

"That might explain the sadness."

"Not a chance." Sam reached out and touched her shoulder, but she didn't look his way. "This is the man who brought me up in the game. And the number one rule he always preached above everything else was to look out for number one." He shook his head. "Trust me, he doesn't have it in him to sacrifice himself. There's no way he'd walk into a room with Little Vincent unless he knew he was walking out."

Rachel turned to him. "Maybe that's what I'm worried about. You heard what he said. A million dollars. That's a lot to walk away from, even for Porter."

Sam watched her eyes for a few moments, running her words through his mind. The idea had never occurred to him, despite existing in a world that had taught him to trust no one. No one except Rachel.

And Porter, he told himself.

But Rachel's worried eyes bore into him, and he dropped his

178

hand from her shoulder and forced himself to consider the possibility. It only took a few moments for him to reject it.

"Not Porter. He'd never do that to us. Not after what I did for him."

Rachel didn't reply.

"He wouldn't," Sam insisted, but even he heard the uncertainty in his tone.

They sat in silence for a long while, the gaze between conveying more meaning than most words could. Sam allowed the idea to rattle around his brain while he tried to attack it, but he kept returning to the same place.

"No way," he finally murmured, shaking his head even as his quiet words were whisked away by the ocean breeze. "He wouldn't do it."

Rachel's expression turned sympathetic. "This is like when we found the key," she said. "We were thinking about that situation wrong. I think we have to look at this one differently, too."

"No."

"Yes, we do. We have to stop trying to think of reasons why Porter wouldn't betray us, and start asking ourselves why he *would*. What would he gain?"

"Nothing. He'd gain nothing, and he'd lose us."

"Oh, Sam." She touched his forearm. "You don't want to see it."

"There's nothing to see."

"Indulge me."

Sam put his coffee cup down on the wide armrest of the Adirondack chair and rubbed his eyes. "The man is the closest thing I ever had to a father. Light years beyond my real old man. I can't do it."

"You don't have to. But listen to me. If you think I'm wrong after that, fine."

Sam dropped his hands and nodded. "All right. Say your piece."

Rachel took a sip of her coffee. "You said he had nothing to gain. But he does. A million dollars. That's a lot, especially coming all at once. Even for him. He might gross that in a year, or two, but how much of it goes back out to pay expenses, or in the form of someone's cut?"

Sam stared back at her, saying nothing.

"It's not only the money. When that occurred to me, I brushed it aside just like you did. I know the man loves us, so money alone wouldn't be enough. But that kind of money gives him something else, too. It gives him *freedom*. Freedom to walk away."

"I still don't see it," Sam said. "He's been in the game his whole life. It's who he is. He'll die an old man, still running one game or another."

"Maybe he realized that. Really, truly realized it. Could be that's why he's so tired."

Sam considered. "I don't think so."

"But it could be," she insisted.

"I've known the man, even longer than you have. Regret for being who he is, the path he's chosen, that's not in his DNA."

"You can't know that. None of us can." She squeezed his forearm. "Is it so outlandish to think that a man in his sixties—a man with no wife and no children, a man who has been living on the edge of the knife his entire life—is it so crazy to think that he might see an opportunity to get out from under, free and clear, and take it?"

"A man? Sure. But Porter? No."

Rachel stared at him for a few seconds. Then she leaned across and kissed him softly on the scar along the edge of his eye. "You're loyal, Sam. I love that about you." She leaned in, pressing her forehead to his. "And I really hope I'm wrong about this, and that it's only a bad feeling."

Sam wanted to say she *was* wrong, that Porter was too solid, and that the man was everything Sam had always believed him to be. But all he could do was clench his jaw and nod.

That night, after a sparse dinner, they nursed a single drink each, staring out into the dark waves.

* * *

On day four, Sam took to carrying his small .32 in his waistband, covering it with an untucked, loose-fitting collared shirt. He left the bottom two buttons undone. To an untrained eye, he hoped he looked like any other weekend-in-Margaritaville type on vacation with his wife.

Inside, doubt was creeping in. Rachel's words made a terrible kind of sense to him, and he was increasingly concerned she might be right. Still, it tore at him to suspect Porter of anything other than complete loyalty. So, he paced the house periodically, checking that the doors were locked and peering out the windows onto the street.

For her part, Rachel retreated into the book she had purchased in Atlanta. He thought it had been the one about psychology that she'd been leafing through when Porter arrived, but when he'd picked it up absently, he saw it was poetry instead.

He gave her a curious glance. Most of her reading had some sort of application to the life they led, or was outright trashy. Cotton-candy for the mind, merely to entertain. This didn't seem to fit either mold.

Rachel stared back evenly. "It requires all of my attention," she said, answering his unspoken question. "And it makes me think about the same things in different ways."

He grunted. That explained things. Both mental exercises were good for what they did. And as he patrolled the house, never sitting for long, he envied her the escape.

By the morning of the fifth day, both of them were on edge. Rachel set aside her book, and Sam paced relentlessly.

"Hey."

Sam stopped and looked to where Rachel sat at the kitchen table. "What?"

"Stop."

"Huh?"

"With the pacing, and the lighter. Stop."

Sam glanced down at the silver Zippo in his hand. Flicking it open and closed was such an old habit, he didn't even realize he was doing it. He snapped it shut and slid the lighter into his pocket. It was the only thing he owned that had been his father's, and despite the cold hatred that he'd developed for the old man, he'd kept the lighter. He didn't know why exactly, except that over time, he'd come to associate it with other things, too. Meeting Rachel, for one. Lighting fat Cubans for Porter, for another.

"You still got that feeling?" he asked her.

She nodded. "So do you."

"I don't know. Maybe I'm keying off of you."

"Pun intended?"

Sam frowned at the joke and ran his fingers through his hair. "I wish we'd thought about this angle before we called him."

"We were focused on getting the box, and then what was in it."

"And now we have to live with this doubt. It feels like no matter what happens, we lose Porter."

"We do, Sam. If I'm wrong, and he follows through, we're out of his world. And if I'm right..."

Sam thought about it for a while. Finally, he made a decision. "Get your things," he told her. "Just in case."

They turned in the rental car and rented another under a different name, one Porter didn't know. After getting a motel room on the edge of town, they returned to the beach house. Sam parked up the street, and they watched.

Rachel left a couple of lights strategically turned on, and the upper story windows of the house open. The breeze made the curtains sway. They were too far away to hear it, but the soft sound of the radio would further add to the illusion that someone was inside.

Sam stared up the street, watching one direction while Rachel focused on the other. They spoke only a little, lapsing back into their working habit. On the job, words were tools, and to be used only when necessary.

Cars passed periodically, and Sam eyed each of them. They

were situated on a quiet residential road on the beach, so all the traffic was slow, but no cars slowed in a way that drew suspicion. The same was true with the foot traffic. Men, women, and children occasionally strolled past, but no one gave the two of them a second look, and none appeared interested in their empty beach house.

The day wound down. Sam kept the car windows cracked open, both to better hear their surroundings and to let in the sea breeze. As the sun set, he wished they were sitting on the deck of the rental house, staring out at the beautiful waters with a drink in hand, celebrating their freedom with Porter, and wishing him a bittersweet farewell. Pushing the thought away, he took the Power Bar Rachel handed him. Wordlessly, he tore open the wrapper, and chewed mechanically.

"We'll give it until midnight," Rachel suggested. "If no one shows, we'll get some sleep at the motel and check back in the morning."

Sam grunted around a mouthful of carob-covered cardboard. They waited.

Night fell, and with it, darkness. Streetlights sputtered on, and slowly brightened. Patches of illumination appeared within the houses along the roadway. Sam felt himself getting tired, only his irritation keeping him alert.

By eleven, they'd seen nothing.

Sam rubbed his eyes.

Maybe they'd been wrong. He'd hoped that was true.

"What was that?" Rachel asked.

His eyes snapped open. "What?"

She pointed toward the beach house, careful to keep her hand below the height of the car windows. "I thought I saw a shadow."

"Moving?"

"Yes."

Sam leaned forward and peered toward the house. He scanned for any movement, but saw nothing. After a few minutes, he said, "I don't see anything. Did you see it again?"

"No."

"Could it have been the curtain? Or something else getting caught by the breeze through the open window?"

Rachel shook her head, staring intently at the house. "It was on the ground floor. If it was there at all, and not my eyes playing tricks on me."

Sam reached for the keys. "We should go."

"Wait. I want to see—"

Both car doors flew open.

It took a moment for the action to register in Sam's mind. But then a rough hand gripped him by the upper arm and growled, "Out, motherfucker," and his mind processed what was happening.

When the thug jerked on his arm, Sam didn't resist. Instead, he went with it, tumbling out of the car and rolling away. He felt the man's fingers slide off his bicep as he slipped out of the man's grasp.

"Hey!"

Sam lurched to his feet. A small shock of pain shot through his leg, but he ignored it. The man who'd grabbed him stood in the doorway of the car, staring at him in surprise. He wore a dark track suit with a heavy gold chain, both of which stood out against his pale white skin.

Whitey, Sam thought, recognizing him from the time they'd spent running their con on Little Vincent.

On the other side of the vehicle, he could hear the sounds of slaps and strikes as Rachel struggled with her attacker. He had to get to her.

Whitey recovered from his surprise. "Okay, then," he said, and reached toward his waistband.

Sam stepped forward and slammed the car door on him.

Whitey's eyes bulged when the metal of the door connected, first with his leg, and then his pelvis. He let out a cry of pain. His hands shot out to push the door away. Sam heard the clatter of metal on asphalt at Whitey's feet. He ignored the sound, swinging the door open wide.

Instead of smashing it into Whitey again immediately, Sam snapped out a hard, short kick, catching him directly in the balls.

The thug let out a deep groan. His hands dropped from defending against the door, instead cupping his injured groin.

Sam didn't hesitate. He slammed the door into Whitey twice, putting all his strength into the action. Both blows struck Whitey with considerable force. The second one caught him in the head as he leaned forward in pain, opening a gash above his brow.

Reaching in, Sam grabbed a fistful of Whitey's track suit and yanked him forward. The thug staggered, tripped on Sam's outstretched foot, and toppled to the ground.

Frantically, Sam searched the dark asphalt for the gun Whitey had dropped. He spotted the bright chrome almost immediately and snatched it from the ground. Whipping toward the opposite side of the car, he pointed it toward the second gangster.

He didn't recognize the man struggling with Rachel. He was bigger than Whitey, and more muscular. He wore a dark blue dress shirt. Sam saw a fresh injury on his face, a pair of parallel claw marks along his cheeks. He didn't seem bothered by them. He held Rachel by each wrist, attempting to get her under control. Rachel thrashed in his grasp, and Sam could hear the thud of her shoes battering against the big man's shins.

"Get your hands off her!" Sam commanded. He shuffled around the front of the car, keeping the gun trained on the man in the blue shirt. "Let her go, now!"

The man glanced toward Sam, his expression flat. Unlike Whitey, his eyes betrayed no surprise when he registered the gun in Sam's hands. He hesitated a moment before releasing Rachel's wrists.

"Step back," Sam ordered, keeping his voice low. The last thing they needed was vacationers seeing him waving around the gun and calling in the local cops. Jail was as bad as Little Vincent's goons at this point.

The big man took several steps backwards. He kept his hands hovering in the air, not quite shoulder height. He watched Sam without fear.

"Down on the ground," Sam said.

The big man slowly lowered himself to his knees, first one, and then the other.

"Faster," Sam urged. "All the way down."

All he got from the man in response was a defiant, even stare.

"Take the wheel," Sam told Rachel.

Rachel slipped into the car from her side, scrambling into the driver's seat and pulling that door shut and locking it. A moment later, the engine flared to life.

"What's your name?" Sam asked the man in the dark blue shirt.

"Fuck you."

Sam eased around the muscular man, keeping the pistol leveled at him. "Down on your stomach," he said.

"No."

"Do it!"

"Or what? You'll shoot me?" The big man shook his head. "No. I stand up and come at you, then maybe. But you ain't shooting me while I'm kneeling here. You don't want the cops any more than we do. Probably less, you fuck."

Sam kept moving to his left, angling for the open car door. "I blow your head off, who shows up after won't matter much to you."

A small smile of contempt curled on the man's lips. "Listen to you, trying to sound all hard. You fucking candy ass."

Sam reached the doorway. Keeping the gun leveled, put one foot onto the floor of the passenger side, letting his knee rest on the seat.

The big man glared at him. "You know that broke-ass moolie sold you out, right? Took the money and ran. But you had to know that was going to happen, right?"

Sam wanted to shoot him right in his face. His finger tensed with the desire. He took a deep breath, trembling with adrenaline.

The man watched him, showing no fear.

Sam moved his finger from the trigger. He eased himself the rest of the way into the car, contorting his body to keep the gun pointed at the thug. "Go," he said out of the side of his mouth.

Rachel goosed the accelerator, and they pulled away. Sam kept his eyes fixed on the big man's descending figure on the street. He made no effort to rise up from his knees, only slowly lowered his hands as he watched them go.

"Are you hurt?" Sam asked Rachel as she took a hard left turn.

Rachel gave him a curt shake of her head.

"Good," Sam said, more to himself than her. He kept watching out the rear window of the car as she drove. "Good."

Rachel drove as fast as she could without attracting attention, taking a series of turns before reaching a main arterial. Then she slowed to the speed limit.

"I'm sorry," Rachel whispered.

Sam stared out the window and said nothing.

They left Myrtle Beach without stopping at the motel and drove westward. After almost four hours, they finally stopped at a diner on the western outskirts of Charlotte, North Carolina. Both ordered coffee and pancakes. The pancakes were sweet, the coffee bitter. Neither of them spoke until the meal was almost finished and the waitress had refilled their cups for the second time.

"You were right," Sam finally said. "About Porter. I should have listened to you."

"Being right doesn't make me happy," she said.

Sam shook his head slowly. "I didn't want to believe it."

"Neither did I."

"But you saw it. I couldn't."

Rachel took a sip of her coffee and grimaced. "Everyone has a breaking point. A million dollars is a lot of money."

"I didn't figure it was enough."

"Would it have been for you?"

Sam glanced up at her. "To betray Porter? Not a chance."

"Not even to save me?"

"That's different."

She shrugged. "I'm just saying. He had a choice. He made it.

That's the game. Now we have to make our choice."

"What to do next," Sam mused. He took the last few bites of pancakes and chewed thoughtfully. Rachel stared into her cup, lost in thought.

"We could try to use the key ourselves," Rachel said.

"The copy, you mean."

"It doesn't matter. It still opens whatever it opens."

"We run into the same problem as before. Him believing us."

"How hard is it to believe we'd make a copy?"

"True," Sam admitted. "But how do we make the deal? We can't use an intermediary again. Little Vincent would either buy off or kill the messenger."

"I agree."

"Then what?"

"One of us has to go."

"No!" Sam snapped, dropping his fork on the plate with a clatter. The vehemence in his voice surprised even him.

Rachel gave him a look of concern, then glanced around to see if anyone noticed. "Easy, babe," she whispered.

Sam reached for the water glass and took a drink. Then he said, "We're not doing that."

"It could work."

"All it would do is give him a hostage."

"We have the leverage as hostage."

"So it's a Mexican stand-off. At best." Sam shook his head. "That move is a loser. We need to stick together."

Rachel thought about his words for a while. Finally, she nodded in agreement. "All right. Then we have to go to ground."

"That's what I think, too. We raid some of the honey pots we've got sprinkled around, and we lay low for a long while."

"How long?"

He gave her a pointed look. "I'm talking a year, at least. Probably longer."

"That's why the honey pots, then."

"Exactly."

"But where?"

Sam reached for his coffee cup. "It has to be someplace we haven't worked. Big enough to hide in, but not big enough to be an obvious choice."

"San Diego?"

He shook his head. "Too close to Mexico. They might search there thinking we try to get below."

"True. But L.A. is too obvious, and Northern California is still a little hot for us. Seattle?"

Sam thought for a moment. "Seattle might be the same problem as L.A. Besides we ran that violin scam there, what? Three years ago?"

"You think he's still watching for us over that one?"

Sam recalled the mark, a Chinese importer/exporter they'd taken for a little north of a hundred thousand. "That guy is going to keep his eyes peeled for us for a long time." He thought some more. "But Portland, maybe?"

"Maybe." Rachel sounded doubtful.

"It's what? Half a million people, more or less? Big enough to hide in."

"Probably."

"We don't know anyone in the city," Sam continued. "We've never pulled a job there. As a place to keep under the radar, it makes sense."

"I know."

"But you don't like it."

"I didn't say that."

"I can tell."

Rachel pursed her lips. "It's a smart move. It makes sense, like you said. But I think it makes *too much* sense."

Sam considered her words. "It's what they'd expect us to do," he finally said.

"Exactly."

"So what do we do instead?"

"We go where they least expect it," Rachel told him.

Sam frowned. "Shit. That means Philly."

"It does."

"Shit," Sam repeated.

"Not the city," Rachel said. "But close. Right under their noses."

"It's dangerous."

"Everything we do is dangerous these days."

Sam nodded in agreement. "You're right."

"At least it's where they'd least expect us," she argued. "If we're smart…"

"We better be goddamn brilliant."

Rachel didn't answer.

Sam thought it through, considering how it might fail miserably. Then he thought about how it might work. If she cut her hair and colored it. He'd have to color his, too, and wear some glasses. Even with a make-over, they'd have to be hermits, without seeming to be so. They couldn't work, not even online.

"It'll take money," he finally said.

"Then let's go collect our honey pots."

There were at least a dozen, scattered across the country. They raided the couple that were accessible online, netting a little over ten thousand in cash. That gave them money to travel on.

"Porter knows about a couple of these," Rachel pointed out as they approached Nashville. "He set up the one in Detroit. After that union thing with Richie."

"I know."

"How much is there?"

"Sixty or so."

Rachel consulted her notes. "We could definitely use it."

"Someone could be watching."

"I thought about that. But would he give them the emergency stashes?"

Sam snorted. "He gave them us!"

"Yes, and that should have been the end of it. Would he go

on to give them this kind of information about us? Would they even think to ask?"

Sam thought about it. "I see your point. If he told them where we were in Myrtle Beach, why would they ask about anything else?"

"They wouldn't. They'd send their goons to finish the job, which they did."

"And Porter skates with the million." Sam ground his teeth in frustration.

"We gotta let that go," Rachel said. "Focus only on getting enough money together so we can go to ground."

Sam didn't reply, but he knew she was right. He kept grudges, but he stored them on the back shelf of his mind's closet, not in plain view where they could distract.

"We should hit Detroit early," Rachel suggested. "To be safe."

"After Nashville," Sam agreed. "And the bank in Indianapolis."

The boot store in Nashville was on Broadway. They mingled with the tourists along the street. Country music blared out of the bars as they passed, and buskers plied their trade on the corners. Rachel didn't like country, but the Iowa boy in Sam held out a special place for a little twang once in a while. He dropped a couple of ones into the guitar case of a red-haired, freckled singer strumming his way through a rendition of a Johnny Cash classic.

"Don't encourage them," Rachel teased.

"It's Nashville," he told her. "They're already encouraged."

At the boot shop, they entered separately. Rachel posed as a shopper for several minutes, browsing the selection. The place was busy enough that none of the salesclerks approached her right away. Sam remained on the sidewalk, listening to the faded, broken snippets of "Ring of Fire" up the block. Once she'd made a loop through the store, she gave him a subtle signal, and Sam went inside.

He browsed until there was a momentary break at the register. The clerk there was older than most of the staff, but Sam didn't recognize him. He wore a baby blue western shirt with navy blue pockets and lapels, along with pearl snaps. His broad face bore a harried, irritated expression.

Sam stuck out his hand. "I'm Evan. How ya doing today?"

The man took Sam's hand gave it a perfunctory shake, then dropped it. "Cade."

"Pleased to meetcha, Cade," Sam said. "Is Rodney around?"

"Rodney?"

"Newsome," Sam added. "The owner of the place."

Cade gave him a derisive look and snorted. "Hell, son, he's two owners ago." He looked Sam up and down. "We still got the same boots, though, if you're looking."

"I might be." Sam gave him a disarming country smile. "But Rodney was holding something for me. A special order from a while back. You think you might still have it?"

"Not a chance. We did a clean sweep through everything when we bought the place."

Sam smiled. "I guess I'll go check with Rodney, then. You got his number?"

Cade shook his head. "He ain't got no number, son. Rodney died over a year ago."

Rachel found the obituary on her phone. Rodney died of a heart attack, with little fanfare. Sam looked over her shoulder as she scrolled down the screen, reading the rote words, looking for what they needed.

"No wife," he observed. "Survived by a son, Reginald."

"I suppose we'll need to meet him," Rachel said. "But for now, let's get a room. I need sleep and a quiet place to research."

Sam considered suggesting they move on to Indy and then Detroit, and circle back for the Nashville pot afterward. But this was a large one, and they needed to land it.

Plus, there was the time factor. Porter didn't know Rodney, at least as far as Sam was aware. They'd met Rodney through an introduction by Finch. Those two had partnered on a number of long cons in El Paso years before, until they made the mistake of taking money from a visiting narco and had to leave for more northerly climes. Finch landed in St. Louis, Rodney in Nashville. But just because they hadn't met Rodney through Porter didn't mean for certain that Porter didn't know him. He almost certainly did, as he seemed to have a line on everyone east of the Mississippi if they had any stature in the game. But even if Rodney was on Porter's radar, Sam didn't think the man knew of Sam and Rachel's connection to him.

Didn't *think* so. There was always a chance, and that made him want to move things along as quickly as possible.

At the hotel, Rachel collapsed onto the bed and was almost immediately asleep. Sam lay next to her, watching her as he tried to doze. He didn't think he would and planned on heading down to the bar for a drink, but inside of five minutes, his eyes drooped, and he slept.

Reginald Newsome's house was opulent, but in a way that Sam could tell was meant to look casual. Reggie wanted to play like he was blue collar country, but make sure you knew he was only playing at it, because he was better than you.

A housekeeper had let them in, seeming unsurprised by the visitors. She led them to a patio, offered them coffee, and promptly disappeared. Sam scanned the veranda, which was spotless despite several trees and bushes that he knew shed their leaves regularly. The late morning sun hit the area perfectly, and he gave a mental nod of appreciation to the architect who imagined the layout.

The coffee arrived before Newsome did. The housekeeper placed their cups and a pot-sized French press of the brew on the table. She poured for each of them, and hurried away, all wordlessly.

Sam took a drink. The distinct, rich blend was delicious, and somehow that irritated him. He stood and walked to the edge of the patio, looking out on the expanse of the back yard.

Ten minutes later, the door opened and Reggie Newsome made his entrance.

The first thing that struck Sam about the man was that he looked nothing like his father. Rodney had been a smaller man, slender and weathered. His energy was canny but peaceful, and while his personality didn't fill a room, Sam had noticed an important trait: Rodney paid attention to you. He made whoever he spoke to feel like the most important person there was in that moment.

His son was a study in opposites. Much taller and bigger, with the beginnings of a gut, Reggie projected a contentious air. His expression was a whisper away from a sneer, and his eyes held a hard, contemptuous expression. Whereas his father had dressed in plain western shirts and jeans, Reggie's black slacks were accented by a black belt with interlaced rhinestones, and his pearl-buttoned shirt was a loud salmon color. More than all of that, it was clear to Sam that Reggie never believed that anyone was more important than him at any moment.

"Sorry I kept you waiting," he boomed insincerely. "I had to take a call from New York."

"No problem," Rachel said with a disarming smile.

Sam walked back to the table. He understood their roles immediately. They fell into them with practiced precision, each of them having taken a read on Reginald Newsome that would be nearly identical. Rachel the coquettish one, Sam the good old boy. Her job was to make him want to sleep with her largely because he wasn't sure he could, and Sam's was to seem to be the kind who could run with him, but only as a sidekick.

Reggie gave Rachel a look that was a little longer than what was polite. He returned her grin. "Aren't you just a vision, doll?"

Sam knew how much the word "doll" made Rachel bristle, but no one else in the world would know it by her reaction. Instead, she turned up the wattage on her smile for a beat, then looked away.

Reggie glanced at Sam. "Your girl?" he asked, motioning

toward Rachel. A heavy gold chain bracelet swayed on his wrist when he did so.

"Sister, actually," Sam said.

"Really?" Reggie made a satisfied look. "Well, then…" He sat down between the two of them and reached for the French press. "You said when you called that this was about my father?"

"It is," Sam said. "But first, we both want to express our condolences for your loss. Your father was a good man."

Reggie snorted while he poured. "He was a son of a bitch. That's why my mother left him."

Sam glanced at Rachel.

"A woman has to do what she thinks is best for her child," Rachel offered.

Reggie snorted again. "A woman might, but not my mother. She left me with the old man." He gave them both a measured look. "Y'all don't know much about my family, do you?"

Sam gave him a sheepish look. "If I'm being honest, I only knew your father professionally."

"That explains it. Everyone loved Boot Store Pop. He was oh-so-popular there, and over at his beloved bar." Reggie set the French press down with a little extra force.

"Sometimes," Sam ventured, "the face a man puts on for business is different than the one he wears for his family."

"No shit." Reggie took a sip of the coffee. Sam wondered if he noticed or appreciated how fine it was, or if he was too used to it. After the round-faced man swallowed, he fixed Sam with another pointed look. "Did you come here this morning to philosophize on fathers and sons, mister? Because this is Nashville, and there are plenty of places I can go to get words of wisdom on family. Only difference is it'll be put to music, so it'll be a whole lot easier to listen to than what you're peddling."

Sam didn't miss a beat. "I'll get to the point, then. We knew your father a few years back. He held onto a package for us. We're here to pick it up."

Reggie showed no surprise. "Package, huh? I knew Pop was

195

into some low-level shady shit. Even when I was kid, I knew."

"There's nothing shady about holding onto something for a friend," Sam said.

"You mean being a bank?"

Sam shrugged. "Call it what you like."

"Since it's my house, and my father, I will." The tone in Reggie's voice had bordered on derisive since he sat down, but now it sharpened. He gave Sam a hard stare.

Sam waited. Across from him, Rachel sat poised to interject if she could help, but he knew she wouldn't yet. She had to realize that Reggie was doing some old school chesting up.

"What's this got to do with me?" Reggie asked eventually. "I mean, it seems to me, you had business with my pop, and that old boy has gone to glory. So why are we talking?"

"Because you're his son," Sam said.

"Maybe so, but I'm not your bank."

"Are you telling us you didn't come across our package after Rodney passed?"

A sly grin creased Reggie's lips. "I inherited *everything*. The shitty boot shop, the beat-up house, and a whole gun safe full of odds and ends."

"Including our package."

"Probably. Can you identify it?"

"It was wrapped up like a gift," Sam said. "Pink paper, white bow."

Recognition registered in Reggie's eyes. "Sure, I found it."

"Good." Sam kept his eyes locked onto Reggie's. "We're here for it."

"Are you, now?" Reggie growled.

The two of them stared at each other in a dark silence for several long moments. Then Rachel's voice broke in.

"We paid a broker's fee up front to your father," she said. "That's standard practice. But there's no way you could know that for sure, so we'll pay it again. To you."

Reggie broke eye contact with Sam to cast a leering glance at

Rachel. "How much?"

"Ten percent is standard."

"I want twenty," Reggie said. "Call it an inheritance tax, but in reverse."

Rachel considered. Sam knew it was mostly for show. Eighty percent of their stash was better than zero, and they didn't have the time to put in the kind of work it would require to take the money by other means.

"Fine," Rachel agreed. "But for that kind of a cut, we get the money right away."

"Darling," Reggie said, "I would give you whatever you want, whenever you want."

Sam willed his jaw not to clench. Reggie was baiting him and he could tell the man was watching him out of his peripheral vision.

"What I want is our money, now." She smiled at him, but managed to put a little danger into it.

Reggie leaned back. He stroked the bristly goatee on his fat face, thinking. Then he glanced over at Sam again, before returning to Rachel. "Tell you what. Out of respect for Pop, I'll take the original ten. But for that, you have dinner with me tonight."

Rachel appeared to think it over. Sam kept his breathing even, his expression correct. He ran through scenarios while Rachel let Reggie's offer hang in the air. If she declined, if she accepted…possibilities flitted through his mind.

"I'll have dinner with you," she finally said.

A triumphant grin spread across Reggie's face.

"But I want half our package up front," Rachel added.

That cut Reggie's smile short. Irritation flickered in his eyes, then disappeared behind a hard mask of disappointment. He shook his head slowly. "Half is better than nothing, huh?"

Forty-five percent isn't ninety, Sam thought, *but it's better than zero.*

"Half shows your good will," Rachel countered. "It shows me you have our package, and that you can be trusted."

"It also gets you a bit further up the road, don't it?"

"I want our entire package, Mr. Newsome. I have no plans to leave until then."

Sam thought he might come back with a "Call me Reggie" and continue to push the dinner angle. But the man surprised him by remaining silent for a short while. He took a drink of his coffee and studied both of them. When he finally spoke again, his tone started out sounding almost contemplative.

"You both know the kind of things my pop was into," he said. "Me, I'm into more respectable business ventures. Construction, mostly. But that can be a cash business, too. And as much as it is above board, there's still some slippery sons-a-bitches involved. You can make a little money without dealing with them, but if you want to make the kind of money that buys a place like this?" He motioned at the house behind him. His tone slowly turned into something with more swagger to it. "That requires some connections. And going in, I never would have thought they were the same kinds of connections my pop had, but lo and behold, they ended up being exactly that."

"Is that so?" Rachel asked him.

Sam didn't react to the subtle code. All it did was confirm that she knew what he'd already realized himself. This con was blown.

"It is, darling." Reggie eyed Rachel without any shame. "You are a beautiful woman, you know that? You stand out. And this one?" He thumbed toward Sam without looking his way. "With that fresh scar next to his eye, and that limp? He sort of stands out, too. A few phone calls, and I found a fella in Philadelphia who—"

Sam grabbed the French press and swung it at Reggie's head, hard. The heavy glass smashed into his cheekbone, shattering. Hot coffee splashed all over his face. Bright red blood flowed from a gash next to his eye. Reggie let out a scream of pain and toppled backward in his chair.

Rachel was already up and moving past him. Sam hurried after her. They moved through the house, watching for armed gunmen. All they encountered was a shocked housekeeper, who stared at them in wonder while Reggie howled in pain from the veranda.

At the car, Sam started the engine and chirped the tires as they headed down the driveway. Rachel scanned for suspicious cars.

"Anything?"

"No. It's clear."

Sam drove out of the neighborhood and onto a main arterial. After a mile, he pulled into a Target parking lot, and stopped. He looked over at Rachel, who was finishing up a visual sweep of the area. With that completed, she returned his gaze.

"Hotel?" he asked.

She shook her head. "Nothing there we can't leave behind."

Sam nodded his agreement. That was per their usual methods. Travelling light was the code, and they adhered to it.

"How could he figure us out so quickly?" Rachel asked. "I only called him three hours ago."

"He told us. He's connected."

She snorted. "He's a general contractor, not Michael Corleone. In Nashville, no less. How connected could he be?"

Sam thought about it. "Maybe he doesn't have to be that connected. Maybe things are just loud where we're concerned right now."

Rachel considered, then agreed. "They missed a big chance, and Little Vincent paid handsomely for that opportunity. There's no choice but to turn up the volume. It's a matter of pride now."

"It's a matter of reputation."

"Same, same." She fingered the stitching on the seat, thinking. "How close was that, do you think?"

"No idea."

"I mean, he only had *three hours*. Three hours to find out who we were, find out who to call, to make that call...There's no way Little Vincent's people could be there that fast."

"Unless they're already close."

She looked into his eyes. "You feel like that's it?"

Sam pursed his lips, then shook his head. "No."

"Me, either."

"Of course, that's the gut talking. Could be that we just want to believe it's true."

"You ever lie to yourself like that, Sam? Because I don't."

Sam sighed. "I didn't used to think so. But I did with Porter." He thought for a few moments. "Maybe LV made a call to friends in Nashville. They could have been the ones coming."

"Maybe. But I don't think so. I think that Mister Hotshot Reginald Newsome messed up. I think he was supposed to find a way to delay us until they could get their people here."

"All of that might be true. But what now?"

"The only way out of the woods..." Rachel began.

"...is through the woods," Sam finished. He took a deep breath and let it out. Then he leaned toward her for a kiss. It lasted a while, another dialect of their secret language, saying things they hadn't given voice to, but which were nonetheless true: love, lust, respect, and a healthy gratitude for having escaped the most recent danger.

When she broke away, Sam watched her for another second or two. Then he gave her a light smile and dropped the car into gear.

"Indy?" he asked.

"Indy," she said.

In Indianapolis, they discovered that the small regional bank where they kept a safe deposit box under the last name of Tinker had been absorbed by Wells Fargo. Sam worried a little as he handed over the Michigan license that read Dan Tinker. He'd deposited funds elsewhere under the same name, but always in local institutions—a credit union in San Diego, a family bank in Boise. He supposed it probably didn't matter anymore in this day and age, with the level of interconnectivity surrounding everyone and everything, but it still felt like it had been a smart precaution at the time.

The bank employee was a wizened manager in a crisp white shirt who could probably tell stories about taking deposit deliveries from a stagecoach. Sam forced himself to remain calm throughout the process, which proceeded so slowly that he wondered if the old man was gaming them. He half-expected to see cops come through the front door of the place, or goons disguised as the same, coming to get them both.

Eventually, they found themselves alone with the box. Sam flipped open the metal top. Rachel let out a small sigh of relief at the contents.

"You thought it might have been raided?"

"Who knows?" Rachel said. "Maybe Gina knew about it."

They'd worked with a part-time madam and full-time black-mailer here in Indianapolis named Gina on the job that eventually allowed them to carve off the money for this honey pot. While she knew what their take had been, he was pretty sure she had no idea about the account.

"She's solid," Sam said.

"Only because no one offered her money. Or threatened her."

"Gina wouldn't..."

"If Porter can turn, anyone can." Rachel's voice was both weary and resolute.

Sam lifted the money out of the box. A quick count revealed what he remembered putting in almost three years ago. If they lived modestly, this would get them through for about six months.

While he counted, Rachel cleared out the rest of the box. Four fake identifications, two each, all complete with multiple documents for each identity. She opened the remaining item, a manila envelope. Inside were the damning photos of the marks from the con they worked with Gina. She riffled through them as Sam glanced over her shoulder. The photos were no good for any further blackmail. They didn't have the time, plus they didn't work that way. But might come in handy as insurance if they ever got in a bind in the region.

From her pocket, Rachel took out the copy of the seven-oh-seven key that she'd given to Porter. She gave Sam a questioning look. He nodded, and she placed the key into the safe deposit box. They locked up and left the bank.

They stayed the night in Indianapolis. Sam slept fitfully, the specter of Little Vincent and his thugs making him restless until morning.

On the way to Detroit, they stopped off in Toledo. While Rachel dealt with the real estate broker where they'd parked some funds, Sam sat in the reception area and watched them bargain through the glass walls of the broker's office. While he waited, he considered trying to contact a pimp he knew in the area, a man named Bigs. Bigs wasn't as plugged in as Porter had been—no one was—but he traveled a circuit throughout Ohio with his girls and kept his ear to the whisper stream.

He wondered how smart it would be. The chance that Bigs knew something had to be weighed against the danger that he'd inform on them, or had already. It was a sad state of mind to be in for Sam. He and Rachel had always claimed to live under the mantra of *trust no one*, and they'd mostly stayed true to that. But they'd bent the rule where a few people were concerned. Other people in the game. People that had helped them, or worked with them, and who seemed to be rock solid.

That had been a mistake.

After Finch was killed in St. Louis, they'd sworn to each other that it was time to tighten their circle. The action was as much for the protection of their colleagues as it was their own. Little Vincent had shown he wasn't above killing others to get to them, and that started with poor Finch.

But what had they done, only weeks later? Answered a call from Aunt Sally, one of Sam's earliest mentors. Despite the experience with Finch, they went to Raleigh for the job with Sally. And the resulting chaos almost cost all of them their lives.

Yet, they still didn't seem to learn from that. They used Joseph O'Rourke on the next con, and that one was another close call, this time with the feds.

Eventually, the two of them adapted. Aside from working

loosely with Bigs a few months later, they limited their collaboration as much as possible. Sometimes they required expertise neither of them had, so it was a necessity. Mia's computer skills were one example. In those instances, they tried to insulate their cohorts as much as possible. Finch's death had been their fault, and neither of them wanted to go through that again.

So *trust no one* had really meant *trust only some*. Some who'd proven themselves true, or were vouched for by someone who had. People like Sally, like Mia.

Like Porter.

Porter had been the most trusted of all. For years, he provided information, arranged jobs, given advice, and looked out for the two of them. His betrayal cut deep, and really drove the point home.

Trust no one.

Rachel returned from the office. Her purse, which had been empty when they arrived, was now unable to close around the stuffed manila envelope inside it.

"How'd it go?" he asked her as soon as the door to the suite closed behind them.

"The bastard chiseled us for fifteen percent."

"I thought the deal was ten."

"It was. He bitched about the impact of taxes and risk from new regulations and the goddamn lack of world peace. Then he asked for twenty-five."

Sam grunted. *Bastard* was right. She'd done well to get it down to fifteen.

"Anything else in Toledo?" she asked as they made their way to the car.

"No," Sam said. "We're done here."

Detroit. A nearly-broken city. Sam hadn't been there for more than five years, mostly because of a job that had gone badly. The marks weren't the problem, but they'd chosen the wrong partners. Sam hadn't particularly trusted them, but he had trusted that they'd do the job and not be so greedy as to want the whole take. He'd been wrong.

It was a shame, too, because the piecemeal resurgence of Detroit would have provided them with a multitude of con opportunities. The place was fertile ground, but there were too many landmines for them to risk working here.

The honey pot was in a house on Rosemary Street off of Gratiot Avenue. They waited until night fell before heading over. On the way, they passed the Gethsemane Cemetery, something Sam thought was fitting. All things end, and their run on the con was no exception.

As they cruised through the neighborhood, the stark contrasts of what they saw was disconcerting. Some homes were vibrant, well-cared for, with signs of life spilling out toward the street. But only a few houses away, they encountered boarded up vacants, still and skeletal. The two images alternated sporadically along the block. It seemed like gentrification was happening, but only randomly.

"I wonder if Richie even still lives here," Sam said.

"Maybe we should have called."

Sam shrugged. "Better that he not know we're coming."

He'd befriended Richie while running a game on a string of grocery stores, right before the deal that killed Detroit for them. The chain had treated Richie poorly and then fired him for trying to unionize the workers. His motivation for helping Sam was classic revenge. The fact that he'd come out of it with some cash hadn't hurt, of course. After the job, Sam had wrapped up over sixty thousand dollars and put it in a box, and asked Richie to keep it at his house for them.

If he was being honest with himself, Sam had to admit that he'd trusted Richie. The man made six figures for his contributions, but that was revenge money, not something he sought out of greed. He wasn't in the game, and the union would make sure he caught on elsewhere. Sam didn't think it was likely he'd even touch the box, much less steal their money.

These days, though, he wasn't so sure.

When they approached the address, Sam slowed and pulled to the curb in front of a vacant three lots away. He eyed Richie's house carefully.

"Looks lived in," he said.

"Definitely," Rachel agreed. "How do you want to play it?"

"It's Richie. He either has the money or he doesn't."

"So just knock on the door?"

"That was my thought."

Rachel gave the idea some consideration, then agreed. "I'll hang back a little. You take lead, since he was your mark."

He was more friend than mark, but Sam didn't bother correcting her. Instead, he got out of the car and started toward the house at a purposeful, easy gait. Rachel fell in beside him. They walked along the sidewalk, which was cracked and had weeds pushing through in places, but at least wasn't buckling.

The narrow driveway housed a blue Subaru, parked up close to the house.

"Richie's?" Rachel asked.

Sam shook his head. "He had a Dodge Charger."

Rachel motioned toward the small pink bicycle with training wheels that leaned against the side of the porch. "Maybe he got domesticated."

Sam frowned. Family, kids, all of that cost money. If Richie's kid needed braces or something, that could change the rules for him.

"Smile, babe," Rachel reminded him, her own expression open and warm.

Sam smiled, too, trying it out on her first. Then he saw something mischievous flash in her eyes, and his smile broadened into something genuine.

"That's my guy," Rachel said. "Game face and all."

Sam mounted the concrete steps and rang the doorbell. Inside, he could hear a television playing what sounded like a sportscast. He waited and was about to ring the bell again when he heard footsteps.

The door swung open. A tall man with sandy hair and a precisely trimmed mustache stood in the doorway. He wore slacks and a blue dress shirt and while he still wore the tie, it was loosened and the top button no longer fastened. It took a few moments for recognition to register in his eyes.

"Evan?" he asked.

"Hey, Richie." Sam smiled widely.

"Wow, man. I haven't seen you in years. What are you doing here?"

Sam glanced over his shoulder at Rachel, who gave him no sign of trouble. He turned back to Richie. "You remember my wife, Tara?"

Richie looked at Rachel. "Oh, yeah. We met over dinner. How are you?"

"Fine, thanks." Rachel answered.

"Mind if we talk inside?" Sam asked.

"Sure, sure." Richie stepped to his right, swinging the door wide. "Come on in."

Sam walked inside, followed by Rachel. As he came through the threshold, he scanned the hallway and what he could see of the living room. "You alone tonight?" he asked.

Richie nodded as he shut the front door. "Kristyn took Sydney to visit her mom out in Livonia." He motioned toward the TV. "I was watching the afternoon game, having a beer. Can I get you one?"

"That'd be great," Sam said.

Richie led them into the living room, where he muted the television before heading into the kitchen. "Bottle okay, or you want it in a glass?"

"Bottles are fine."

Richie rummaged in the refrigerator and returned to the living room holding a pair of dark bottles. He handed one to each of them and sank onto the couch. He lifted his own bottle and took a drink. "Please, sit," he said, waving at the couch and an overstuffed chair.

Rachel took the chair, and Sam sat down next to Richie on the couch. An uneasy silence hung in the air. Richie took another drink from his beer, but neither Sam nor Rachel drank any of theirs.

Sam let the silence drag a little while he watched Richie. The man was definitely nervous and trying not to show it. The question that ran through Sam's mind was why. Was it the money, or something else? Did he steal from them, or do something worse?

"So..." Richie finally said. "How've you been?"

"Good, mostly," Sam said. He glanced around the house. "You've updated the place."

"A little." Richie's voice was strained.

"It's not a single's pad anymore."

"No."

"Kristyn, you said? Your girlfriend?" Out of his peripheral vision, he noticed Rachel scanning the room, glancing at the windows and open doorways.

"Wife now." Richie lifted his left hand, displaying the gold band.

"Wow. Congratulations."

"Thanks."

"You two have a daughter, too."

"Sydney." Richie leaned over to the end table nearest him and picked up a framed photo. He handed it to Sam. "That's her right after she turned two."

Sam glanced down at the beaming child. He didn't bother to hand the frame to Rachel. "Where's my money, Richie?"

Richie slumped on the couch, seeming to collapse into himself. "I..." he started to say, then stopped.

Sam waited, staring at him.

"I still have it," Richie said quietly, his voice wavering. "Most of it."

"Most?" Sam put an edge into the word.

Richie nodded apologetically. "It's a little light, is all."

"How much?"

"Eighteen."

Sam kept his hard stare boring into Richie, but inside, he felt relief. Relief that it was only eighteen thousand and not the whole amount. Even with the eighteen missing, that still left them over forty. Money equaled time, and forty grand bought them months. Mostly, though, he felt relief at knowing why Richie had been nervous in the first place.

"It wasn't for me," Richie continued. "It was for Sydney. She had to have an operation. Insurance covered some of it, but not all. I was short, so I borrowed it, that's all."

"Without asking?" Rachel interjected. "That's not borrowing, that's stealing."

"It's stolen money, anyway," Richie said.

"So was your cut of it," Sam reminded him in a warning tone.

Richie held up his hands. "You're right, you're right." He paused, then said, "But I wasn't stealing it. I borrowed almost thirty thousand for Syd's medical bills. I've been paying it back for almost a year now."

"Get it," Sam ordered.

"Okay." Richie rose and left the room, heading for the same basement door he'd led Sam through years ago in order to hide the box.

As soon as Richie left the room, Rachel said in a hushed tone, "We should go."

Sam motioned after Richie and stated the obvious. "He's getting the money."

"He's hinky."

"It's a lot of money. Months' worth."

Rachel pressed her lips together doubtfully. "I don't like it."

Sam considered. They'd walked away from more money than this before on less of a gut feeling. But that was a different situation. Then, there was always another job on the horizon, even if they didn't know what it was yet. Now, they needed the money to lay low.

"It's worth the stretch," he told her, a phrase they'd both used on more than one occasion. The words carried their own message. *I trust you. I know you're right about the risk, but it's one we've got to take.*

Rachel gave him a short nod, and they waited.

Richie surprised him by returning to the living room with the same oversized shoe box Sam remembered packaging the money into years ago. He put it down on the table in front of them. "I'm sorry," he said. "You can count it. It's eighteen light, and I'll get that to you. I just need some more time."

"How much time?"

Richie swallowed nervously. "A year? Maybe a little more."

"Kids don't stop costing money, huh?"

"No, they don't." Richie laughed at Sam's comment, but it had an unnatural feel to it. Too fasted and too forced.

Maybe I was wrong, he thought.

Sam stood and picked up the box. "This is good for now."

Richie gave him a worried look of surprise. "You don't want to count it?"

"No. Why would you lie about it? Besides, we'll count it later. And we'll be back for the rest."

Rachel rose and started for the door. Sam followed.

"Wait!" Richie called after them. He scrambled around the living room furniture to catch up.

Sam paused, glancing back at Richie. His old accomplice had a slightly frantic look to him. "What?"

"Do you have to leave so soon?"

Sam glanced at Rachel, who was already looking at him, her expression clear. Then he returned his gaze to Richie. "Yes, we do."

"I thought you might stay for dinner or something." Richie licked his lips. "For old times' sake."

"Sorry. We're pressed for time."

Sam turned to go.

"I have the rest of the money," Richie blurted.

Sam hesitated near the entrance to alcove that led to the front door.

"No, Sam," Rachel whispered from behind him.

Sam didn't turn around. "Don't worry about it, Richie," he said. "We'll be back for it another time."

He took another step.

That was when he heard the metallic click of a gun hammer.

Sam froze. He sensed Rachel stop moving as well. Slowly, he turned around to face Richie. The former grocer held a small revolver leveled at them. His eyes were shiny and frantic.

"Don't make me shoot," he begged them.

"No one's making you shoot," Sam assured him, his tone soothing.

"I can't let you go," Richie said in a broken voice. "I can't."

"You can."

Richie shook his head. "No, I can't."

"Richie—"

"Put the box down."

Sam hesitated, but when Richie jabbed the gun in his direction, he relented. "All right, easy," he said. He bent at the knees and lowered the box to the floor, then stood upright again.

"Back to the couch," Richie ordered.

Sam felt Rachel's eyes on him. He knew what she was waiting for. However he played it, she'd make the complementary move. "Any way you want it, man," Sam said to Richie, but letting her know with the phrasing what his intention was.

He took a step into the room, but before he put his plan into motion, he had to know something. "Why?" he asked. "Why, Richie?"

Richie swallowed hard. "They came this morning. They knew everything. I didn't have a choice."

"Everyone has a choice."

"They *took* them. Kris and Syd both." His voiced cracked. "They said all they wanted was the two of you."

"So you gave us up."

"They have my wife and daughter!" Richie yelled at him. "They said someone was going to die behind this, and if it wasn't the two of you, it would be them. I had no choice!"

210

"You had a choice," Sam said. "And you made it."

Richie didn't answer, only gestured toward the couch.

"How'd they know?"

"Sit down," Richie said, motioning again. "You're going to sit down, and we're going to wait."

So they're on their way already. Richie must have called them on a cell when he went to retrieve the money.

Sam took a step to his left, exaggerating his limp as he shuffled slowly along the back of the couch. Rachel remained motionless.

"It's gotta be the union, I figure," Sam said. "The mob still has its hooks into the locals."

"My union's independent," Richie said emphatically. "It's clean."

"Maybe. But there's still a pipeline. A clean union bumps up against a dirty one once in a while, and a dirty union deals with an owned one every single day. Information finds its way to them eventually. It just takes longer."

Richie shrugged. "I don't know, man, and I don't care. All I know is that they are going to come here and pick up the two of you, and then I get my family back. Now, sit down."

To his right, Rachel was moving now. She circled in the opposite direction. At first Richie didn't notice, but as she reached far edge of his peripheral vision, he swept around and pointed the pistol at her. "Stop it," he ordered.

"Stop what?" Rachel asked, her voice a practiced purr.

Sam stepped around the edge of the couch.

Richie swung around to direct the gun at him. "Don't move. Sit on the couch."

"Which is it?" Sam asked, angling to his left. "Don't move, or sit on the couch?"

They weren't quite to six and twelve o'clock on him yet, but getting close. Call it seven and eleven-thirty. Sam risked closing the gap between himself and Richie, even as he slid to his left a little more.

"Stop!" Richie took a step toward him and extended the

pistol.

Sam stopped.

Behind Richie, Rachel sidestepped and closed distance. He heard the movement and whipped around. "I said, stop—"

Sam took two quick shuffle steps and plowed into Richie, wrapping his arms around him and driving him forward. He heard the man grunt upon impact, and then let out a cry when they crashed into the television. Sam tried to wrestle him to the ground, but Richie was too strong. He stood his ground, trying to thrash his way free of Sam's grasp.

"Let me go!" he cried out.

Sam kept expecting to feel the hard butt end of the pistol on his head, but Richie seemed more intent on getting free. Sam stepped one of his legs behind Richie and attempted to push him backwards, but Richie spun to his left, slipping out of Sam's grasp. He took a step to follow, but Richie recovered and raised the gun.

"You son of a bitch! I said, don't move or—"

Rachel smashed a table lamp over Richie's head from behind. The blow stunned him. He staggered forward, a dazed and slightly surprised look in his eyes. Sam side-stepped, grabbed his wrist with one hand and pried the gun away from him with the other. As he pulled the weapon away, Richie sank to his knees with a groan.

Sam backed away, keeping the gun trained on Richie.

"You all right?" Rachel asked him.

Sam gave her a terse nod.

Richie went to all fours, shaking his head. Then he retched. Vomited splattered against the wood floor.

"Let's go," Rachel said. She moved away, and Sam heard the light scrape of cardboard against the wooden floor as she recovered the box of cash.

He thought about shooting Richie. The man had betrayed them, after all. But murder for the sake of it wasn't their style, and there was nothing more that he could do to hurt them now, anyway.

"You're lucky," he whispered, and turned to go.

"Wait!" Richie rasped. He clambered to his feet and staggered around the couch. "Wait!"

Sam stopped, lifting the gun again. "No closer," he growled.

Richie stopped short, raising his hands in the air. "You can't go," he wheezed, heavy tears coming into his eyes. "If they come and you're gone…"

"Turn around," Sam ordered. Behind him, he heard Rachel move to the door.

"Please," Richie begged, the word ending in a sob. "Kris, and Syd. They'll do horrible things to them. They told me they would. They described them to me."

That sounded like Little Vincent's boys to Sam. They were playing for keeps now.

"And then they'll kill them," Richie continued. "Please, you gotta stay."

Sam took a backward step, keeping the gun leveled at Richie's chest.

"Please," the crying man repeated. "Please, Evan."

When Sam heard Richie use the name of the persona he'd used for the job, any pity he had for the man evaporated. He was reminded of the stark truth of it all. Richie was just another mark, another accomplice that couldn't be trusted. He was outside the circle. There was the world, and there was Sam and Rachel. That was how it was now, how it always should have been.

He heard the door swing open.

"You made your choice," Sam said.

Richie sank to his knees, weeping and begging.

He backed his way to the front door, then turned and was through the doorway in a flash.

As soon Sam was down the steps, he slipped the small revolver into his back pocket and broke into a trot. Rachel was already halfway down the pathway, her pace a rapid walk. He caught up and fell into step beside her. Rachel clutched the shoebox like a football, cradling it under her arm. Her eyes scanned the street.

"He called them when he went to get the box," Sam said.

"Or sent a text when he saw us on the porch. It took him a while to answer."

Sam didn't respond. She was probably right, but it didn't matter now. What mattered now was getting to the car. He didn't know how much time they had, but he didn't think it was much.

He was right.

Five seconds later, a dark blue sedan rounded the corner, its tires screeching. The car barreled toward them, engine revving.

Sam and Rachel instinctively moved in different directions. She sprinted thirty feet to the yard of a vacant house, taking momentary refuge behind a tree. Sam bolted straight across the street, forcing the driver to make a decision.

He chose Sam.

The bump clipped him on his left leg and threw him several yards in the air. The world tilted and spun while he flew, disorienting him. He crashed onto the road, skipping along asphalt for a few feet.

He heard car doors opening, and men cursing.

"Hello, motherfucker," said one.

"Get that bitch!" yelled another.

His head swimming, Sam reached for his back pocket. His fingers found the handle of the small revolver. He wrenched it free and rolled onto his back, pointing the gun upward.

Two men stared down at him. The one of the left was the muscular man who'd pulled Rachel out of the car in Myrtle Beach. The second face was also familiar. It was Rocco, the man who had accosted them in St. Louis, who Porter said had been pursuing them across the country.

Both men were slightly surprised at his action, and Sam took full advantage. He snapped off three quick shots. He aimed the first shot at Rocco's heart, but his angle was too sharp. By the man's reaction, the bullet seemed to graze him along the chest on its way into the sky. Rocco let out a cry and staggered backward toward the car.

Sam was already moving the barrel toward the muscular man, firing twice. The first slapped into his chest, but the second blasted into his jaw. The man crumpled to the ground, falling toward Sam.

Rolling out of the way, Sam pushed himself to his feet. He stepped purposefully toward the rear of the sedan. A slice of pain cut through his leg with every step. His mind told him that he had to be injured worse than that, but at the moment, everything seemed to be working.

To his left, Rocco clutched at his throat as he slid down the side of the car. *"Figlio di puttana..."* He spat the words at Sam. When he raised up the gun in his other hand, Sam fired twice more into his midsection. The enforcer howled in pain. The gun in his hand went off, but was pointed harmlessly away from Sam.

Across the street, a form of macabre tag was taking place. The single thug pursuing Rachel wore a tan track suit fringed in gold. A gun dangled from his hand as he tried to get around the thick tree to grab her. For her part, Rachel kept moving and ducking back and forth, dodging his flailing grasp and keeping the trunk of the old oak between them. Sam saw the pale white skin of the reaching hand and knew it was Whitey, the same man who'd pulled him from the car in Myrtle Beach.

Whitey was so intent on Rachel that he didn't notice Sam approach. Rachel gave no indication that she saw him, either. She just kept juking the pale bastard right out of his Nikes, ignoring his threats and curses.

When Sam was ten feet away, he leveled the gun and shot the Whitey in the back of the head. He fell abruptly, collapsing to the ground in a lifeless heap.

Rachel didn't miss a beat. She stepped around the tree and past the fallen thug. Her eyes swept up and down Sam, taking in his condition.

"Are you okay?"

"We gotta go," he said.

They turned toward their car, which was still more than two

lots away. Several blocks up, an SUV swerved onto the residential street. The frame leaned to the side as it turned, then seemed to jostle on the shocks as the vehicle accelerated.

"This way!" Sam shouted, grabbing Rachel by the hand and tugging her. He sprinted toward the blue sedan, his pronounced limp mimicking a crazy gallop. Rachel outdistanced him, getting to the car first. She flung open the passenger door and climbed in, scrambling across the center console. Sam got to the car right as she pulled her legs to her chest, swiveled and planted them on the driver's side floor.

"Get in!" she hollered at him.

Sam collapsed into the passenger seat. He pulled the door closed as she gunned the engine. The sedan lurched forward, tires screaming.

He glanced at Rachel, whose eyes were intent on the road in front of her. She clutched the steering wheel with a death grip.

Sam turned in the seat, looking backward. The SUV had rolled to a stop near the two bodies in the street. He watched as a thick figure clambered out of the SUV and checked on the downed men.

"We've got a chance," he said aloud. "They're stopping for their friends."

Rachel whipped to the right at the first intersection and accelerated up the street. At the next opportunity, she turned left. She kept at the serpentine route for several blocks while Sam kept watch out the back window. There was no sign of the SUV.

Finally, Rachel turned left onto a thoroughfare road. A horn blared at her. Sam looked over his shoulder to see a woman in a green mini-van holding her hands up at them in a what-the-hell gesture, before slowing slightly and creating a couple car lengths of distance between them.

He turned his gaze back to Rachel, realizing what she'd done. It was a risk, circling around and going back in the same compass direction they'd come from, but it was also not what their attackers would expect. He admired her guts.

"I love you," he told her, the words springing to his lips before the surge of emotion was even fully realized in his chest.

She shot him a sideways glance. "I love you, too"

"We're going to be all right."

Rachel patted the shoebox full of money on the console between them. "For a little while, at least." She was quiet for a moment, then looked his way again. "How badly are you hurt? Do we need to find a doctor?"

Sam glanced down at his body and took a quick inventory of his injuries. The front of his shirt was streaked black with rub-off from the street. Blood was smeared across it in places. He lifted his arms and examined them. Road rash on his left arm bled slightly, but he didn't see any deep cuts. His pants were torn and his left knee bloody, but when he leaned forward to inspect the wound, it seemed minor. Carefully, he stamped his feet against the floor. Dull pain was the response, but the structure felt solid.

"I think I'm good," he said, turning toward her. "I'll need some doctoring from you, but—"

He saw the flash of black through her window as the SUV leapt toward them from the cross street. A brief second of eternity hung still in the air, like his brain took a snapshot of the approaching grill. He wanted to do and say a thousand things in that moment, but all he could do was stare.

Despite him seeing it first, the crash was sudden and powerful. The car spun slightly. The force of the impact hurled Rachel's body toward him even as it slammed him into the door. Somehow she kept her hands wrapped around the steering wheel.

It took a moment for him to realize that the sedan was wrapped around the front corner of the SUV. He heard the distinctive grind of metal on the roadway. Sparks showered up around him. All of this happened in about a second, and yet it seem like it when on for an hour.

He heard another loud crash and saw the grill of the SUV pull away in the opposite direction. Then they slammed into something on his side of car and were rolling. Sam flailed for something to hold onto. Then he was flying.

* * *

When he could think again, he was aware of sounds first. One sound, really. A rhythmic scream, he thought. Then his hearing sharpened and he opened his eyes. A horn blared repeatedly, like an old-style car alarm was rigged to it. No human sounds, no sirens.

Not yet.

Sam pushed himself to his feet. He was on grass that was slick with blood. He didn't bother to look for why. He knew he couldn't allow himself to panic. Instead, he scanned the scene in front of him. His shocked mind struggled to take what he saw.

Twenty-five yards up the street, a green mini-van sat motionless in the middle of the street, its front end demolished. The rear brake lights flashed. The horn sounded in time with the flash. A dozen yards further up the street, a black SUV lay on its side amidst shattered glass and a pool of fluid. Small flames danced on the surface, licking against the underbelly of the vehicle's frame.

Sam could see the windshield opening of the SUV, but didn't bother looking further.

It didn't matter.

Only one thing did.

To his left, ten yards away, a crumpled mess of twisted blue metal rested in the unfenced front yard of a home. The vehicle was upright.

Sam limped toward the car in a lurching gait. What felt like a handful of needles stabbed into his ankle with each step. His left arm hung nearly limp at his side, swinging as he walked. Without looking down, he flexed it and lifted. Sharp pain greeted him. He gritted his teeth and worked it again.

Not broken. Not severed.

That was all he needed to know.

At the driver's door, he panicked when he didn't see her. The he leaned in and saw her lying across the center console. Her head rested on the passenger seat.

Sam tried to work the door handle, but it was broken. He

tugged on the door. Nothing. He pulled harder, but it didn't budge. Then he reached inside and pushed the latch. He was rewarded with a metallic click.

With all his strength, he pulled on the door. The metal screeched as it swung open halfway. He pulled again, and it opened only a little more.

It's enough, he told himself. *Get her.*

In the distance now, he could hear sirens over the top of blaring horn.

Sam pawed at Rachel's legs, swinging them around toward him. They were heavy. Lifeless. He leaned inside the car and took her by the elbow. Carefully, he cradled her head with his other hand. Her hair was matted with blood. He couldn't see the cut.

Easing her up into a seated position, he struggled to keep her from flopping back down. Her head lolled to the side.

"You're all right," Sam told her. "You're all right."

He pulled her toward him into an embrace and backed out of the car.

"You're going to be fine," he whispered.

Rachel didn't answer. Her warm cheek pressed against his.

"We're getting out of here," Sam told her. "You and me, babe."

He lowered his weight slightly, letting her slide forward onto his shoulder. Then he dropped his hands below her buttocks and heaved her upward. His ankle cried out in protest, but he winced and ignored it.

Sam looked around for the best escape route. Up the street, people were already out of their houses and standing on their front porches. Soon they'd be running up to help, he knew.

He looked back the other way and saw more of the same. The flames surrounding the SUV had grown. He wondered if the gas tank would ignite. Maybe a Hollywood explosion would keep the do-gooders away.

The faraway wail of the sirens pushed him forward. He decided the direction of the SUV was safer. At least a fire would keep people at bay or attract more of their attention. He didn't want a Good Samaritan, or a fire truck or an ambulance any more than he wanted the cops. It all eventually led back to Little Vincent. He had to get Rachel out of here. Somewhere safe, where they could regroup and recover.

He thought of the money suddenly and stopped. They still needed it. Now more than ever. He started to go back for it. Shouts from residents up the street and the nearing sirens changed his mind.

A sudden huffing sound caught his attention. He turned toward the SUV. With a benign *fwoop*, the vehicle was fully engulfed in flames. No explosion, at least not yet. And no screams from inside, either. Maybe they were already dead or unconscious from the crash.

Pity, Sam thought. He'd always heard that burning was a terrible death.

"Get back!" Someone yelled.

Sam adjusted Rachel's weight over his shoulder, turned and walked toward the vacant house. A plan began to formulate in his mind. A simple one, but it might work. Disappear behind the vacant. Get out of the immediate area. Check on Rachel. Get her awake. Then work his way back to Richie's. He can tell the man that they changed their minds and took on the gangsters. That his family was safe now. It would take some doing, but Sam knew he could con him. Once he and Rachel were safe, they'd doctor each other up well enough to travel, and then it was goodbye, Detroit.

"We've got enough to lay low," he said. "Long enough to catch our breath."

Rachel didn't answer. Her slack arms swayed and bounced off his buttocks as he walked. He wanted to stop and check on her, but he couldn't. Not yet. Sam thought he heard a weak moan come from her, but the sound of his own voice and his exertion made it impossible to tell for certain.

Just keep moving.

"It's going to be okay, baby," Sam told her. "We're going to make it."

There came no reply.

He took one step, and then another. There were yells of confusion and shouts behind him. Sirens drew closer. He stumbled on, waiting for the darkness to take him. A flash of despair went through him at the thought, but Sam refused to quit.

It's been a good run.

That's what Porter said. Sam could hear the deep, gravelly voice in his head when he thought the words. He should have known it then, should have heard the resignation in the man's tone. But he conned himself that it wasn't true. Like the best cons, he never even knew he'd been conned until it was too late.

Sam kept walking. The game wasn't over yet.

FRANK ZAFIRO was a police officer in Spokane, Washington, from 1993 to 2013. He retired as a captain. He is the author of numerous crime novels, including the River City novels and the Stefan Kopriva series. He lives in Redmond, Oregon, with his wife Kristi, dogs Richie and Wiley, and a very self-assured cat named Pasta. He is an avid hockey fan and a tortured guitarist. You can keep up with Frank at FrankZafiro.com, where you can score a free book just for signing up for his newsletter.

COMING IN JANUARY 2021

A GRIFTER'S SONG
SEASON THREE

SERIES CREATED AND EDITED BY FRANK ZAFIRO

The Rule of Thirds by Matt Phillips
The Down and Out by Lawrence Maddox
Travel Money by Jonathan Brown
Rocky Mountain Lie by Michael Pool
Open Up Your Heart by Carmen Jaramillo
Ride Like Hell by S.A. Cosby

Plus a Bonus Episode by Frank Zafiro
exclusively for subscribers.

BOOKS

On the following pages are a few
more great titles from the
Down & Out Books publishing family.

For a complete list of books and to
sign up for our newsletter,
go to DownAndOutBooks.com.

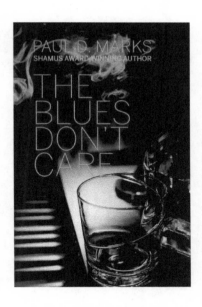

The Blues Don't Care
Paul D. Marks

Down & Out Books
June 2020
978-1-64396-050-0

Bobby Saxon lives in a world that isn't quite ready for him. He's the only white musician in an otherwise all-black swing band at the famous Club Alabam in Los Angeles during World War II—and that isn't the only unusual thing about him...or should I say her? For Bobby was born Roberta and is trying to live as a man—no small thing in the 1940s.

And if that isn't enough to deal with, in order to get a permanent gig with the band, Bobby must first solve a murder that one of the band members is falsely accused of in that racially prejudiced society.

Driving Reign
The De La Cruz Case Files
TG Wolff

Down & Out Books
July 2020
978-1-64396-087-6

The woman in the stingy hospital bed wasn't dead. The question for Detective Jesus De La Cruz: did the comatose patient narrowly survive suicide or murder?

Faithful friends paint a picture of a guileless young woman, a victim of both crime and society. Others describe a cold woman with a proclivity for icing interested men with a single look.

Beneath the rhetoric, Cruz unearths a twisted knot of reality and perception. A sex scandal, a jilted lover, a callous director, a rainmaker, and a quid pro quo have Cruz questioning if there is such a thing as an innocent man.

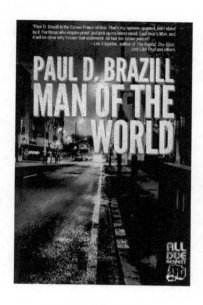

Man of the World
Paul D. Brazill

All Due Respect, an imprint of
Down & Out Books
April 2020
978-1-64396-099-9

Ageing hit-man Tommy Bennett left London and returned to his hometown of Seatown, hoping for respite from the ghosts of the violent past that haunted him. However, things don't go to plan and trouble and violence soon follow Tommy to Seatown.

Tommy is soon embroiled in Seatown's underworld and his hopes of a peaceful retirement are dashed. Tommy deliberates whether or not to leave Seatown and return to London. Or even leave Great Britain altogether. So, he heads back to London where violence and mayhem await him.

Shotgun Honey Presents Volume 4: RECOIL
Ron Earl Phillips, editor

Shotgun Honey, an imprint of
Down & Out Books
May 2020
978-1-64396-138-5

With new and established authors from around the world, Shotgun Honey Presents Volume 4: RECOIL delivers stories that explore a darker side of remorse, revenge, circumstance, and humanity.

Contributors: Rusty Barnes, Susan Benson, Sarah M. Chen, Kristy Claxton, Jen Conley, Brandon Daily, Barbara DeMarco-Barrett, Hector Duarte Jr., Danny Gardner, Tia Ja'nae, Carmen Jaramillo, Nick Kolakowski, JJ Landry, Bethany Maines, Tess Makovesky, Alexander Nachaj, David Nemeth, Cindy O'Quinn, Brandon Sears, Johnny Shaw, Kieran Shea, Gigi Vernon, Patrick Whitehurst.

CPSIA information can be obtained
at www.ICGtesting.com
Printed in the USA
LVHW050731210620
658569LV00006B/1130